Chapter 1

One glass of cheap California chardonnay cost me my husband, my job, and my best friend. Unfortunately, that was only the beginning of my troubles.

I slowly regained consciousness when a cold nose nuzzled my ear and then a warm, wet tongue licked my cheek. I squinted against the sunlight streaming through the small window as I tried to open my eyes, but they stopped at the halfway mark. My head pounded even more from the bright light. My face was pressed into my guest bathroom's chilly white subway-tile flooring, and my entire body ached. I shivered when I realized I was still dressed in a sheer blouse and teeny-weeny leopard-print skirt. The ensemble had been an unwanted early birthday gift from my best friend, Tori. I groaned with the effort of trying to remember what had happened the night before but was rewarded only with brief, fleeting flashes of memory.

Piper, my rescue Labradoodle mix, nudged my face again and whined. I couldn't remember how I'd gotten home and had no idea how I'd ended up sleeping on the bathroom floor. I hoped my husband, Philip, hadn't come home from his graveyard shift yet. I raised my left arm and squinted at the blurry numbers on the watch sitting on my wrist. Seven thirty. Philip would have come home an hour ago, and I prayed he'd gone straight to bed and hadn't seen me.

Piper whined again and walked into the hallway, trying to tell me she wanted her breakfast and time outside. A moan escaped my lips when my head and stomach started feeling like they were on a Tilt-a-Whirl ride. I crawled to the sink, pulled myself up, and washed my face and mouth. Looking in the mirror, I decided my wild red hair needed a stiff brush to calm the frizzies. Piper nudged my foot with her nose and whined again, but I ignored her. Red, puffy eyes peered back at me, but what made me want to lunge for the commode was the purple, almond-shaped bruise on the side of my neck. A love bite? How in the heck did I get that?

Uh-oh. I suddenly remembered sapphire-blue eyes that made me feel warm and fuzzy. Randall. Tori's mysterious cousin who I hadn't even known existed until last night. How would I explain Randall to my husband when I couldn't explain him even to myself? It would be worse if he saw me in these party clothes.

After I removed the sheer black blouse and hid it between the extra towels in the vanity cabinet, I yanked a fluffy pink bath towel off the bar and wrapped the towel around me. I hoped I could sneak into the laundry room and get dressed, preferably in something that went with a scarf wrapped around my neck, before Philip noticed me. Nope, that wouldn't work. A scarf in August would make him even more suspicious.

The carpeted hallway muffled my tippy-toe walk while my dog practically danced beside me. When the sliding glass door that led to our condo's patio and the postage-sized patch of grass that was part of the unit opened, Piper raced past me. The fringe on my towel caught on her collar, and suddenly, my dog became Piper the Super Dog, complete with a pink cape. I, on the other hand, was left standing in broad

2

daylight, wearing nothing but a small lacy black bra and miniskirt that had inched up over my ample derrière. I didn't need one of my neighbors seeing my lack of clothing over the half walls that surrounded our small piece of land. Why did Tori think she should give me this outfit? And how had she managed to talk me into wearing it to meet Randall? The image of his face pinballed around my head as I slunk back down the hallway. Why had Tori invited him to go out for drinks with us?

I eased the accordion laundry room doors open. I paused when one of them squeaked, then rummaged through the laundry basket sitting on top of the washer. Dirty clothes would be better than these party clothes when it came time to face Philip, my husband of seven years. After getting dressed in capri-length yoga pants and a very wrinkled, slightly stained T-shirt, I tiptoed to the kitchen and opened the cupboard, looking for antacids and pain relievers.

My head screamed, and my stomach threatened to send me running back to the bathroom. Once I popped the pills, I hunted for my purse and my emergency stash of concealer. Maybe Philip's drowsy state and the dim lighting in the bedroom would cause him to overlook my new bruise, especially if I had enough makeup on it.

I finally found my purse hidden behind the sofa. My mind struggled to remember how it got there, but the only thing I remembered from the night before was drinking a glass of chardonnay with Tori. Oh yeah, and Randall. I would dearly love to forget he was there. My hand went to the love bite. Tori would know what happened. I needed to call her.

While I tried to cake on the concealer, Piper came back in, without her Super Dog cape, and nudged my hand with her slightly muddy nose. Breakfast time. I cut open a package of lamb-and-brown-rice dog food and dumped it into her ceramic dish. The sloppily painted dish made me smile. I remembered taking my towheaded, preschool-aged nieces to the ceramic painting store and their efforts to make Piper's food and water bowls as colorful as possible.

After refreshing her water dish, I tiptoed back down the hallway to the half-closed master bedroom door. I slid my head into the crack and waited for my eyes to adjust to the dim light, since the blackout roman shades had been pulled down. My stomach flip-flopped when I saw our bed hadn't been slept in. In fact, my husband, with his short wavy-black hair, was nowhere to be found. I rushed back to my purse and pulled my phone out. Had Philip left a message for me? Nothing.

Perhaps he had to work overtime and couldn't call me. It happened once in a while, so I didn't worry too much. Actually, I was a bit relieved, if I were honest with myself, since I needed to figure out what I'd done last night before I felt ready to face Philip. The niggling doubt that, instead of working, my husband and his partner, Officer Amy Doyle, were having an affair swirled around my brain. I had no proof, just suspicions that something or someone was tearing our marriage apart. Randall was someone I didn't need to think about right now.

I quickly called Tori's cell number, hoping she'd be able to tell me how I got so drunk that I blacked out. I rarely drank more than a glass of wine and had two at the most, since more than that gave me the world's worst hangover. One party during my senior year of high school cured me of binge drinking. I had a very low tolerance for pain and suffering.

Her sultry voice, an imitation of Marilyn Monroe, announced I had reached her voice mail. "This is Tori, and you know what to do. *Ciao*, baby."

I hung up without leaving a message.

Tori never, ever missed answering her phone and slept with it even when she had a boyfriend in her bed. I found it annoying when we were together and I was trying to carry on a conversation, but several times in the recent past, I was grateful she answered my call when I needed to dissect Philip's inattention or his more frequent hurtful remarks. I wouldn't take her advice, though. She had told me repeatedly to move on and find someone new. Perhaps that was why she had introduced me to Randall.

I waited a few minutes and called Tori again, this time leaving a message. "Tori, it's Em. Call me as soon as you can."

I started to get worried, letting my imagination run away from me. What if Randall had drugged us or tried to poison us? I shouldn't let my mind wander like that, but then again, I couldn't explain my blackout. What happened last night? After a cup of hot herbal tea and a slice of dry toast, I called Tori. Again, I reached her voice mail. Something was definitely wrong.

After giving Piper a new chew toy, ruffling her golden fur and telling her to be a good girl, I grabbed my purse and headed to the garage. I needed to make sure Tori was safe. When I walked into the garage, the empty space where my car should have been gave me pause. What had I done with my Honda Accord? Oh, yeah, I had left it in the parking lot where I worked as an accountant when Tori picked me up for drinks.

I eyed my rusty beach cruiser and sighed. Five miles from Huntington Beach to Tori's house in Costa Mesa on a bike wasn't that far unless you were already in agony. But that was what friends did for each other, and I was becoming certain Tori needed my help.

As I pedaled, I huffed and puffed while sweat dripped down my cheeks, and I cursed myself for not thinking to bring a bottle of water. When I climbed off my bike, I stood with wobbly legs at the end of Tori's block. Her four-plex building was located six houses down from the corner where I had stopped, and I saw her red Mini Cooper parked in her driveway. My husband's white Tahoe SUV was parked right behind it.

I wasn't a Peeping Tom, or a Peeping Jane, if that was

what they called women who peered into other people's windows, but I knew I would have to resort to that if I wanted to find out the truth. I really wanted to think Philip was there because something bad had happened to Tori. But wouldn't he have called me if that were the case?

Other images sprang to mind of Philip and Tori not making eye contact when all three of us spent time together, acting like they were ignoring each other. And the bottle of perfume he had given me for Valentine's Day this year was Tori's fragrance. A wife knew when another woman was on her husband's mind, but how could I have been so blind thinking it could be Officer Amy Doyle? Why did Tori do this to me?

I looked up and down the street to make sure no one saw me, then tiptoed across the dying grass bordering a cracked cement walkway. I ducked under a withered ficus tree that barely provided any shelter from the hot morning sun. The tree grew next to her unit's front window. Even though it wasn't a good hiding spot, it was the best I could find.

I looked up and down the street again and observed no one. It was very quiet for a Saturday. I turned, stood slowly, and pressed my nose against the dusty screen and held in the sneeze that tried to erupt. I quickly ducked back down and almost cracked my head on the windowsill. My husband reclined on Tori's sofa, which faced the window I had peeked into.

Worried he might have seen me, I waited a moment before cautiously peeking back in. Philip had his eyes closed. I stretched up onto my tiptoes and saw perfectly proportioned, size-two, platinum-blonde Tori in an intimate pose with my husband that would, unfortunately, be forever burned into my brain. I wished I could unsee it. But it was too late for that.

A sudden puff of wind swirled and caused one of the branches from the tree to hit the window with a loud clunk. I squatted down, but the wind had pushed my frizzy hair into the screen and caused it to get entangled on some of the protruding broken wires. When some of the hairs were yanked from my head, I yelped, although the pain from my scalp was nothing compared to my heartbreak. I rubbed the sore spot and then crept to the front door, ready to tell them to go to you-know-where—but in a polite way because, after all, my mother raised me to have manners.

By the time I reached the glass front door and saw them together, all thoughts of etiquette fled from my brain. Instead of knocking or ringing the bell, I twisted the door handle and burst into Tori's unlocked house. Later, I concluded that I had experienced a red-mist moment because my actions weren't those I would have thought myself capable of. The details were still kind of fuzzy, but somehow, after Tori fell through the screen door and stumbled down the steps, pulling me along for the fall, we ended up on the front lawn.

Chapter 2

W hen we both landed, I ended up on top of her and pummeled her with my fists, screaming at the top of my lungs, "You lying, cheating hussy. I'm gonna make you sorry you were ever born!"

Tori was giving as good as she got. When I tasted blood from my busted lip, I shrieked even louder.

"Meow…. Hey, dude, look, a cat fight." The slow drawl of Tori's stoner surfer neighbor finally pierced my brain.

I rolled off Tori and lay panting in the dusty grass. Her wheezes sounded loud in my ear.

"Hey, don't stop fighting yet. It's just getting good." Stoner Dude's roommate and brother, a game software developer, had popped open a beer and now leered over the railing of their rooftop patio. "We haven't finished taking bets yet."

Tori gave him a middle finger wave. "Bug off, Steve."

"C'mon, Tor. You and Em need to do some real World Wrestling Federation stuff." Steve was practically drooling as he brushed his shoulder-length sun-bleached wavy hair away from his eyes.

I had a hard time telling the two brothers apart, even

though they insisted Steve was two years older than Stan. They looked like twins.

I shook my head as I pushed myself up to a shaky standing position. "Steve, you know that's all fake wrestling, right?"

"No way, dudette. That stuff is real." Stan, aka Stoner Dude, lit up a cigarette and passed it to his brother. The pungent smoke drifted down. It was a wonder they were successful in developing game software.

A siren wailed at the end of the block, and the brothers and their Maui Wowie quickly disappeared back into their apartment without another word.

I felt like kicking Tori in the ribs while she still sprawled in the grass, but I thought I'd better not when I saw the black-and-white police sedan pull up behind Philip's SUV. I glanced back at the apartment, wondering where Philip could be. Apparently he was a coward, hiding in there somewhere, away from the drama.

The officer unfolded his long legs from his cruiser. He stepped out, and his dark-blue uniform showed sweaty rings beneath his arms while his prematurely balding head threatened to send beads of sweat rolling down his face.

"You ladies having a problem here?" Officer Larry Callahan, an old high school friend of Philip's, couldn't tear his gaze away from Tori's scantily clad, perfectly developed, golden-tanned chest. He didn't even notice me.

"No, we're good, Officer." Tori gave him a smile and batted her eyelashes, but instead of looking sexy, she looked creepy with blood dripping from her lip. "I just tripped and fell."

"Can I get you medical assistance?" Officer Callahan asked her chest.

"No. I'll be okay. Right, Emory?"

Officer Callahan finally looked at me. "Emory? What are you doing here?"

"Hi, Larry."

He peered at my bloody lip. "Are you okay? Where's Philip?"

Good question. Where could that chicken husband of mine be?

"I'm fine. I accidentally tripped when Tori did." I looked back at the house and mumbled, "Philip's using the bathroom. We'll get cleaned up as soon as he's out."

Larry looked back at Tori's chest. "We got a call about a fight going on. Disturbing the peace."

I opened my mouth to tell him nothing had happened, but he glared at me and shook his head, so I closed it just as fast.

"Now, if you ladies will take it back into the house and keep it quiet, I'll be on my way. Make sure Philip calls when he's available."

Officer Callahan adjusted his sunglasses and then got back in his vehicle. Once he had driven out of sight, Tori turned and limped up the steps to her house. I followed close behind but stopped short when she slammed the screen door in my face.

"Get off my property," Tori said with a snarl. "I don't ever want you here again."

"I need to talk to Philip first."

"If he ever wants to see your ugly face again, he'll call you."

I couldn't help it. My voice escalated to a shrill shriek as I tried to yank open the screen door. "You'd better watch your back, Tori! I'm not going to let you get away with this!"

"Go away. You don't want the cops to come back. What would your mother think if you got arrested?"

She knew me too well. My mother would be mortified. I backed down the steps and began the walk of shame to my bike.

"Oh, Em?" Tori opened the screen door and stuck her head out. "You're the one who's going to regret this."

I limped down the block to my bicycle, happy to see it was still where I'd left it. I had dropped it to the ground in the middle of the sidewalk when I first spied Philip's vehicle. I wheeled the bike around the corner and found a low concrete wall to sit on. Thick shrubs had been planted behind it to shield the house from the street. I touched my lip gingerly and winced when the gash stung. I imagined how swollen my lip must be. My bones ached, and I couldn't fathom riding the bike home, so I whipped my cell phone out of my pocket and called my sister.

"Carrie? Can you come pick me up?"

"Where are you? What's going on?"

Behind the shrubs, a lawn mower sprang to life, the buzzing noise cutting a path of pain through my pounding head. The smell of sharp green grass floated on the air as the mower moved toward me. A sneeze exploded from my mouth, and I walked farther down the street.

"I'm around the corner from Tori's house. Can Thomas stay with the girls?" I touched my swollen lip again and shuddered. "They shouldn't see me in this condition."

"What are you talking about?"

"Just come pick me up, and I'll tell you then."

I gave her directions then found another shady spot to sit under, away from the piercing whine of the lawn mower. It sounded like it had been supercharged, which wasn't something you needed when mowing Southern California's postage-stamp-sized yards.

Carrie finally pulled up in her dark-blue minivan.

"What the heck happened to you?" Carrie reached into her purse and retrieved a pack of baby wipes then handed them to me. "Don't you dare get blood in my van."

"I'll try not to." I sounded whiny, even to my own ears.

Grateful that Carrie would drop everything to pick me up, I was still annoyed that her life seemed so perfect. Her shoulder-length red hair wasn't frizzy like mine, and her makeup appeared always in place, even though she didn't have to cover up a generous number of freckles like I did. My eyes were green with flecks of brown, which often looked muddy, whereas her eyes were a gorgeous solid green. And she didn't have a husband carrying on an affair with her best friend.

Carrie shook her head at the tone of my voice, jumped out, opened the cargo hold door of the van, and helped me stow my bike. She carefully avoided getting tire dirt on her impeccably clean white shorts and then used one of the baby wipes on her hands before getting back into her vehicle. After peeking at the love bite on my neck, Carrie kept her lips pressed together in a grim line. She didn't say a word until I asked her to stop by my work to retrieve my car.

"Okay, but you've got some explaining to do."

"I'll tell you once we get to my condo," I promised her.

Once we reached my home and unloaded my bike into the garage, we got comfortable on my sofa. I told my sister, who was older by a few minutes, my entire torrid tale.

"I knew Philip was bad news the minute I met him." My twin shook her head. "Tori too. I never understood why you liked her. She's just not our type."

Our type. Caucasian Presbyterians. Did everything by the book. Didn't color outside the lines. Pretty much summed up how my mother and Lars raised us. Whatever my sister might say about Philip, my mother had adored him from day one. She might have even loved him more than she loved me.

"I put the blame completely on Tori. She's the one who ruined my marriage." I wiped my eyes with the back of my hand. Faced with the reality of Philip's betrayal, I needed to make some hard decisions. Right now, though, I didn't want to voice those choices out loud.

"I don't know why you're defending the bas… um, the guy."

We didn't swear either.

"He gives you a love bite then runs to his tawdry girlfriend for more? And what is Mom going to say about all of this?"

"Probably the same thing you're saying right now." I glared at her. Why couldn't my sister be more understanding? "Except I'm sure it will somehow be my fault."

"You remember, don't you, that you're supposed to help me with the party tomorrow?" Her sigh was loud. "How am I supposed to explain your appearance? I can't tell people you were in a fight. I have a family-friendly reputation to uphold."

Of course Carrie would make the situation all about her. I loved my sister dearly, but she was often self-absorbed. Maybe it had something to do with being the oldest, even if only by a few minutes.

"I'm sure telling people I fell off my bike will work." I pulled some dried grass from my hair, a reminder of my fight with Tori. "Everyone knows what a klutz I am, anyway."

"You want me to lie?" She looked like she'd seen a snake slithering in the street.

"No. You don't have to say a thing, Carrie. I'll lie." Might as well add that to my growing list of sins. "Don't worry about it. I'll be there to help, and it will be fine."

"And you've just about finished the cake, haven't you?" My sister, the professional party planner and caterer, was on top of every detail. "I've promised my friend that your horse-themed cake will be spectacular. We can't disappoint her little girl."

"I know that. Stop worrying." A five-mile bike ride would have been preferable to this chat. "I've got it under control."

"Okay, as long as you're sure. I've got to run and get Sophie and Kaylee to their ballet class." She turned, put her arms around my shoulders, and pulled me into a hug. "I really am sorry this happened to you. I'm just angry that jerk hurt you and I can't fix it for you."

"Thanks." I returned the hug. "And thank you for picking me up and letting me spill my guts."

"You need to call Mom and tell her."

I groaned. "Can't you tell her for me?"

"No way." She grinned. "I'm not about to face the firing squad for something I didn't do. That's your responsibility."

Chapter 3

I had told my sister another little white lie. The cake wasn't under control, and it would take a long day and most of the night in the kitchen to finish it. If I had stayed home last evening instead of going out with Tori, I wouldn't be facing some of my current problems.

Decorating cakes was a hobby I discovered when my sister became pregnant with my twin nieces. Twins ran in our family. I wanted to do something special for my sister's baby shower, so I made the cake and then got hooked. Thanks to all the cake-decorating shows and competitions aired on cable TV, I'd pushed myself to try more difficult designs using different techniques. People told me I was talented, and I even won ribbons at last year's Orange County fair for both my decorating and unique cupcake flavors. I dreamed of opening my own bakery and specializing in cupcakes, especially on the days when I was fed up with crunching numbers at work. Who would have thought an accountant could be so creative?

I spent the rest of the afternoon and evening working on horse-themed decorations using gum paste, fondant, and royal icing. The hours flew by as I lost myself in the sweet world of creativity, and I blocked out the ugly scenes I had participated in earlier that day. I wasn't about to let the drama in my life disrupt the happiness my cake would bring to a little girl. My heart felt nothing but pure joy whenever I witnessed a child's face light up upon seeing their birthday cake.

When the doorbell rang, I jumped, nicking my thumb with the blade of the X-Acto knife I used to cut cowgirl boots from pink fondant. I glanced at the clock and figured that only two people would visit this late. I hoped for Philip and not my mother.

Apparently, I was a bad girl and God didn't listen. My mother, Addie Gosser Whitendale, stood on my porch. Her flawless face, illuminated by the carriage lights flanking the front door, barely concealed her anger. She brushed past me into the house before I even had a chance to invite her in. I took my time closing the door and securing the lock before I turned to face my mother.

"Emory Danae Martinez, just what do you think you're doing?" Her voice sounded two octaves higher than normal, and her face had turned scarlet. "What are people going to think about you? About your family?"

"It isn't my fault. It's Philip." I rushed to get my words out when I saw her take a deep inhale, ready to launch more disapproval my way. "Besides, Tori started it. Carrie's right. I shouldn't have trusted her."

"Don't you blame this on Philip. You're the one who should be ashamed of yourself." A sob escaped her lips, which was unusual because my mother was a very stoic woman. "And then to post it on Facebook. I am utterly humiliated!"

"Mother, what the heck are you talking about?" She wasn't making any sense, which irritated me, since I always seemed to get blamed for anything bad that happened. Plus, I had at least a few more hours of work left before the cake would be finished, so I didn't have time for this. "Why didn't you call me?"

"Don't you take that tone of voice with me, young lady.

Your calls just go into voice mail. Why can't you ever answer your phone?" Her voice lowered, and she enunciated each harsh word. "You march yourself to your computer right this instant and take that, that… that photo down right now. Do I make myself clear?"

"Yes, ma'am." Even though I had no idea what she was talking about, I knew I'd better not argue. I grabbed my cell phone, remembering I had turned it off so I wouldn't be disturbed while decorating. After the phone powered up, I saw that twenty-five messages cluttered my voice mail. This couldn't be good.

I turned on my heels and marched to the guest room, where we kept our computer. While waiting for it to boot up, I sucked on my nicked thumb. I sensed my mother watching me from the doorway. Her perfume, Chanel No. Five, drifted into the room, but I noticed her keeping distance between us. Perhaps she was avoiding the computer?

"Where did I go wrong with you, Emory?" She sighed and tucked a strand of her shoulder-length salon-colored ash-blonde hair behind her diamond-laden ear. My stepfather treated her like a queen. She favored St. John Knit suits and casual wear, but tonight she wore jeans and a T-shirt, which made her appear much younger than her fifty-five years. "I know it was hard on you when your dad left, but I've tried to make up for that and give you a good life."

My dad, Joel Gosser, took off before I turned ten years old, abandoning us. He packed up his stuff while we girls were at school and my mom was at work and disappeared. Didn't say goodbye or even leave a note. My mom eventually found out he had run off to Reno with a twenty-something-year-old hooker. Well, I called her a hooker, but I was sure she was one of his students in the night-school math class he taught at the local junior college.

Right after we married, Philip found out Joel lived in Las Vegas and thought I might want to contact him. I declined.

Until he left us, I had been Daddy's girl, while Carrie was Mama's girl. Essentially, I felt blame for his abandonment. Maybe if I had been as perfect as Carrie, he might have stayed. Almost eighteen years had passed, and I still struggled with his leaving if I allowed myself to think about him.

A few years later, my mom married Lars Whitendale, who loved her to the moon and back. He'd treated us like his own daughters, taking us on lavish vacations and giving us top-notch educations. My twin adored Lars from the very beginning, and they developed a close bond. I respected him and what he did for my family, but from the beginning, I resented him. Irrational as it might seem, I wanted no one stepping into the spot where my dad should have been. Despite my growing respect and fondness for Lars over the years, my mother probably sensed my earlier attitude, which resulted in our relationship becoming strained at times.

"This has nothing to do with you or Dad." I looked back toward the computer, which was still going through the boot-up cycle. I couldn't bring myself to tell my mother about my cheating husband. "Philip and I are going through a rough time right now."

Addie almost choked. "As if your behavior isn't to blame. I'll be surprised if Philip ever forgives you."

Uh-oh. How did they find out about Randall already? I didn't even really know….

Finally, the Facebook login screen came up, but when I tried my password, the page failed to load. I tried again, but access was denied.

"Something seems to be wrong. It won't accept my password."

"Try my account. It should work." My mother wouldn't look me in the eyes as she gave me her password.

Addie's Facebook page loaded quickly, and a scream erupted from my lips. My vision started going black, and I almost threw up. In bright living color, I stood against a wood-paneled wall with my sheer black blouse unbuttoned and half of the tiny lacy black bra on full display. Randall nuzzled my neck as his hand caressed me. One of my hands rested on his shirtless back, while scratch marks, obviously left by my nails, showed across his rippling muscles.

"Oh my god! That can't be me," I screeched, my hands shaking as I tried to log out of my mother's account and access my account so I could delete the photo. I couldn't believe my mother had witnessed this. "There are hundreds of likes and over ninety shares on this photo already. Oh. My. God!"

Nothing I did would allow me to access my own Facebook account. Whoever posted the photo had also changed my password. And that person must have been Tori.

"Emory, do something now." My mother sounded close to having a heart attack. "What if your grandparents see this?"

"Okay, don't panic." I felt panicky enough for the both of us. "I'm going to run over to Tori's house and have her straighten this out. She's a computer whiz and can fix it."

"You said Tori is part of your problem with Philip." She looked at me from the corner of her eye. No way would she look at the computer screen and risk seeing that picture.

"Oh, nothing so serious that can't be fixed. She'll help me out." I seemed to be getting good at lying, even under pressure. I should probably worry about myself.

"All right, if you think that's a good idea." She went quiet for a moment. "I'll call your grandparents, have a nice long chat with them this evening, and keep them away from the computer. Text me when it's fixed."

"I must have been drugged last night. Nothing else makes sense, and I don't remember this or how I got home." After making sure I had fully logged out of her Facebook account, I powered off the computer and turned toward my mother. "It's not my fault."

"You can worry about that later, young lady. Right now,

you get that thing off of Facebook." She still wouldn't meet my gaze. "Expect a serious discussion about this. You've got a lot of explaining to do."

As I drove the five miles to Tori's house, I tried to figure out who had drugged me. It was the only explanation for why I blacked out. And why would someone do that to me? Even if Tori was having an affair with my husband, I didn't see her doing this. If Randall had drugged me, wouldn't Tori have noticed?

I pulled into Tori's driveway and parked behind her Mini Cooper. I slowly got out of my car and wondered what to do since there weren't any lights on in the house. Dim streetlights barely illuminated the area, so I gave myself a moment to let my eyes adjust to the darkness. Tori might have gone out with Philip or with other friends and left her car here. I fervently hoped she wasn't home.

All of a sudden, Jimi Hendrix music pierced the silent darkness, pulsing from Stoner Dudes' balcony. Pungent smoke drifted down. Maybe she was partying with them. I had never been invited to a party at their apartment, thank goodness, but they had shown up with Tori at a barbecue Philip and I hosted earlier this summer. My husband had been beyond angry about them crashing the party.

I searched my purse and found the house key Tori had given me months ago. I rang the doorbell and knocked several times, just to be sure no one was home, before using the key. No one answered the door. The inhabitants upstairs wouldn't be able to hear me over the blaring music, so I felt somewhat safe. I decided to let myself in for a quick look at her computer, hoping to delete the offending photo, change my password, and leave without her ever knowing I had been there. I really didn't want to get into another fight with her, but I didn't trust myself not to try to finish what I had started earlier.

The key slid the lock open silently, but the door made an

unearthly squeal when I pushed it open. I startled then stumbled into the house when a car came down the street. I didn't need anyone seeing me sneaking in.

The worn shag carpeting muffled my footsteps, and I could barely make out the shape of her glass coffee table, dimly illuminated by the microwave light in the kitchen. I still nearly cracked my knee against the table since it stood at an odd angle from the sofa. Perhaps it had gotten shoved to the side when… I tried to think of something like pixies and fairies so I could ignore the images of Philip with Tori. It didn't work, and I'd never be able to forget that memory. Ever.

I made my way to the left hallway, toward Tori's bedroom. She usually kept her laptop hooked up to a larger monitor in her room. Tori needed glasses to view the small laptop screen, but being too vain to wear them, she'd resorted to an auxiliary monitor instead. I prayed she had left my Facebook page open so I could get out of there without being caught.

Her bedroom door was shut, and I almost ran headlong into it. I mentally smacked myself for not bringing in my cell phone. The flashlight app would have been handy right now, since I didn't want to risk turning the house lights on. I turned the doorknob as slowly as possible and inched the door open. I held my breath and listened for a full minute but heard nothing except Tori's kitchen clock. *Tick tock, tick tock.* Until now, I hadn't realized it made such a loud noise. Stoner Dudes' music came back on with a faint thump, thump. It sounded like rap. I shook my head. First Jimi Hendrix, now Snoop Dogg.

I pushed the door farther open, took one step in, and then spent another minute holding my breath and listening. My eyes were still blind inside the pitch-black room, and I couldn't determine whether Tori was in bed or not. I took another two steps into the room and my nose wrinkled involuntarily. Something metallic and funky stifled the air. Tori wasn't the best housekeeper, but I'd never smelled this in her house before.

Not hearing any other sounds, aside from my pounding heart, I tiptoed toward the desk I knew sat beneath the window. Tori hated any light coming in through her window when she wanted to sleep in, so she'd covered it with foil, topped that with duct tape, and finished with a black satin roman shade that hid the ugly mess.

Feeling a bit more confident that no one else was here, I took three quick steps and immediately tripped over something, pitching face first. Luckily, the top half of my body caught the edge of her king-sized bed, but then the satin comforter dumped me to the floor. My hip bone landed first with a thud, and I envisioned the large purple bruise that would show up tomorrow morning. Gravity made sure the rest of my body followed suit.

"Oomph." The noise escaped my mouth when my ribs landed on something hard, yet it gave a little with my weight.

I rolled onto my side. As I pushed to my knees, my hands touched an arm. A stone-cold human arm.

Chapter 4

Shivering uncontrollably, I crab walked backward then fumbled for the light switch by the bedroom door. Bright light flooded the room, and I squinted against the glare. I couldn't control the screams that erupted from my mouth when I saw Tori lying on the floor, with a trickle of blood oozing from her chest and pooled beneath her body. My shrieks echoed in the room, but I couldn't stop them.

The room twirled, and dark spots danced in front of my vision. Afraid of passing out, I slumped down on my hands and knees and angled my head toward the floor. I gagged when I saw the sticky red fluid covering my hands, but at least that stopped the earsplitting noises coming from my mouth.

In a panic, I crawled out of the room, leaving handprints in my wake. I needed to call someone; I needed to get out of there. I switched lights on, found Tori's phone on the coffee table, and dialed 9-1-1 with hands that wouldn't stop shaking. I waited for a dispatcher to answer.

"What's your emergency?"

"There's a body. Tori's been, been…." I couldn't finish my sentence. My teeth chattered together, and I wondered if the dispatcher would consider this a crank call.

"Ma'am? Do you need an ambulance?"

"Yes, yes, send an ambulance." I closed my eyes, knowing an ambulance wouldn't help.

"What's your address, ma'am?"

"Um, um. It's a friend's house. Pine Street in Costa Mesa." The phone almost dropped because I had no idea how to control the shaking going on in my hands and knees. "I can't remember the street number, but there's a Honda Accord and Mini Cooper in the driveway."

"What's the nature of the injuries?"

"Um, she's been…." I gulped air. "I think someone stabbed her. I think Tori is dead!"

My knees finally gave out, and I collapsed onto Tori's sofa, the same sofa where she'd been with my husband just hours before. I didn't want to sit there. I sprang back up and paced.

"Ma'am, ma'am, are you still there?"

"Yes, sorry, I'm here."

"Do you want me to stay on the line with you until the police arrive?"

Police? Oh no. I needed to call Philip. He was going to kill me.

"No. I'll wait outside for them to show up."

As soon as the emergency dispatcher disconnected, I called Philip's cell phone.

"Babe, I told you not to call me." Philip's low voice filled the phone. "It's over. There's nothing left to talk about."

I took the phone away from my ear and looked at it. How did he know it was me? I was using Tori's phone. Could there have been trouble in paradise and he had broken up with Tori?

"Philip, it's Emory." It would have been easier to get mad and yell at him than to envision the body in the next room. On the other hand, I understood that I probably shouldn't piss him off because, as my shock wore off, I realized I needed his help. With Tori's blood all over me, I knew the authorities would suspect me.

"Why are you on Tori's phone?" I pictured his thick black eyebrows pulled into a V-shape.

"Philip, you need to come over right now." My voice quivered, and tears leaked from my eyes. "Something terrible's happened to Tori, and I need your help."

"What are you talking about? What happened?" His cop voice took over—in charge, in command of his wife, who sounded on the verge of falling apart.

"There's blood all over her chest, but I swear I didn't do it." My voice turned into a wail. "I need you."

The piercing scream of sirens came down the street, and flashing red and blue lights pulsated through the living room windows.

"The ambulance and police are here. Just come. Please?"

Philip's own siren screeched to life. "I'll be there in a few minutes."

The cacophony of police, ambulance, and paramedic sirens split the air. Strobes of red and blue lights oscillating in the darkness overwhelmed me as I stepped outside and made my way to the sidewalk. The sudden onslaught of emergency personnel carried me in their wake, back into the house, and I found myself once again sitting on Tori's sofa.

"Miss, where are you hurt?" A young mustached man in a white uniform squatted in front of me, studying my face. He shivered when his eyes strayed to the blood covering my hands and clothes.

My sour mouth dried up, and I pointed toward the bedroom. "It's not me. It's Tori."

A police officer, one I vaguely remembered being introduced to at some long-ago Christmas party, replaced the white uniform. "Can you tell me what happened, ma'am?"

"I don't know. Tori was just lying there." My sticky red

hands caught my attention, and I grimaced. "I tripped and fell on top of her arm. I didn't know she was...."

"What's your name?" He had inched away from me. "What's your relationship to the deceased?"

"Philip!" I jumped up from the sofa and rushed to him, my arms held wide. "I didn't do it. I swear."

He frowned but didn't push my hug away, so I rested my head on his chest. I clasped my hands behind his back and held on tight. Hoping I'd wake up to find this was only a nightmare, I wanted to be wrapped in his arms and embraced. Except, as I hugged him, I felt how soft he'd gotten around the middle. How had I not noticed that before? How long had it been since we'd been this close?

"Mrs. Martinez? I guess I didn't recognize you." The officer scratched his head and looked toward Tori's room then back at Philip. "Um, I'll go check on the status of the crime scene techs. You'd better not touch anything else."

Philip stepped away from me and examined my blood-stained clothes and hands. "What the heck happened? What did you do?"

"I didn't do anything. I just found her." Everyone's assumption that I had something to do with Tori's demise terrified me.

"What are you doing here? You should have left things alone." His voice, low and angry, buzzed in my ear.

I realized he didn't want anyone to hear about his affair with Tori. I stepped away from my husband, afraid. What if he told people I killed Tori? He witnessed my fight with her and heard my threats. Would he blame me?

I shook my head and tried to settle all the thoughts swirling around in there. Despite what I'd seen this morning, I was having a hard time reconciling her betrayal with the vivacious Tori who, only yesterday, made me laugh when she brought me an early birthday gift in my office. It had tickled me, watching the young statistic-analyst guys in my accounting department pop their heads above their short walls when she entered the room. They reminded me of prairie dogs as she sauntered like a catwalk model, her curvy hips swaying in her tiny, low-cut blue jeans. Her wavy platinum-blonde hair bounced against her shoulders, keeping rhythm with her impressive chest jammed tight into a tiny hot-pink sequined T-shirt. She created a bobble-head effect on the guys watching her. Long after she'd left the room, her signature honeysuckle scent lingered on the air-conditioning-generated breeze, reminding those boys of her presence.

She captivated everyone who came across her path, and while women might want to envy her, Tori managed to make them friends instead. Including me, despite our differences. Physically, I was the exact opposite of Tori, with my frizzy red hair and short stature. I was chubby, thanks to my sampling the goodies I loved to bake, yet my chest remained flat. My clothes were comfortably conservative, and I wore flat shoes instead of the colorful ensembles and stilettos Tori favored. What mattered was our common interests. We enjoyed the same kinds of music, movies, books, and food. Tori's devil-may-care attitude about life balanced my overly cautious outlook. Now she was gone. Forever.

"Officer Martinez, what do you think you're doing here?" A deep voice, sounding like the owner chewed gravel for breakfast, barked right behind me, and I jumped.

"Captain Newman. My wife is the one who found the body." Philip edged a bit farther from me, looked at the floor, then shook his head when he noticed Tori's blood on his uniform. "I came as soon as she called me."

"Captain?" a uniform called from Tori's room. "You've got to see this."

"Martinez, I trust I don't have to tell you not to touch anything." He nodded toward me. "You either."

I looked at my husband, whose chocolate-brown eyes

glared at me. "Why did you get me in such a mess, Em? Why couldn't you have left things alone?"

"You're insinuating I did this?" I stamped my foot, my anger getting harder to contain. My voice rose an octave. "You realize you're the one who started it, you idiot."

"Officer and Mrs. Martinez," the gravelly voice boomed across the room, "there's something you need to see in here."

I didn't want to go back into Tori's room, and I really didn't want to see her body again. Philip must have sensed my reluctance because he placed his hand on my lower back and propelled me down the hallway toward the room of death.

I told myself not to look at the body, but my eyes betrayed me. Tori looked like she'd been ready to go clubbing. Hiked up, her short leather miniskirt allowed a glimpse of lacy red panties. Black Manolo Blahnik stilettos were strapped to her feet, and her painted toes played peek-a-boo out of them. Perhaps the killer had surprised her while she was getting ready for an evening out—on her upper body, she only wore a plunging lacy red bra that didn't hide the gash in the top part of her torso.

"Oh no," Philip groaned.

I turned to comfort him, despite his betrayal. I knew it was a shock to see someone you cared about lying with her life snuffed out. But instead of looking at Tori's body, he fixed his gaze on Tori's large screen computer monitor.

There I was, black lace bra and all, with Randall's lips planted on my neck, in living color.

"You've got some explaining to do, Mrs. Martinez," barked Captain Frank Newman.

"It's Philip and Tori's fault. If they hadn't had an affair"—I paused and gulped air—"none of this would have happened."

A muffled moan sounded behind me. I turned to find the noise. Officer Amy Doyle stood there, glaring at Philip. Her short, curly brown hair shook back and forth, while her lips pressed tightly together. Her hands, bleached white from gripping her water bottle so tightly, quivered. Moisture glittered in her almost-black eyes. Maybe the lighting made me think it could be tears. I glanced over at Philip, who looked like a deer caught in headlights. His normally olive-toned skin turned pale, drained of color. Amy stomped from the room. Had something been going on between them after all?

The captain's barking orders made me turn back toward Tori, and then his rough hands gripped my arm.

"Emory Martinez, you are under arrest for the murder of Tori Carlton. You have the right to remain silent…."

Chapter 5

I stopped listening to the rest of my Miranda Rights. My mind buzzed, trying to make sense of it all. Who had killed Tori, and why was I being set up for it? I allowed myself to be led to the captain's car and placed gently in the back seat. He retrieved a silver Mylar blanket from the trunk and placed it over my lap, tucking it around my quivering legs.

"Officer Martinez, I suggest you stay away from this crime scene and take the night off. Be in my office at eight sharp tomorrow morning."

"Yes, sir." My husband's voice sounded low and mournful.

I tried to get Philip's attention, but he wouldn't look at me. I wanted to make sure he took care of Piper but couldn't get the words out. Instead, my husband turned his back on me and walked away. His head hung low, and his feet scuffed the sidewalk while he walked to his patrol car. Amy sat in his passenger seat, her nose buried in a wad of tissues.

That lying son-of-a-you-know-what would get everything he deserved for cheating on me with not one but two women. At least I hoped he didn't cheat with more than two women. How could I have been so blind? Captain Newman drove, but all I noticed was how blurry the streetlights were and how quiet the evening had become.

"Young lady, I didn't want to arrest you." He ran a hand through thin graying hair. "What a mess."

"I'm sorry, sir." Tears stung my eyes. "I didn't kill her. Please believe me."

A heavy sigh came from the front seat. "I know. But you were getting ready to incriminate yourself back there, and I had to get you away before you said anything stupid."

"I didn't mean to, Frank." My hands shook, so I squeezed them together. "The shock kind of made my mouth run on its own."

"I'm not going to lie. This looks bad, and I shouldn't be helping you. My retirement is in five months, and this might blow up in my face." Captain Newman cleared his throat, which did nothing to help his rough, gravelly voice. He fumbled with the volume on his scanner. "As soon as we get to the station, call your parents and have Lars get the best lawyer he knows. Say nothing until they show up, and please don't say a word about my advice. Do I make myself clear, young lady?"

"Yes, sir." I shivered.

Mother was going to kill me, and Lars would be pretty angry too. They played golf with Captain Frank Newman and his wife several times a month, and everyone at their country club would find out he had arrested me for murder.

I had even made his silver wedding anniversary cake four months ago. It was a five-tier chocolate cake with white chocolate and Oreo cookie filling. I had covered four tiers with wedding white fondant and accented the middle tier with lilac-colored fondant billows. It was my first try at making gum paste flowers, and I had to say my pale-pink anemone flowers turned out perfect. I was at the anniversary party serving all one hundred and fifty of his guests, so everyone knew me. To say this might blow up in his face was an understatement.

Once we reached the police station, Captain Newman had the desk officer take photos of my hands and clothing and then allowed me to visit the ladies' room to wash up. Three rounds of soap and scorching-hot water later, my hands felt somewhat clean, although what I really needed was a stiff brush to get the rusty-brown gunk out from beneath my fingernails.

My reflection in the mirror looked as bad as I felt. My hair had partially escaped the ponytail I had pulled it into while working on the party cake and looked frizzier than normal. Dark bags sat beneath my eyes, and the whites of my eyes looked like small red arteries on a road map. I tried to tame my hair with water and secure it in the scrunchie again. That effort didn't help much. I thought about trying to rinse some of the blood out of my favorite pink T-shirt, which had a cartoony cake silk-screened on the front, but I decided I would never wear this shirt again. It was destined for the trash can if I ever made it back home.

I stepped out of the bathroom, and the captain led me to his office. His rubber-soled shoes squeaked beneath his lumbering gait on the graying linoleum flooring that covered the hallway. He apologized for the mess as he removed stacks of Australia and New Zealand travel books from the burgundy-tufted upholstered chair sitting opposite his leather executive chair. Even though the wood desk was small, his office felt crowded. He placed his phone in front of me.

"I'll give you a moment while I start the paperwork I've got to fill out." Captain Newman paused, his liver-spotted hand resting on the doorknob. "Open the door when you've finished your call."

Once I could no longer hear his squeaky footsteps, I picked the receiver up and made the hardest phone call of my life.

"Hello?" My mother answered after the first ring, sounding groggy.

I glanced at the clock hanging on the military beige-painted wall and noticed plaster chipping in places. It was ten forty-five already? That explained why she sounded groggy.

"Hello? Is anyone there?" My mother sounded impatient.

"It's Emory. Can I talk to Lars?"

"What's wrong? Please tell me you got that… that picture down." My mom's voice got louder. "I spent half the night waiting for you to text me. Why are you only now returning my phone calls?"

I rolled my eyes. A little over two hours had passed since I'd left her at my house to go visit Tori. She was really trying to pour on the guilt. "Can I talk to Lars? Please?"

"Young lady, don't you take that tone with me. What's going on?"

Oh lord, I didn't want to be the one to tell my mother. Much better to have Lars gently explain my predicament to her.

"Um, I need an attorney." The bile in my throat threatened to choke me. "I've been arrested for murder."

Too late, I pulled the phone away from my ear when her shriek blasted my eardrums.

"Emory, what did you say to your mother? She looks like she's going to pass out." Lars was generally soft-spoken, but he now had panic in his voice.

"I'm so sorry to bother you, but can you get an attorney for me? I've been arrested for murder."

A sharp intake of air followed by a slow exhale filled the phone. "Where are you now?"

"Costa Mesa. Captain Newman has me sitting in his office."

"Okay. I'll call Mel Shearwood. He's a good criminal defense attorney, and I went to law school with him. We still play golf every now and then." He covered the speaker and mumbled something to my mother before getting back on the phone. "Hang tight, kiddo. We'll be there as soon as we can."

I opened the door as Captain Newman had requested and sat back down to wait, this time in a visitor's chair.

Shortly thereafter, he came back in and set a cup of hot tea in front of me. "Are they on their way?"

I nodded my head as I blew on the tea to cool it. "He's bringing Mel Shearwood."

"Good choice." He sat behind his desk and swiveled his chair back and forth while seeming to study the photographs of himself and local dignitaries hanging on the wall. "I spoke with District Attorney McMann. He agrees with me, and we won't charge you at this time."

A sigh of relief escaped my lips. "Thank you. Someone set me up, and Philip was cheating…."

"Enough, young lady." The captain held up his hand, palm facing me. "Didn't I tell you to not say a peep until your attorney arrives?"

"Yes, but you're not charging me. I thought I should explain what happened so you can catch who killed Tori." I scowled. Didn't they want to catch the murderer?

He locked his hazel-colored gaze onto my muddy green eyes and over-enunciated every word. "You are the number-one suspect. Do I make myself clear?"

"Yes, sir." Oh boy. This wasn't going the way I thought it would when he said I wouldn't be charged.

"Wait here and finish your tea. I'll send Lars and Mel in when they get here." Captain Newman stood abruptly and left the room. I suspected he was making sure I wouldn't accidentally incriminate myself again.

It seemed like I had waited forever, with nothing to do but browse through the captain's retirement travel brochures, when my stepdad finally poked his head into the office. When he stepped into the room, I jumped up from my chair and hugged him. The wrinkles around his light-blue eyes were deeply creased, and his tan skin made his white hair seem even more vivid. He said he looked much older than his sixty-five years because he spent a lot of time on the golf course before anyone knew about sunscreen. Even though it was close to eleven thirty, he still dressed in carefully pressed khaki slacks and a wrinkle-free golf polo.

"Emory, this is Mel Shearwood. He was kind enough to meet with us on such short notice."

Mel stepped around Lars and held out his hand, which I shook. He was a head shorter than my stepdad, bald, and in serious need of a shave. A thick gray five-o'clock shadow covered the lower part of his face, while bushy gray eyebrows perched over his pale-blue eyes. His skin was leathery, and he also looked like he spent a lot of time in the sun. Unlike sharply dressed Lars, Mel had hastily dressed in a wrinkled river bar T-shirt that stretched tight over his large belly, faded blue jeans, and flip-flops. I tried not to notice he needed to cut his toenails. After all, he was here to help me.

"Mrs. Martinez, you need to change out of your shirt and leave it with the front desk for evidence." Mel scratched his chin. "You'd better get a move on before they change their minds and decide to detain you."

I looked at my bloodstained shirt. "I don't have anything to wear home."

"You can wear one of your mother's shirts. She keeps a change of clothing in the trunk of my SUV just in case."

Of course she did. Addie would never appear in public with as much as a drop of coffee staining any part of her clothing. "Okay, I guess that works."

After changing into my mother's Ann Taylor white crepe cap-sleeved top, which was carefully wrapped in tissue to prevent wrinkles before being stored in Lars's Escalade, I handed Mel my bloody shirt. The stained garment was wrapped tight in a white plastic bag.

"Captain Newman has agreed to give us until Monday at

ten to answer questions." Mel led me to the front of the station.

"But I have to work Monday." It seemed inconceivable to skip work. I never called in sick, and since Philip had started working graveyard shifts three years ago, I had taken no vacations.

"This is more important than crunching numbers, Mrs. Martinez. You must call in sick or take a personal day." He paused and made eye contact with me. "You can plan on spending most of Monday with me. Now, what do you say we stop off at Denny's for a midnight snack and discuss your case?"

The restaurant was only a block from the police station, and it didn't take long for us to make our way to an empty table. I plopped down onto the brown plastic banquette seat, which sank beneath my weight, until my chin practically rested on the table.

"Are you ready to order?" The waitress sounded tired and more than a little annoyed. It was just after midnight, and she probably resented us making her work at this ungodly hour.

"I'll take your waffle breakfast, eggs over easy, bacon, and coffee." Mel handed her the menu.

"Nothing for me." Lars handed the plastic-covered menu to the waitress.

"Um." I fiddled with the menu, trying to decide whether I needed to eat or not. I couldn't remember having dinner, aside from a few licks of buttercream and maybe a cookie or two. Or was it three? Plus, I was sure I'd have to pull an all-nighter to get the cake done.

The waitress impatiently tapped her pen on the order form after she smoothed her mousy-brown, limp hair away from her lined face.

"I'll have what he's having." I pointed at Mel. "But make mine scrambled eggs."

As soon as the waitress had shuffled away and out of

hearing distance, Mel leaned in and rested his elbows on the table. "Start at the beginning and tell me everything. Even if you think it's incriminating, you need to tell me up front. I can get pretty pissy if I find out you've omitted anything or tried to cover up something."

"Yes, sir. Before I get started, is there any way you can get a picture removed from my Facebook account? Someone seems to have changed my password and posted a, um, a not-so-nice picture of me."

"It will take some work, but yes, I can do that. Does this picture have anything to do with the case?"

"I'm not sure. But that's why I was at Tori's house. I think she may have posted it."

Mel nodded and took out his cell phone. "I'd better take a look and see what we need to preserve. What's your username?"

"You don't need to see this. I just want it gone."

He cleared his throat and narrowed his eyes until his bushy eyebrows practically touched each other. "Did you not understand what I told you only a moment ago? I get pissy if you try to hide anything from me."

Lars patted my arm. "I promise I won't peek."

"You know about this? Please tell me you haven't seen it."

Lars shook his head. "No, I haven't seen it, nor will your mother tell me what it's about, except that it's making her crazy. I had to promise her I wouldn't get on Facebook until she said it was safe."

I glanced back at Mel, who had his fingers poised over his iPhone. He looked ready to type my name. "Okay, it's Emory Gosser Martinez."

As he entered my name, I covered my face with my hands and rested my head on the table.

"Excuse me, miss." The waitress juggled two cups of coffee and three glasses of iced water and looked for a way to put them on the table without drenching me.

I straightened up and stared at the ceiling.

Mel exhaled noisily. "I hope this is your husband."

"No. That's the problem."

Mel kept his gaze on the tiny screen.

"So… how many likes are there?"

Chapter 6

"Over five thousand."

"Sh… yikes!" I looked at Lars and shrugged. "Oh, sorry. I mean, that's terrible."

"That's probably the right word, since your mother's not here."

"How can there be that many, though? I don't even know that many people."

"The photo was tagged for public viewing, which allowed it to be shared over nine hundred times. That means all those people's friends have it showing up in their news feeds, who then like and share it." Mel finally tore his gaze away from his phone and redirected his eyes to my chest. "I've got a techie who can block the image. We can't permanently delete it since the police will consider this part of their evidence trail."

Upon realizing I was wearing my mother's white blouse over my hot-pink sports bra, I wrapped my arms across my chest, hoping he'd get the hint. "Whatever it takes. I don't want anyone else to see it."

My attorney punched a couple of buttons and put the phone to his ear. His techie's loud voice boomed out of the phone. "Yo, what's up?"

"Kurt, I need you to block a photo from the Facebook account of Emory Gosser Martinez."

The techie mumbled something I didn't quite understand.

"Trust me, you'll know which photo it is. We need it done immediately." After more mumbling from the tech, Mel disconnected and laid his phone onto the table as the waitress placed our waffles in front of us.

"He'll take care of it, but if someone downloads the photo to their hard drive, there's nothing we can do." My attorney took a huge bite of his eggs and then crammed a full piece of bacon into his mouth. He chewed, swallowed, and then put his fork down. "Kurt will reset your Facebook password so you should be able to log back in. Use my last name, Shearwood, all lower case, for the password."

I nodded and hoped no one thought it worthwhile to permanently save my infamous photo.

While my attorney devoured his waffle breakfast, I started from the beginning and told my entire wretched story. Lars appeared uncomfortable and even embarrassed at times, but he didn't interrupt.

I nibbled at my waffle while talking, but the eggs were much too cold to consider eating. "Can you help me?"

"I'll admit it's not looking so great for you, especially since there are witnesses who heard you threatening the deceased and you were at the scene of the crime with evidence all over you." Mel shoveled another bite of waffle topped with egg into his mouth. Yellow yolk dribbled down his chin. "However, I've gotten clients off with worse cases."

"But I'm innocent! Don't you think the police will find the real murderer?"

"You're a very convenient suspect, so, unless there's other evidence left at the crime scene, you'd better be prepared for a hard battle to clear your name." Another huge bite of waffle disappeared into his maw. "It sounds like someone went out of their way to let you take the blame."

It was almost two in the morning when Lars dropped me off at my condo. The streetlights glared in the darkness, and a coyote howled mournfully in the distance. When I opened the front door, I expected Piper to be whining by the door, eager to go out. Instead, even after I called for her, silence greeted me.

Switching on the kitchen lights, I saw Piper's leash missing. I assumed Philip picked her up, but I didn't see a note. His empty closet confirmed he'd stopped here and packed up all of his clothing and toiletries. I briefly wondered where he was staying but then decided I didn't care. Instead, I headed back to the kitchen, started a pot of coffee, and tackled the birthday cake and cupcakes I promised my sister I would finish before the party began at noon today.

I started with the Cowgirl Quencher Mocktail Cupcakes. Since I used a cake mix as the base, these were pretty foolproof and easy to make, despite the list of ingredients. Pineapple juice, peach nectar, orange juice, and coconut extract provided the tropical flavors in the cupcakes. I replicated the flavors with a glaze after they baked, which helped keep the cupcakes moist, and included the same flavors again in the frosting, which provided layers of yumminess. Grenadine and a drop of pink food coloring made the frosting the perfect color for a little girl's birthday party. I would add colorful rainbow sprinkles to the tops of the frosting for this party, but if I made these cupcakes for a tropical-themed party, I might garnish them with slices of pineapple or a colorful paper straw or umbrella.

While the mocktail cupcakes cooled, I started in on the adults-only cupcakes. The flavors were similar, but I swapped in peach schnapps and coconut rum for a little boozy flavor. I wouldn't put pink food coloring into the frosting, nor would I use sprinkles on the adult cupcakes. I needed to keep them looking different from the cupcakes prepared for the children.

By the time six rolled around, my kitchen looked like a

disaster zone. Pink buttercream decorated the cabinets, the walls, and even my hair. All I had needed was a gentle whip to fluff the frosting back up before I piped swirls onto the cupcakes to hold the multicolored sprinkles. Instead, a twirling vortex opened when I accidentally switched the KitchenAid mixer to super-high from a standstill all at once. Then I knocked over an open container of the sprinkles, and they crunched beneath my feet while I frantically tried to finish the cupcakes. I blamed it all on lack of sleep.

For once, I was glad I didn't have Piper underfoot. She often came wandering into the kitchen when I baked and licked up the crumbs and frosting that found their way onto the floor. With this mess, she would've needed to be crated so she wouldn't get sick from being a doggie vacuum cleaner. She was one of the reasons I didn't sell my cakes. I would never pass inspection for a business license. So, instead, I gave my cakes and cupcakes as gifts to friends and family while building up a portfolio and turned down requests from those who wanted to hire my services. If I wanted to go into business full-time, I needed to find a bakery, and realistically, we didn't have the money for that, thanks to my husband.

Philip was adamant about buying our Huntington Beach condo three years ago, located just a few blocks from the beach. The down payment wiped out our savings, and between the two of us working full-time, we made the mortgage payments with just enough left over for other moderate bills. As an accountant, I should have known better, but Philip was very persuasive, and I caved. It seemed like we were always short of money. I cringed as I remembered our many arguments over Philip wanting to buy the latest and greatest gadget and my attempts to be the voice of reason. How would we manage financially when our marriage ended? I didn't want to think about it, but a reckoning would come sooner rather than later. His betrayal would never be forgiven.

. . .

AN INCESSANT RINGING and pounding pulled me reluctantly from the deep sleep I had finally given into around seven. I rubbed my eyes and grimaced when I realized it was already ten thirty. Carrie would be angry I wasn't ready to go. She lived by her schedule and wouldn't appreciate my tardiness.

I shuffled to the door and opened it. Before Carrie could give me a piece of her mind, I cut her off. "Give me five minutes, and I promise I'll be ready."

"Fine, but put a bandana over that thing on your neck. I can't have you around the kids looking like that." Carrie looked me up and down and exhaled in resignation. "You have pink frosting in your hair."

I reached up and tried to feel for the sticky mess, wondering if I could find time to wash my hair.

She breezed past me and started loading up the cake I had barely finished a few hours before. "Come on, Em. Get a move on. Mom told me a little about your night, so I've got a triple-shot latte in the van for you."

"You're a lifesaver. I was wondering how I would get through this party without falling asleep on my feet." My blurry eyes stung, and I tried to rub the sleep out of them with the palms of my hands. My hands started shaking when I remembered the blood that had covered them. I needed to shove all thoughts of finding Tori the night before out of my head. There would be plenty of time for that later, but for now, I had a party to cater.

While I crammed my body into too-tight blue jeans and a short-sleeved red plaid western-looking shirt, I hunted in my bureau for a bandana. I tied it around my neck and tried to strategically position the knot to cover the red mark. The glint of my gold wedding band sitting on my ring finger caught my eye. I tugged the ring off, threw it into a drawer, and decided I'd throw it off the end of the pier the next time I walked to the beach. Satisfied with my decision, I brushed the tangles from my hair the best I could, grabbed a scrunchie, and twisted my hair into a messy bun. After shoving concealer and mascara into my purse, I picked up my decorating tool box, along with extra frosting and gum paste decorations. I always took them with me in case the cake needed minor repairs after the drive.

Carrie was sitting in her van with the engine running. I looked back and saw my cake already in the cargo area, as far away as possible from anything that might fall onto it or bump it.

"How did you get that heavy cake in here all by yourself?"

She said nothing and instead drove off before my seat belt was even secure. I sipped on the latte and stared out the window. Brown hills rolled by as we headed south on the 73 toll road. I waited for Carrie to answer me. Instead, I heard blessed silence, except for her fingers tapping on the steering wheel… a sure sign she was mad at me.

"Carrie, it wasn't my fault." I gulped the latte, waiting for her response, but there was nothing except more silence. Uh-oh. This wasn't good.

"I mean, I didn't know Philip was having an affair, and I would never have thought Tori would stab me in the back like that…" I shuddered when I realized my bad choice of words. "You have to believe I'm innocent. I didn't kill Tori!"

Carrie let out a long sigh and shook her head back and forth. "Mother called me at five this morning, waking up the twins. Do you know what it's like dealing with her when she's having a meltdown over your situation? On top of dealing with twins who are demanding breakfast? And needing to get organized for this party?"

The van sounded extra-quiet once my sister stopped screeching at me. She clamped her lips together so tightly they started to turn white.

"You should have told Mother to call me instead." To be honest, I was very glad she hadn't.

Carrie rolled her eyes. "And risk you not being able to finish the cake?"

"How did you…?" Of course she knew. I think she understood me better than I did myself.

"I don't understand how you find yourself in situations like this. Trouble always seems to find you."

Okay, that was an exaggeration… kind of. One time in high school, I tripped over a huge canned goods display at the supermarket, and the entire thing came crashing down. The manager claimed I did it on purpose and called the police. Even reviewing the store's video footage didn't exactly exonerate me, but Lars somehow managed to get me off the hook. Seriously, it was an accident. But things like that happened to me more often than I liked, and they never happened to my sister.

I glanced back at the cake and yelped. "Pull over, Carrie. It's going to fall!"

Chapter 7

"What?" Despite not knowing what could be wrong, Carrie slowed the vehicle and steered the vehicle toward the right shoulder.

"The cake. It's leaning over!" I whimpered when I envisioned all my hard work collapsing into one sticky, crumbly mess.

As soon as the van came to a complete stop, I jumped out, ran to the back, threw open the doors, and surveyed my cake. I apparently missed the mark on my first attempt at a topsy-turvy design. Even though I had studied several YouTube videos on how to do it, I hadn't figured out how to keep the cake stable. Now it tilted at a decidedly unplanned angle, ready to topple over.

"What frosting did you use between the layers?" My sister stood right behind me.

"My normal fluffy buttercream." That buttercream tasted light and airy, unlike the heavier, cloying sweet versions favored by bakeries. My clients loved it.

"I think that's the problem. It's too hot, and the frosting isn't firm enough to hold up the weight of the cake on top of the heat."

I sighed. She was right. With everything involving Philip and Tori going on, I didn't think about the supporting structure for the cake design.

"I'll sit in the back with the cake and try to keep it steady while you drive." I climbed in and tried to squeeze myself between several food bins. "If we put it in the fridge when we get there, I can cover up the sags with more decorations. Maybe it will hold up until we serve it."

"I hope you're right." Carrie shook her head and grimaced. "I'm glad we're not charging anything for the cake. It would be embarrassing."

I scowled but said nothing. Despite the near accident, I could repair the cake, and no one would be the wiser… I hoped.

Carrie climbed back into the driver's seat, cranked her air-conditioning to as high as it would go, and carefully pulled into traffic. I found a stack of napkins and wedged them beneath a corner of the cake board to raise it so the cake would be more level. With a napkin in each hand, I steadied the top layer to keep it from sliding even more, but the heat of my hands made the fondant soften until indentations marred the surface where my fingers touched. I hoped I had enough extra decorations with me.

The party was being held at a therapy riding stable for one of the little girls who rode there each week. Alina Hansen, turning seven, loved horses, so Carrie planned a western-themed party. Not only was there a barbecue with a horse-themed cake, my sister had finagled a country-western band into donating an hour of their time to play for the party.

When we pulled into the parking lot, my sister backed up to the loading dock space, and we jumped out to unload. An older man, who looked to be in his late seventies, ambled our way. Dressed in a red western-style shirt, blue jeans, and highly decorative cowboy boots, he was the epitome of a cowboy.

"Howdy, ladies." The white handlebar-mustached man offered us his hand to shake when he reached us. "I'm Bill, and I've volunteered to help you unload and set up. Can you show me what you'd like me to start with?"

My sister and I eyed his thin limbs and somewhat unstable walk. I didn't want him getting anywhere close to the cake I had worked so many hours on, especially given its precarious state. Carrie gave me a quick look, thanked Bill for his help, and handed over plastic sacks that contained tortilla chips and plastic- and paperware. While the elderly man tottered off, my sister grabbed the edge of the heavy cake board and slid it toward me.

"Let's get the cake into the refrigerator, and then I'll try to find the light stuff for Bill to help carry in."

"Thanks. I was worried he would want to help with the cake, and I could envision what might happen if he lost his balance."

With the heavy cake board between us, we crab walked through the party room and made our way to the kitchen, which, fortunately for us, wasn't very far from where we parked.

The party room was already decorated with pink gingham covering each table. Mason jars filled with pink and white daisies and garnished with straw raffia bows dotted the room. Hot pink and white balloons floated in bunches, secured by horse-shaped wood carvings. The buffet table boasted a pink gingham tablecloth while a couple bales of hay bookended the fabric-covered slab of wood. A large wagon wheel sat at the center of the table, with raffia and daisies woven through the spokes. Pink bedazzled cowgirl boots were placed next to the wheel, along with a chalkboard menu of our food offerings written in an old-fashioned font. Alina's mom and her friends had gone all out for this party.

After getting the cake stashed into the walk-in refrigerator, we hustled back to Carrie's van. I grabbed the cupcakes while

Carrie collected a large ice chest to take to the kitchen. Apparently, Bill had picked up several more bags from the back of the van.

The cupcakes in the party room were arranged on wagon-wheel-shaped stands. I added more colorful sprinkles to the kids' cupcakes and then spread a large handful on the table below the stands for decoration. I made sure to carefully label the adults-only Cowgirl Colada Cocktail Cupcakes. Coconut and pineapple flavors mingled in the little cakes, while peach schnapps and peach nectar added a zing of sweetness. Even though the grown-up version appeared somewhat plain without the colorful sprinkles, they still looked delicious with the rosette tip I used to pipe the buttercream frosting. I took plenty of photos of the cupcakes and the decorated table to download to my digital portfolio. Eventually I would have the photos professionally edited and printed for a book to show prospective clients.

I fetched the serving container of the matching Cowgirl Colada Cocktails and placed it on a tall table, along with the cocktail cupcakes. That arrangement made them difficult for little hands to reach accidentally. I made sure the label "Adults Only" was prominently displayed. Carrie and I kept an eagle eye on the table so underage guests couldn't help themselves.

One of our catering secrets was after mixing up large amounts of nonalcoholic drinks for parties, I always froze a couple of large blocks of the mixture to use instead of ice to keep the drink chilled. We could then add alcohol to the remaining mixture for an adult party or leave as is for a children's party. That way the drink could sit out as long as necessary without being diluted with melting ice.

Bill ambled into the party room and admired the table. "Anything else I can do for you gals?"

"If you don't mind, would you be able to keep your eye on the adults-only cupcakes and cocktails?" I pointed at the separate table. "Even though guests aren't here yet, I don't want a child to wander in and help themselves."

"No problem, ma'am." He settled down in one of the chairs dotting the room and pulled out his cell phone. "I've got arthritis in my knees, so it'll be good to rest them for a while."

"It's nice of you to volunteer and help us out, especially if you're in pain." I walked over to the cupcake tower and plucked a cupcake from the stand. "Can I offer you a cupcake and a cup of coffee while you're sitting here?"

"That's mighty nice of you, but I'll wait until after lunch." Bill held his phone up. "My grandson loaded a new book on that Kindle thing and showed me how to read on this phone. What'll they think of next?"

After I left Bill to guard the cupcakes and read his book, I entered the walk-in refrigerator and worked on making the topsy-turvy horse-themed cake presentable. The short time under refrigeration had helped firm it up, and I inserted three dowels for extra support. I hoped it would keep the cake from completely toppling over. A few extra pink gum-paste cowgirl boots and pink-and-brown paisleys covered up the indentations and minor cracks. After taking photos of the cake with my cell phone, I followed the smells of smoked barbecued ribs to help Carrie prepare the food.

"What do you want me to do?" I asked my sister, who frantically opened containers of her famous Rootin' Tootin' Potluck Beans and dumped them into a huge soup pot.

"You can finish filling up the pot and heat the beans for me. I've got to find out where to turn on the air-conditioning in here. This heat is making me melt."

My sister's face looked beet red, and a sheen of moisture dotted her forehead. I reached out and touched her cheek. "It's not that hot. You're not getting sick, are you?"

"Bite your tongue. I can't afford to be getting sick. It's just hot in here, is all." She was already halfway to the door.

I plucked more containers out of the ice chest sitting on the floor. Then I opened and added the beans to the halfway-full pot then turned the flame to medium heat.

"Be sure to stir the beans. You'd better not let the bottom of the pot burn." Carrie must have thought she needed to remind me, since she'd returned to the kitchen without starting the air-conditioning.

I sighed but ignored her comment. After spending so much time helping Carrie with her catering, I knew what to do without her telling me. Since Philip usually worked on the weekends, catering was a good way for me to make a little extra money and gain experience. She even helped cover the costs of the ingredients I used for the cakes and cupcakes I provided. Because the kitchen was unlicensed, I couldn't sell the baked goods, so we told Carrie's clients it was our birthday gift or anniversary gift to them. While my labor for creating the cakes and cupcakes was essentially free, I looked at it as a great opportunity to build up my portfolio. When I finally had the chance to open my bakery, I'd have lots of photos, recipes, and expertise for my clients.

When the beans reached a simmer, I turned the flame down to low and covered the pot. Next, I unpacked Grannie's Colonial Coleslaw, placed it in decorative serving bowls, and put Mama's Cornbread Muffins and my Cowgirl Cookies into large baskets lined with pink and white gingham napkins. Carrie had the air-conditioning on full chill, which wouldn't be a bad thing by the time we had the ovens cranked on and the cooktop simmered pots of food.

"It looks like the band just got here. Go show them where we want them to set up and make sure they can find the electrical outlets." Carrie pointed out the window toward a white van.

We had toured the stable facility several times while planning this party. We wanted to be sure we knew where everything needed to be set up so the event flowed smoothly. I walked to the covered picnic area, which had a small stage set to one side. The band's van had backed into the parking space close to the gate that led to the picnic area. A man, bent over at the waist, was fumbling with mounds of equipment in the cargo area of the van. I noticed the backside of his blue jeans fit just right, and though he wore a plaid cowboy shirt, you could tell he had a V-shaped torso. Even if this band wasn't any good, I would at least enjoy watching them.

"Excuse me." I tapped the cowboy on the shoulder. "I can show you where to set up your equipment and where the electrical outlets are located."

The cowboy turned around. My heart dropped as I stared into his deep sapphire-blue eyes.

Chapter 8

"Emory! What are you doing here?"

Randall…. What in the heck was he doing here? My mouth refused to talk, and I was sure it hung open like a fish gasping for air as I bent my neck backward to look at him. I should have been angry he had taken part in the compromising photo Tori had posted. But somehow, as I peered into those sapphire-blue eyes, my irritation was replaced with an unexpected attraction. I wished I could remember what it had been like to kiss him.

"Are you okay?" His eyes darted to the handkerchief tied around my neck.

I finally stuttered as if I had no control. "Um, um…yeah, I'm okay, okay?"

He looked at me like I should be saying something more than "okay," but my mind was still whirling, and I wasn't ready to talk to him, especially after what happened between us last Friday night. Oh my god, Tori! Tori is—or was—his cousin. Shouldn't he be in mourning instead of playing at the party?

"What are you doing here?" His eyes flashed again to my handkerchief.

I noticed that he also had a bandana tied around his neck. I hoped he wasn't wearing it for the same reason I was.

I licked my lips. "My sister is the caterer for the party, so I help out when I can. I'm the one who made the birthday cake and cupcakes, so be sure to give them a taste."

I mentally slapped my forehead, wondering why I had to tell him that. Why was I letting this man rattle me so much?

"Cool," he answered in a voice that was anything but cool. In fact, it was hot... smokin' hot.

My sister stood at the corner of the building, frantically waving at me. I turned to Randall, tried not to stare at the handkerchief tied around his neck, and instead focused on his close-cropped chestnut-colored hair. I wondered if he had been in the military. "The band can set up over there by the picnic tables. You'll find plenty of electrical outlets if you need them. I'm really sorry about Tori. Please know it wasn't my fault."

Randall looked at me like I was out of my mind. "What?"

I glanced back at Carrie, and even from a distance away, I saw she had gone pale. She waved at me again, in the manner of telling someone to hurry.

"I need to go help my sister with the food. Truly, I'm sorry about Tori."

He glanced another time at my neck. "We need to talk. Can we get together after the party?"

"Um, I don't think that will work. I have to help my sister clean up, and then my job is to go home with her and do all the dishes. It's going to be a late night. Let me give you my phone number, and you can call me tomorrow."

A Cheshire-cat grin appeared on his face as he rolled up a sleeve on his plaid cowboy shirt. He thrust his forearm in front of my face, and I almost fainted. In hot-pink, bold Sharpie, someone had written my phone number accompanied by the words, *For a good time call Em xoxo!*

"I didn't write that," I choked out.

Carrie waved even more frantically.

"But that is my phone number, so call me. I've gotta go help my sister."

I didn't give Randall the chance to respond and instead hurried away toward my sister. She wasn't looking so good. Her pale skin looked a little green, and sweat droplets beaded on her forehead.

"Carrie, you're sick!"

"You'll have to run this party without me. I need to get home, but Thomas will be here in a while to help you."

"Please don't tell me you have the flu." My mind was going a mile a minute, thinking of everything that needed to be done. "What about the food? Is it safe?"

My sister's skin turned even greener, and tears gathered in the corners of her eyes. "It's perfectly safe. It's not the flu."

"Well, what's wrong? Are you contagious?"

"I sure hope not." A small smile played at the corners of her perfectly glossed lips.

"What?" I peered into her face. "What aren't you telling me?"

"Nothing."

"Liar." I poked her in the arm. "I've seen this color on you before. You're pregnant."

Carrie practically beamed. "But you can't let Mother know you found out before she did. Promise?"

"I can be quiet for a price." I giggled, but inside I panicked when I thought of everything that I had to do. "Go home and rest. I'm sure I can handle this."

I glanced back and watched Randall walk around the band's stage.

"He's one fine-looking man, isn't he?" Carrie whispered in my ear. "Don't forget your marriage is ending. Doesn't hurt to look around now. Especially at a guy who's willing to volunteer at a party for a little girl he's never met."

My mouth fell open. I'd never heard my sister talk like this before. Must be the pregnancy hormones. "Um, I'm not sure how to break the news to you, but that's Randall… Tori's cousin."

"OMG! How? Why? Shouldn't he be home in mourning or something?"

I felt a sudden chill. Randall had acted surprised when I expressed sympathy over Tori's death. "I don't think the poor man knows about Tori. What should I do? I can't be the one to tell him. Don't you think Tori's mom would have called him?"

"Maybe the poor woman is too distraught to make calls yet." Carrie groaned. "I need to get out of here before I cause a scene. This morning sickness had better not last as long as it did with the twins."

After I hugged my sister goodbye, I went back to the kitchen. I dished up platters of heated baked jalapeño poppers and bowls of Cowgirl Caviar. With Carrie out of the picture, I decided we would serve the appetizers on the table with the rest of the food.

Thomas came as promised, his pudgy body dressed in tight Wrangler jeans and a blue plaid shirt that brought out the blue in his eyes. His cowboy hat was perched tight around his moon-shaped head, and his dark-blond hair curled at the edges, where it brushed the tops of his ears. We quickly placed bowls of Mouthwaterin' Melon, Campfire Corn on the Cob, and the last chafing dishes filled with Git Along Little Hot Doggies, Wagon Wheels Mac & Cheese, and barbecued ribs on the long serving table. After we centered the birthday cake on the cake table, I took more photos, and the party guests arrived. I smoothed my hair and went out to the party room to greet them, wishing all the while I had thought to put on some lipstick and comb my unruly hair.

Alina and her mom, Madison, were the first to arrive. Alina's hot-pink wheelchair was decked out with balloons and wrapped with sparkly tulle. A glittery crown sat on the birthday girl's shiny black curls, and her sparkling brown eyes, framed with the longest lashes I'd ever seen, scanned the room. A huge smile lit up her face when she saw her birthday cake.

"Happy birthday, Alina!" I bent down and gave the slight girl a hug. "I love your cowgirl shirt and boots."

She turned her beaming face at me, clearly happy with her hot-pink paisley cowgirl shirt and blinged-out matching cowgirl boots. Her jean shorts had miniature pink horses embroidered around the hemline.

"You've outdone yourself, Emory," Madison gushed. "The cake is fantastic. It's too pretty to cut into, though."

"I took lots of photos, so don't feel bad. Let me know when you want to serve lunch, and I'll get you and Alina plates."

"You're a doll. Thank you." Madison swiped at her dark-brown eyes. "I'll take Alina to get pictures of the cake and visit the horses for a few minutes. Most everyone should be here soon, so let's serve in about twenty minutes. Will that work for you?"

"Sounds good. We're ready when you are."

It warmed my heart to see Alina's happy expression at the prancing horses decorating her cake. The young girl was nonverbal, one of the many symptoms of Rett Syndrome. However, as I had found out long ago, the eyes were truly the window to your soul and could speak volumes even when your lips couldn't.

I gave Thomas a thumbs-up and then directed arriving guests where to place the birthday girl's gifts. I also answered questions about the cake and the party food. It didn't take long for the fifty guests to arrive and fill the room with their laughter and happy chatter. Some of the small children chased one another around the gingham-covered tables while a few others whined to their parents that they wanted to pet the horses. Several other Rett girls had arrived, each decked out in pinks and purples and each pushed in equally girly wheelchairs.

I was relieved to see Bill had moved his chair right next to the adult-only cupcake stand so he could keep a close watch while the kids zoomed around. I walked over and stood next to him. "As soon as guests go through the chow line, feel free to get a plate of food for yourself. My brother-in-law and I will take turns watching the cupcakes so you don't need to."

"I'm happy to help out, ma'am." Bill pointed at the long table of food. "I'll have to admit my mouth is sure waterin' smelling your cooking. I appreciate the offer."

As soon as Madison and Alina returned and greeted their guests, I grabbed my rustic chow triangle to call everyone to lunch. The clanging metal got everyone's attention. Once the noise level settled, I welcomed everyone to the party.

"I want to wish Alina a very happy birthday and thank all of you for joining her to celebrate." I hated being in front of a crowd and wished my sister were here to do this. "The food will be served buffet style, and there are picnic tables outside with plenty of shade. For the girls using wheelchairs, we have special tables set up for them, so please be considerate and use the picnic tables if you can. I'll start the chow line for Alina, and then I'd like to let her Rett sisters go next. Thanks for coming, everyone."

I jangled my triangle one last time. Then I grabbed two of the heavy-duty disposable plates with hot-pink plasticware wrapped in pink gingham napkins tied with raffia. Thomas had opened the lids on the chafing dishes, and savory smells filled the room. My mouth watered.

I quickly filled the plates and wandered out to the patio, where the picnic tables were. I stopped suddenly when Randall dropped to one knee, in front of Alina. His deep baritone voice sang the birthday song while he held her tiny hand in his dark tanned hand. Alina had the biggest smile on her rosebud lips, and she peeked shyly through her long lashes.

Not only was the man hot, he could sing too. I tried to clear my head of that thought and placed the plates down in front of Madison when he finished the song.

"Thanks, sweetie." Madison gave my hand a squeeze before she tucked a strand of her long, curly black hair behind an ear. "Have you met Randall Burke? He's part of the band that will play for us after lunch."

I tried to avoid looking at Randall, but my gaze was drawn to his mesmerizing blue eyes. "Uh, yes. We met earlier."

"I can't thank both of you enough for making this party so special for Alina." Madison swiped at her eyes again. "Alina says thank you too."

Apparently, Alina couldn't stop looking at Randall either. Her smile was huge, and she swung her bedazzled boots back and forth.

"It's my pleasure, ma'am." He tipped an imaginary hat, winked at Alina, and, much to my chagrin, winked at me. "I'd better go grab a plate of that awesome grub before we play. Thanks for feeding the band, Emory."

With that, he turned and strolled to the banquet room, and my gaze followed those perfectly fitted blue jeans.

"Wow, just wow." Madison fanned her face once Randall moved out of sight.

"Yeah, I know what you mean." My hand touched the knotted handkerchief around my neck. The problem was I had kissed him, and it looked like I had enjoyed it immensely. Unfortunately, I couldn't remember a single darn second of that kiss. It hit me right then that it could have been Randall who drugged me. All along I had assumed a random person at the bar slipped something into my glass of wine while it was waiting for delivery to our table. Until now I'd assumed Tori would have been watching out for me, but what if she left for the restroom and he doctored my drink? How did I know Randall was safe to be around?

Chapter 9

"**A**re you okay, Em?" Madison asked with concern. "You looked like you were spacing out for a minute."

"Sorry. I was going through a mental list about everything I need to do at the end of the party. I don't want to leave anything behind." The lies seemed to be slipping off my tongue much too easily these days.

"Alina and I can't ever thank you enough for the amazing party, especially the birthday cake." Madison fed a small bite of the wheel-shaped macaroni and cheese to her daughter. "You really need to let me pay you for the cake. I can't even imagine how many hours you put into creating it."

I waved her off. "It's my gift to the birthday girl. You're actually doing me a favor and helping me build my portfolio, so I'm happy to do it."

"Oh?" The mother speared a small piece of watermelon and fed it to Alina. "Are you opening a bakery?"

"One of these days. I need to work out some things, but in the meantime, it will be nice to have a portfolio to show prospective clients." At the top of my list of priorities needed to be clearing my name as a murder suspect. I looked up to see Thomas waving at me. "Time go help my brother-in-law, but please let me know if there's anything else you need."

"You've done so much for us already. We'll be fine." Madison stood, gave me a hug, and winked at me. "Well, maybe send that cowboy back on over here for a bit."

I hurried back to the banquet room, where I found Thomas scurrying to freshen up the chafing dishes.

"Sorry about that." I grabbed the container of extra watermelon. "I didn't mean to chat with Madison so long."

"That's okay." He placed more ribs in the silver warming tray. "The band members are heading in. I figure they'll have large appetites, so I want to make sure we're prepared."

I had hoped Randall had already been through the chow line, but as I glanced around the room, I saw him talking with four other men, all dressed in tight blue jeans and blue plaid shirts. Darn! I didn't want to face him yet.

As if he sensed eyes on him, Randall turned his head and gazed right at me. Flustered, I spilled the container of watermelon. Fortunately, most of the fruit stayed on the serving platter, but a few unlucky skewers slid to the floor. Heat flooded my face. Why, oh why, did I let that man get to me?

I picked the skewers up off the floor and headed to the kitchen to dispose of them. My sister was a generous caterer, so I knew we should have plenty. When there were leftovers after a party, Carrie boxed them into individual servings and dropped them off at church, who delivered the food to some of the elderly parishioners living alone. She was thoughtful like that.

When I came back to the banquet room with wet paper towels to wipe the floor, my face heated even more. Randall knelt on one knee, cleaning up the watermelon. Could this get any worse? I wanted to turn around and hide in the kitchen. But, of course, that wasn't possible.

"Thank you. You really didn't have to do that."

"No problem. Accidents happen." He grabbed the wet

paper towels from my hand. "It's the least I can do for getting a free lunch."

"Well, it's not exactly free. You're donating your time to play for the birthday girl."

His rich baritone voice laughed, sending sparks down my spine. "The band is brand new, and we're anxious to play. We need to get some Yelp reviews and word of mouth going."

Yeah, I got it. Kind of like my portfolio. "It's still a nice thing to do."

He stood, tipped his imaginary cowboy hat, and strolled to join his band mates in line for the chow. My eyes drank in the sight.

Someone cleared their throat right next to my ear, making me jump.

I turned and almost screeched when I saw Thomas's flushed red face staring at me. "You don't have to sneak up on me like that."

"I didn't sneak up on you. In fact, I said your name a couple of times, but I guess you didn't hear me."

"Uh, no. Guess my mind was elsewhere."

"Your sister filled me in." Thomas smirked and jerked his head toward Randall. "Can you take over so I can call Carrie and see how she's doing?"

My face heated up again. Great. Why couldn't my sister keep our conversation in confidence? I'd also hoped to sneak out of the room before Randall made his way through the banquet line, but that wasn't going to happen. "Sure. I hope she's better."

"Me too. I'm guessing this morning sickness will run its course like it did with the twins. A couple months of discomfort and then she'll be fine."

I shook my head. Carrie seemed to have experienced more than a little discomfort today, but what did I know? "Don't worry about the food. I've got it covered."

After I checked the chafing dishes and refilled the ones

that were getting low, one of the elderly guests needed my help to take their plate to the seating area. Thomas was standing next to the cupcakes while talking on his cell, so I knew he wouldn't let any little hands swipe a cupcake they shouldn't have. As it worked out, I left the food station just before Randall came through the line. I chatted with several of the guests, and when I saw Randall exit the banquet room, I made my way back to replenish the food. We needed to prepare for the onslaught of people wanting seconds.

I kept myself busy washing out empty containers (I wanted less work to do after the event) and keeping an eye on the food levels. Thomas checked on me a couple of times in between talking to guests and sitting with the birthday girl and her mom. I had forgotten that Carrie and Thomas were friends with Madison from their college days, which explained why my sister had comped so much for this party.

While the band played their toe-tapping music, I went to the door to watch. Randall's band sounded good—really good. Randall not only sang but played the guitar too. Their music seemed a bit like George Strait at times and more contemporary, like Luke Bryan, on other songs. Some of the guests wheeled the birthday girl out onto the makeshift dance floor and danced with her. My eyes got a little misty seeing Alina's smile light up her face as she was surrounded by friends and family to celebrate her special day.

I got Thomas's attention, and he came back to help me place the cake and cupcakes on a rolling cart. The plan was that the band would play three numbers and then we would take the cake out to Alina for her birthday song. While guests ate their cake and ice cream, the band would play for another forty-five minutes.

The cake, which thankfully hadn't toppled yet, was secured in place on the rolling cart with the plates, napkins, and forks stowed on the lower shelf of the cart. I put the ice cream into a specially designed ice chest to keep it from melting too quickly. Dry ice rested inside a secured bottom compartment so no one could accidentally touch it while we served the frozen treat. The moment we finished our preparations, I heard Randall announce that it was time for cake and then immediately launch into the birthday song.

Thomas and I wheeled the cart out to oohhs and aahhs and stopped in front of Alina. She clapped her hands in delight. As soon as the song ended, I cut pieces of cake while Thomas scooped the vanilla ice cream. Randall jumped off the small stage and helped serve the guests who sat in wheelchairs and the elderly who had difficulty getting around. Next, he offered the cocktail cupcakes to adults and brought back a single leftover cupcake, which he ate in two bites. The guy was almost too good to be true. I shook my head and concentrated on the knife in my hand, making sure I didn't hurt myself or Thomas, who stood next to me.

Once the band started on their second set, I began the cleanup. Extra cake got boxed up for guests to take home, the leftover food got placed back in the coolers, and the dishes were washed, all to toe-tapping music. As the party wound down, I wiped off the last table, grateful Thomas hadn't grilled me over whatever Carrie had shared with him. I had almost forgotten the murder, and I preferred to keep it that way for as long as possible. Call me an ostrich, but there was something to be said about ignorance being bliss.

"There you are!" My back was toward the door, and while I recognized the masculine voice, I couldn't place its owner. "Don't you ever answer your cell phone?"

I turned and saw my attorney.

"The police want to talk to you about the murder weapon. Does a silver-plated cake knife with the monogram EMP mean anything to you?"

I became lightheaded, and my head spun. How had my wedding-cake knife ended up being used to kill Tori?

Chapter 10

"Seriously, Emory, don't you understand you need to be available and not flitting off to parties and ignoring your phone?" Mel Shearwood rubbed the white stubble liberally covering his jaws. "You're lucky the police didn't come find you with sirens blaring and haul you off in handcuffs."

"How… where? What do you mean, my knife is the murder weapon?" I shuddered. My sister would be in line to kill me after my mother killed me if I was arrested in front of all these people. "For your information, I'm not flitting around to fun parties. I'm actually working."

He finally saw the dishcloth and antibacterial spray in my hands. "You still need to keep your phone on at all times."

"Sorry. Why do the police think it was my cake knife that killed Tori?"

"For starters, it has your monogram, and Philip confirmed your knife is missing at home."

My head spun again. Philip seemed ready to throw me under the bus, so to speak. "I have no idea how someone could have used my knife. It must be a coincidence. Did they check for fingerprints?"

"They were wiped clean."

"Where did they find it?" I turned to finish the table I had been cleaning. There had to be a mistake. The knife couldn't be mine.

"In a dumpster behind a convenience store a couple blocks from Tori's house." Mel reached over and grabbed the dishcloth from my hand. "I don't think you understand the gravity of the situation. You need to collect your belongings and go for your interview with the investigator right now."

"You mean now, like right this minute?" My voice squeaked. I blamed my foggy, sleep-deprived brain. Of course my attorney wouldn't show up at the party just to check on me. "Coffee. I need coffee before I talk to them."

"Well, get a cup, and let's go."

"First, I need to tell my brother-in-law I'm leaving."

I scurried to the kitchen, grabbed my purse, and headed out to find Thomas but stopped short when Randall walked in.

"Can we talk for a minute?" If he had been wearing a cowboy hat, he would have clutched it between his hands.

"Sorry, I don't have time." When his shoulders drooped, I took pity on him. "Call me tomorrow. Just not early."

I didn't give him a chance to say anything else. Instead, I rushed past him and quickly found Thomas still chatting with Madison and the birthday girl. I whispered my predicament in his ear.

"No problem. I've got it covered." He patted my shoulder. "Call your sister when you can."

"Sure."

I found my attorney waiting—quite impatiently, it appeared, if his tapping foot and his looking at his wristwatch were any indications, by the gate. He ushered me to his running car, and before I latched my seat belt, he gunned the engine and peeled out of the parking lot.

I didn't know what to say to this man who I obviously

annoyed, so, for once, I kept my mouth shut and watched the rolling hills whiz by. All the scenarios of what might happen kept flashing through my brain. Were they going to arrest me? Would my mother post bail? And, oh god, would they force me to wear an orange jumpsuit? It was the color that clashed the worst with my red hair. I checked my voice mail and found three messages from Mel, who sounded increasingly annoyed with each one left, and two from a Detective Jackson. I assumed he was the detective assigned to Tori's case.

Mel didn't turn music or a news station on. What did liking silence say about a person? A few miles from the police station, I couldn't stand the quiet anymore.

"I didn't kill Tori."

"It doesn't matter." He kept his gaze glued to the road. "My job is to keep my client from being charged or get the charge dropped. If that doesn't work, I need to give a jury reasonable doubt so you can get on with your life. In exchange, I get a nice fee that I split between my ex-wives."

Ex-wives? I wondered how many he had.

"But I still want you to know I'm not a killer." I shuddered. I couldn't even watch the slasher movies Philip liked, and I would never forget the sight of all that blood covering Tori.

"Okay, fine. You do realize, though, that's what they all say." He exhaled, like he was sorry he had to take care of my mess. "When we get in there, do not say a word aside from confirming your name and any other identifying questions. Do I make myself clear?"

"Yes, sir." I clamped my lips together, determined not to speak again unless Mel asked me a question.

All too soon an officer escorted us to a drab-looking interview, or as I thought of it, an interrogation room. Beige walls, dirty beige linoleum, and beige plastic chairs. The obligatory two-way mirror lined the far wall. I sat in the chair facing the mirror while my attorney sat to my left. Lights winked in the upper corners above the mirror, while red-and-white signs that read You May Be Recorded hung next to two cameras.

A detective I had never met made his way in and slapped a thick beige folder onto the table next to me. Nerves made my mouth parched, and I licked my lips. He introduced himself as Detective Harper Jackson and appeared to be in his late thirties, with thinning, sandy-blond hair. Although he was clean shaven, his eyebrows were bushy and seemed to encroach on his dark-brown eyes. Thin lips were pressed together in a tight line, like he didn't want to give them a chance to smile. Or perhaps he didn't want to smile at a potential murderer. The detective pulled out the chair across from me and sat down.

After confirming my name, age, and other identifying factors, Detective Jackson opened the file, leaned across the table, and got close to my face. "Tell me what happened Saturday, Mrs. Martinez."

My mouth opened involuntarily to answer when my attorney jabbed my arm.

"Mrs. Martinez has nothing to say," Mel interjected. "Now, if we can discuss what evidence you have to hold her, you might stop wasting my valuable time."

Detective Jackson seemed annoyed but tried not to show it. I watched the two men verbally spar for close to two hours, all the while keeping my mouth closed. Although the murder weapon belonged to me and technically to Philip, no finger-prints or conclusive proof that would convict me had been found. They only had circumstantial evidence I was the killer. The detective tried to get me to explain how strands of my red hair happened to have been on the front window screen, but my attorney cut my reply off with a steely glance. Finally, the detective told us I was free to go but not to leave town. I should have felt more relieved, but instead, I felt terrified they would pigeonhole their facts to convict me.

Once Mel and I were ensconced in his car, he turned and

looked me straight in the eyes. "Now, young lady, suppose you tell me how your wedding cake knife turned into the murder weapon."

"I truly have no idea." I briefly wondered if Philip had killed his lover. He hated to be manipulated, and I began to realize Tori had manipulated both of us. There was no other explanation for what happened with Randall and the photo surfacing on Facebook. Still, I couldn't throw my husband under the bus, so to speak, without any proof.

My attorney's sharp voice pulled me back. "Emory! I need you to focus."

"Sorry. I guess my mind drifted. I didn't get any sleep last night." I rubbed the palms of my hands on my eyes for emphasis. "What did you say?"

"I asked when was the last time you saw your cake knife."

A yawn escaped me. "About four months ago. I made and served a silver anniversary cake for Captain Newman and his wife's celebration."

"Do you remember what happened to it after the event? Did you take the knife home?"

"I honestly don't remember. After the waiters served the cake, Philip brought a bottle of champagne to our table. The rest of the night is kind of fuzzy."

I don't generally overindulge with alcohol. Chocolate, yes! But alcohol wasn't my vice. I remembered wondering why the champagne hit me so hard after I had only a couple of glasses. Had Philip slipped something into my drink so he could take the knife without me remembering?

"Mrs. Martinez, please focus." Mel's face contorted with the effort of trying to contain his anger. "Who helped you clean up?"

"The country club's wait staff boxed up the leftover cake for guests to take home. I'm assuming they put my cake plates and knife into the box I had brought for that purpose."

"But you're not sure?"

"Sorry, that night is really fuzzy."

"Wouldn't you have washed the items and put them away the next morning?"

"Yes, except I had a horrible headache and didn't get out of bed until noon. Philip had everything cleaned up and put away for me." The second the words left my mouth, I paused. Philip never did dishes or helped me with household chores. Why would he have cleaned up the cake plates and knife? Was it possible he had premeditated Tori's murder and then tried to pin it on me?

"You're telling me you have not seen the murder weapon since you served cake to Captain Newman?"

"Yes, that is correct."

"Who else would have had access to the knife in your home?"

"Besides my husband, a lot of people. We hosted a barbecue with about fifty guests earlier this summer. Quite a few coworkers from Philip's station came along with Tori and some of her friends. I suppose any of them might have taken it."

Maybe Philip's partner, Amy, took it. I recalled seeing a sour look on her face anytime she saw Tori—or me, for that matter.

"Where did you normally keep the knife?"

"In my china hutch with my wedding cake topper."

"And you wouldn't have noticed it missing all these months?"

"No. It's stored in a velvet box I keep closed so it doesn't get dusty."

"Do you know anyone else who wanted Ms. Carlton dead?"

Oh boy. I couldn't tell him I considered my husband and his partner as suspects. Without proof, it would only look like I was trying to get back at him over his affair with Tori.

I shook my head. "Sorry, I can't think of anyone."

When Mel dropped me off at home, I found my car sitting in the driveway. I assumed my stepdad and mother picked it up from Tori's for me. My mother would be waiting for a "talk" about my situation, but I wasn't ready to face the music yet. I hoped she wasn't inside, ready to ambush me, since I wanted to forestall that conversation as long as possible.

Silence greeted me when I opened the front door. Philip must have kept Piper, and I hoped he would be reasonable about sharing custody with her. But for now, with my future freedom at stake, I was grateful he had our fur baby.

I found my keys on the kitchen counter with an elegantly penned note from my mother reminding me to call her. Shivers jittered down my spine. I wanted to avoid that phone call for as long as possible. So, instead of calling, I washed the piles of dishes and wiped up the splattered buttercream frosting left from my frantic cake-decorating session early this morning. When I realized the refrigerator was bare except for buttercream frosting, butter, and an assortment of dairy products, I also made a grocery list.

The second I finished cleaning the last countertop, my cell phone rang. Mother. I groaned inwardly.

"Hi, Mother, I was just going to call you." I tried to sound cheerful.

"Emory Danae," my mother said, her sharp voice cutting across the phone. "I know good and well you've been home for over forty-five minutes."

"Sorry. I meant to call you sooner." I looked around my kitchen. Had she installed a camera to spy on me? "I'm exhausted, and once I saw the mess from decorating the cake this morning, I had to clean before I did anything else."

My mother knew I didn't like messes, especially in my kitchen. But seriously, how did she know I'd been home for that long?

"Well, explain yourself, young lady. How did you get

involved in this mess?" Her voice rose an octave. "I've told you all along that Tori person would be bad news."

I sighed, kicked my shoes off, and plopped down onto the sofa. Might as well make myself comfortable because once my no-nonsense mother got on a roll, it could take a while. "It wasn't my fault, and Tori certainly didn't ask to be killed."

"Don't take that tone with me." Her exasperation marred her polished voice. "You need to tell your attorney to make this whole mess disappear so we can get back to normal. You also need to tell him he is free to keep me updated on his progress."

So, that was how she knew when I got home. She had talked to my attorney right after he dropped me off. "Um, sure."

"Your sister is calling, so I need to go." Of course, the perfect daughter would take precedence over me, the murder suspect. "You get this mess straightened out and make up with Philip."

The disconnected call beeped in my ear, and then I looked at my phone, not believing what I'd heard. Make up with Philip? Did she not understand he'd been cheating on me? And if I were honest with myself, the cheating had been going on for a long time.

My lack of sleep caught up with me because when I woke up, it was dark. My neck and shoulders were stiff from napping on the sofa, and I fumbled to turn on the small table lamp. I looked at my wristwatch. Eight already. When the doorbell chimed, I jumped. Had my mother come to harass me in person? I chastised myself mentally for even considering it.

I shuffled to the front door, opened it, and let out a squeak. Randall? Oh my god, what was Randall doing at my house?

Chapter 11

I ran my hand across my hair, trying to smooth it down. It was always a disaster when I woke up, and I was sure I looked a fright.

"Randall, what are you doing here?" My voice still sounded squeaky, so I cleared my throat. "You were supposed to call me tomorrow."

"I'm sorry to barge in on you like this, but I just found out about Tori." He ran a hand across his stubbled cheek. "We really have to talk."

My mind whirled a million miles a minute as I noticed his blue eyes, dark hair, and that bandana still tied around his neck. The stubble lining his jaw made him look like one of those rugged magazine models. Letting him into my house was probably a really bad idea. How had he gotten my address? He seemed surprised when I brought up Tori's name at the party, or perhaps he was a fantastic actor. Could Randall be a killer?

"Can I come in?"

Before I could talk some sense into myself, I opened the door wider. "Sure. Would you like some coffee or a beer?"

"No thanks, I don't need anything."

I sat on my sofa and straightened a couple of throw pillows. Randall chose my grandmother's rocking chair, leaned back, and rocked.

"I'm really sorry about your cousin. I hope you believe me because I didn't have anything to do with Tori's death."

"Cousin?" Randall tilted his head and drew his eyebrows together. "Tori isn't my cousin. Why would you think that?"

"Wait, what? Tori told me." This was getting worse by the minute. I had kissed a stranger? "Well, who are you? What is your relationship with Tori?"

Using Tori's name in the present tense made me wince. It was hard to accept she was no longer alive.

"Ah, Tori. I see she tangled you in one of her sticky webs."

"What do you mean? We were friends." Yeah, that friend-ship was in the past tense, even without her murder.

Randall let out a harsh grunt. "Tori didn't do friends. She had marks."

I shook my head and twisted a few strands of my red hair around my index finger. "I don't understand. We were good friends until, well…."

Randall sat there, rocking back and forth, not saying anything.

"Okay, so she wasn't the best of friends, especially after I caught…." I didn't need to be spilling my guts to a man I didn't know. "How do, I mean did, you know Tori?"

"She was engaged to my brother."

Okay, I didn't see that one coming. Tori? Engaged? I had a hard time picturing the party girl wanting to settle down.

"Why did they break up?" I assumed the brother had gotten wise to the real Tori.

"My brother was murdered."

Me and my big mouth. Why did I need to ask questions? "I'm so sorry for your loss, Randall. How long ago did it happen?"

"Two and a half years ago." He scowled and brushed

some imaginary lint off his blue jeans. Or maybe it was one of Piper's hairs floating around. "Tori disappeared right after his death. I've been looking for her ever since."

I scooted farther away from him. He seemed to blame Tori for his brother's death. Could he have killed her?

Randall must have noticed my movement because he chuckled. "I didn't kill her, and I'm pretty sure you didn't either. But for some reason, someone threw us together, and I need to find out why."

He tugged on his bandana, and I glimpsed a dark-red mark. Oh great.

"I'm sure Tori orchestrated this because of her affair with my husband. She wanted him to leave me, and she used you to make him think we were having an affair."

"For being married, you were quite amorous Friday night." He tugged at his bandana again. "Tori told me about your nasty divorce."

"No, no divorce. Tori made that up." Aware of my own bandana, I scratched my neck. "I'm sure I was drugged because I don't remember anything except having a glass of chardonnay. When I woke up, I had this on my neck."

I wouldn't have dreamed of considering divorce on Friday, but today it was a definite possibility.

"Tori! She must have drugged us both at some point." His tan face seemed to go pale. "You pounded mojitos after the glass of wine. That's when you crawled all over me."

"Please believe I'm sorry because I'm never like that." I pointed at his neck. "That's not something I remember doing to you."

"I don't remember either, and I don't remember reciprocating the, uh, favor." He shook his head. "Everything seemed fine when we dropped you off here, and then Tori talked me into getting a cup of coffee to reminisce about my brother. That's the last thing I remember until I woke up yesterday at home with a raging hangover, which made little sense because I only had two mojitos."

"But what about the photo of us at Villa Havana? Why did you half undress me and let Tori take a picture?"

"I didn't undress you so there can't be a photo." He tilted his head and looked at me. "I would never, ever take advantage of a woman, especially when she's intoxicated."

"How the heck did a photo show up on Facebook with your face buried in my half-undressed chest?"

"Tori!" we both said in unison.

"She was really good at Photoshop back in Florida and must've marked our necks after drugging us."

Why did Tori feel such a need to humiliate me? Why did she post the photo all over Facebook? All she needed to do was make sure Philip found the photo on my phone, and our marriage would have been history.

"You said you drove me home? Did you help her bring me inside?"

"No. She said she'd manage you."

Yeah, she managed me all right. Bit my neck and dumped me on the bathroom floor. But at least that explained how Randall found out where I lived.

I rubbed my face. "This is such an awful mess, and I'm sorry you got dragged into it. I don't understand why she wanted my husband so desperately."

"It was one of her flaws. That's how she hooked my brother." Randall went quiet for a moment.

"If you don't want to talk about him, I understand." I reached out my hand to pat his but pulled it back into my lap. I didn't want him to get the wrong idea, especially after my behavior on Friday night.

"No, that's okay. For whatever reason, you're in the middle of Tori's murder, and somehow, I think her death connects to my brother's death."

"Didn't they catch the person who killed your brother?"

"No." Randall rubbed his face and closed his eyes. "I've been hunting her for over two years, and I'm certain Tori was the killer."

I almost fell off the sofa. Fun-loving Tori? The Tori who shared my love for jazz, pedicures, and good books? No way. Stealer of husbands? Yeah, I could see that. But a killer? No.

My mouth hung open for several seconds before I snapped it closed. I shook my head. "No, I don't see Tori killing anyone. As her friend for almost two years, I'm sure I would have known something was wrong with her."

Randall snorted. "You didn't even know she'd been engaged. Psychopaths can be very convincing that they're normal people."

I shuddered. Had I really been hanging out with a murderer all this time?

"If I tell you about my brother and what happened, you'll see Tori for the monster she is. I mean, was."

This guy seemed bitter, but if I suspected someone of murdering my sister, I wouldn't ever forgive them either. Still, I didn't see Tori killing anyone.

"Earth to Em? Do you want to hear about my brother or not?"

"Sorry. This is a lot to process and take in." I looked straight into Randall's gorgeous blue eyes. "Yes, I want to know about him."

"I guess it is a bombshell, isn't it?" Randall cleared his throat. "Dylan—that was my brother—was on the vice squad in Florida."

"In Miami?"

"What? No, Tampa."

"Sorry. I guess I remember Tori mentioned she moved from Miami, and when you said vice, I thought of *Miami Vice*."

He looked at me like I'd lost my mind… and I probably

had. I clamped my lips together and turned an imaginary key with my hand.

"He worked undercover on drug cases when his fiancée met Tori."

"Wasn't Tori his fiancée?"

When Randall narrowed his eyes, I decided I'd better stop interrupting.

"Sorry. I'll be quiet."

The doorbell rang, interrupting Randall again. I glanced at my watch. Eight thirty. Who would drop by unannounced this late? As I mouthed "sorry" to Randall, I jumped off the sofa and went to the door. Before I reached for the handle, I heard a key inserted in the lock. The door opened. Uh-oh, there was only one person who would let themselves into my house.

"Philip, what are you doing here?" My voice squeaked, and I glanced back toward the family room where Randall sat.

"Darling, I thought you two needed to work this out, so I insisted Philip come." My mother breezed in behind my cheating husband, air kissed my cheek, and then froze in place. She stared over my shoulder.

"What the heck are you doing in my house?" Philip's deep voice sounded threatening, and his strong, square jaw clenched so hard he could've chipped a tooth. His chest puffed up, and his face became red as he turned and scowled at me. "You didn't waste any time, did you? You'll be hearing from my attorney."

"It's not what you think!" I didn't need to explain myself to him any longer, but I wanted to keep my conscience clear.

"I am so ashamed of you." My mother's eyes filled with tears, and she had red splotches on her neck. "Where did I go wrong raising you?"

Randall edged around us, heading for the open door and sanity.

"You're not getting away with cheating with my wife!" Philip yelled, grabbing Randall by the scruff of his neck.

Philip curled his fist into a tight ball and took a swing at Randall. Randall deftly sidestepped the attempted punch and hightailed it out the front door.

"Coward!" Philip yelled at the retreating figure.

Why didn't my mother call me instead of showing up unannounced? I scrunched my eyes together, trying to wish this entire mess had never happened. When I heard my mother huff in that exasperated way only she could do, I peeked through my lashes and hoped Philip would be nowhere in sight.

Instead, my mother frowned at me, gave a small shudder, and walked out into the night without saying one word to me. I was sure she would make me feel extra guilty about this scene tomorrow.

Unfortunately, Philip still stood in the doorway and glared at me. "Nobody humiliates me and gets away with it."

"Excuse me? Humiliates you? I'm the one who caught you in the act with Tori. You lost all rights to expect any respect and courtesy from me."

Philip's eyes narrowed. "Mark my words. You're gonna be sorry for this."

He stomped out the door. I slammed it behind him and made a mental note to change the locks in the morning.

I decided to bake some butterscotch cookies to take to work the next day. Spending time in the kitchen with the sweet smells of sugar and warm vanilla soothed me. My mind kept seeing Tori's dead body, and I worried about how I would clear my name. I also worried about how Philip planned to make me sorrier than I already felt. Beating the butter and brown and white sugars in a bowl with a wooden spoon instead of an electric mixer used some of the energy from my angst. Would he keep me from sharing custody of Piper? I regretted not having the chance to ask how she fared. I missed her but knew Philip provided her with a stable home life… for the time being.

Being curious, I wondered why Randall thought his brother's murder connected to Tori's death, especially if Tori was the murderer. Maybe Randall killed Tori in revenge and wanted to steer me away from suspecting him? I needed to get the full story, but I had no idea how to contact Randall.

I sighed as I measured out the flour and leavening. Instead of sifting them together, I whisked the ingredients vigorously. It wasn't any use. I couldn't lose myself in the baking. My mind wouldn't stop trying to figure out who killed Tori. As I banged the baking sheet holding spoonfuls of butterscotch-chip-laden dough into the oven, I decided I would take Tori's mother cookies and a bouquet of flowers after work. It was time to pay my condolences and find out how to reach Randall.

Chapter 12

Sleep had eluded me for most of the night, so after dumping my purse in my cubicle, I stumbled to the break room for a cup of coffee. The message light on my desk phone had been flashing furiously, but it would wait until I'd had a cup or maybe three of coffee. I had debated about calling in sick, as my attorney had suggested, but after my interrogation yesterday, I wanted to get on with my life. Being overly optimistic, I hoped they'd find other suspects and leave me alone.

After I placed the plate of butterscotch cookies on one of the break room tables, I arranged cute napkins extolling the hardships of Mondays around the plate. With a full cup of coffee, I stumbled back toward my cubicle. I walked the long way around the floor to avoid the statistics section. Heat flamed my cheeks when I remembered Tori parading me around my office in a sheer blouse and short skirt, the outfit she claimed she bought as an early birthday gift for me. I didn't know how she talked me into wearing it, and I didn't think I'd ever be able to look any of those young men in the eyes again.

My phone rang the second I reached my cubicle. I stared

at the phone for a moment and then ignored the call while I booted up my computer. I sipped coffee, willing the caffeine to kick in. Once the computer turned on, I entered my login and password information. It wouldn't let me in. I tried again, slowing down my typing to make sure I had it right. Nope. Wrong again. After the third try, a message popped up stating the username wasn't recognized. What? I'd been at this company for seven years with the same username. This Monday couldn't get any worse. As I picked up the phone to call the IT department, it rang again. Tempted to send the call directly to voice mail, I changed my mind now that other employees milled around. I didn't want my coworkers to consider me a slacker, even though I felt like one.

"Emory Martinez speaking."

"Mr. Wilkins wants to see you in his office. Right this minute," my boss's efficient assistant, Rosa, practically yelled into the phone. "This wasn't the day to be late. I've been calling you nonstop for fifteen minutes."

"I wasn't late. My computer won't log in, and I was trying to fix it." I didn't mention my priority had been coffee.

"Well, hurry and get up here. He's in a mood."

Rosa must have slammed down her phone because the disconnected call made me jump. Really, this was the worst Monday ever. Part of me hoped the summons would be about the promotion I had applied for, but that the owner displayed a "mood" didn't bode well.

I took the elevator up to the sixth floor and hurried to Rosa's desk, where she had been a fixture for two decades. "Do you know what Mr. Wilkins wants?"

"No, but don't say I didn't warn you. He's out for bear this morning." Her midnight-black eyes examined my silk turtle-neck top. She probably wondered about my choice in the middle of summer. Then she picked up her phone and announced my arrival. She bobbed her dark curly-capped head toward the door. "Go on in and good luck."

I entered the cavernous room and blinked at the brightness. Two glass walls from floor to ceiling looked out toward the California coastline. Another wall contained bookshelves with a few books, but most of the shelves held trophies and framed photos of Mr. Wilkins with a variety of dignitaries and actors. His massive glass desk sat at the far end of the room, next to the windows, while a small seating area with a comfortable-looking sofa and chairs surrounded a glass coffee table. My boss sat at his desk, his gaze glued to his flat-screen computer monitor, so I tentatively made my way across the plush carpet. He still hadn't looked up when I reached his desk, so I cleared my throat.

"I'll be with you in a moment, Ms. Martinez."

Uh-oh. He didn't offer to let me sit on one of the buttery-leather captain chairs stationed at the side of his desk, so this couldn't be good. I fidgeted with the button on my blazer. When I realized doing that made me seem nervous, I clasped my hands behind my back. His liver-spotted balding head, rimmed with white hair, intrigued me when it looked like a rabbit-shaped spot peeked out from the fringe of his hair. Bushy white eyebrows that needed trimming flowed over his wire-rimmed glasses, and I wondered if they smudged his lenses. Mr. Wilkins exuded formality and wore a crisply ironed white shirt and a blue tie. His suit coat hung neatly on a hanger on the door leading to his private bathroom.

Mr. Wilkins finally looked up with a scowl. "Ms. Martinez, you've been with this company for over seven years. Wouldn't you say we've treated you with respect and fairly compensated you?"

"Yes, Mr. Wilkins. I've enjoyed working for your company."

"Then why would you try to tarnish my sterling reputation with your feeble attempt to blackmail me?"

A loud buzzing filled my head, and I became dizzy. I gripped the front of his desk to keep from collapsing.

"Excuse me? I don't understand." My voice shook, and I could barely get the words out.

When he turned his computer screen toward me, I screamed. The horrid photo of Randall buried in my chest stared back at me. Except it wasn't Randall's head. It was Mr. Wilkins's head. "Oh. My. God! Where did that come from?"

"The question is, why did you think it would be a good idea to email it to me, demanding a promotion? And then threaten my company with trumped-up charges of harassment if I didn't comply?" Mr. Wilkins's face turned beet-red. Even though he wasn't yelling at the top of his lungs, his quiet rage terrified me.

"I swear I did not email that picture, nor do I have any demands or blackmail plans." I wiped my sweaty palms on my skirt. "Please, you have to believe me!"

"It came from your company email address, so don't try to deny it, Ms. Martinez. I'm considering calling law enforcement to report your blackmail attempt."

"Someone hacked into my account. Mr. Wilkins, I'm telling you the truth! I'm being set up." I didn't want to be arrested again.

He glanced back at his screen then glowered at me.

Not wanting to give him a chance to call the police, I babbled on. "See, my friend, Tori—well, I guess she really wasn't my true friend—set me up because she had an affair with my husband. Then she got murdered, and I found her and got arrested, except I didn't do it, and then I found out she might have killed her fiancé, from her almost-brother-in-law…"

I stopped talking when Mr. Wilkins's eyeballs looked like they might pop out of their sockets. He inched his chair away from me.

He snatched up his phone and yelled, "Get security up here. Now!"

"What? I didn't do it!" The desk gave me something to steady myself against.

"I don't care if you're innocent or not. That's for the police to figure out. But I have the reputation of my company to protect, and you're undermining all my hard work." He lifted his index finger and pointed it at me. "Effective immediately, you're fired! Security will escort you to your desk to collect your belongings. Please see that you leave without causing a scene."

I knew there wasn't any use in arguing or pleading, but I couldn't stop the lone tear from trickling down my cheek. The office door banged open, and a burly man dressed in a uniform strode in, making me jump.

Mr. Wilkins didn't give the man a chance to say anything. "Please escort Ms. Martinez to her desk to collect her personal belongings and then escort her out of the building. Make sure you take away her badge and disable her entry access code."

The security officer touched my shoulder. "It's time to leave, ma'am. Please come quietly."

I wanted to say something to Mr. Wilkins, but he already had his back turned to us, looking out the huge glass window at the distant ocean.

The security guy led the way out, and we passed by Rosa's desk. Her mouth hung wide open. Not one word was spoken between the two of us as the security guy and I took the elevator and then did the walk of shame to my desk. I grabbed a tissue and wiped my eyes before putting photos and a couple of mystery novels into a box I had stashed beneath my desk. A lipstick I'd been hunting for during the previous week was found in a drawer, as was a package of pretzels. I handed my ID badge to the man who stood at attention just outside my cubicle, grabbed the box, and trudged to the elevator. My eyes stared at the carpet, hoping to avoid seeing the look of curiosity mixed with pity from my former coworkers.

Once I made it to my car and stowed my box, Mr. Security Guy stood and waited for me to start my car and drive off the lot. My limbs trembled so hard it was difficult to drive. The tears pooled in my eyes and made the road blurry. I worried about my ability to stay on the road, but I couldn't stop. Not yet. I needed to get home, away from prying eyes. I needed the privacy of my bedroom to give in to a complete sob fest.

Fired? Oh, dear lord, how would I pay my mortgage and bills? Philip, pissed off at me, would probably gloat at my misfortune. My sister had another baby on the way, and I was beyond humiliated at the thought of asking my mother for help. I wouldn't be out on the street, but to have to consider moving back in with my mother at my age? It was more than I could bear. Now the pity party was heading into full swing.

Chapter 13

After fifteen minutes of an uncontrollable crying jag, I pulled my limp noodle of a self from bed. When the horrific image in my mirror threatened to leave me crying again, I ran some warm water over Lipton tea bags, placed them in the freezer for a few minutes, and applied them to my swollen eyes. As I lay on the sofa, waiting for the tea bags to work, I wondered who wanted to set me up for Tori's murder.

With all the questions I'd been asking, I'd learned plenty of people might have wanted her dead. But how did they connect to me? Randall qualified as a suspect, but how did he get ahold of my cake knife? Philip was a stronger possibility. If he found out Tori manipulated him and that I had cheated on him, perhaps he snapped and saw it as a way to get back at us both. I didn't want to think I'd been sharing a bed with someone who was capable of murder. The best solution would be that the killer was a random stranger from Tori's past, connected to Randall's brother. Possibly Tori had swiped my cake knife, and it was a convenient weapon for the stranger.

I shook my head, knowing full well I was grasping at straws, trying to arrange my limited clues so that they made sense. The more I thought about it, the angrier I became that someone had decided to destroy my life.

I hoped Detective Jackson would investigate with an open mind, but given his reaction to me during his interrogation, I suspected he only looked for evidence that confirmed I killed Tori. It was time to put the big-girl panties on and do something to rescue my own life. No one else would do it for me.

I needed to track down Randall and find out why he assumed she killed his brother. My very public catfight with her might have given that random stranger a scapegoat: me! I added talking to the stoner brothers to my list of mental notes and hoped those guys had seen someone lurking around. My visit to Tori's mother would be the best place to start. She might have Randall's phone number. I had yet to offer my condolences, although I wasn't sure she'd be happy to see me, since I was a "person of interest" in her daughter's murder. My eyes teared up as I wondered what people thought of me. But I shook the tears off and grew determined to get busy with my to-do list.

I called a locksmith to change my locks because I didn't want a repeat of Philip wandering in whenever he wanted. They promised someone would arrive within an hour, and they even waived the rush fee. Business must be slow. Lucky for me since my cash flow was drying up, but I knew I would never figure out how to change the locks myself. A handy person I wasn't.

With two dozen frozen, pre-formed ginger crackle cookie dough balls arranged between two baking sheets to defrost, I turned the oven on. My mother considered it good manners to bring food and flowers to a grieving family. I always kept several dozen cookie dough balls in my freezer for emergencies… like a condolence visit, a potluck at work, or if a friend dropped by to chat. Nothing could make people feel special like fresh-baked cookies.

While the oven preheated and the cookie dough thawed a

bit, I added eye drops to the red orbs of my eyes, redid my smeared makeup, and smoothed down my bedhead hair. My eyes were still puffy, despite the tea bags, but I couldn't do anything about it. I didn't want to waste any more time feeling sorry for myself.

Once the oven finished preheating, I slid the baking sheets into the oven and set a timer. My rumpled clothes weren't up to a condolence visit, so I changed into turquoise capris with a frilly white blouse—the perfect outfit for going to the beach and for hot, summery weather. But then again, this was a sympathy visit, so I didn't want to seem frivolous. I changed again, this time into black slacks and a muted burgundy silk blouse and tied a burgundy floral-patterned scarf around my neck. Instead of fun strappy sandals, I opted for sensible kitten-heeled pumps. My mother would be proud of me.

While the cookies cooled on a wire rack beneath a ceiling fan, I lined a basket with a moss-green linen napkin. Once the cookies had completely cooled, I arranged all but six of them in the basket, wrapped the package with cellophane, and tied the top with a silver ribbon. It would have to do. The remaining six cookies went into a clear, treat-sized cellophane bag, which I also tied with a silver ribbon.

The doorbell rang. When I opened the door, I found an elderly locksmith bent over at the waist, looking at my lock.

"Mrs. Emory?" the white-haired man asked with an Eastern European accent. "You called for a locksmith? I am Yuri and at your service."

"Yes. Thank you for coming so quickly." I gestured into the house. "I can show you all the doors that need changed."

He followed me after removing his shoes in the entryway. "It smells so good in here." He sniffed again. "Is that cinnamon and ginger?"

"Yes. I baked some ginger crackle cookies and saved some for you." I grabbed the cellophane bag from my dining table and handed the package to the locksmith. "It would be unkind to let you smell the cookies and not share with you."

The elderly man gave me a short bow. "Thank you. I haven't had homemade cookies since my wife passed away five years ago."

"I'm so sorry about your wife." The conversation felt awkward now that I had dredged up painful memories for the man. Should I offer him a glass of milk to go with his cookies or continue showing him the locks?

Yuri saved me from deciding. "You were going to show me all the locks you need changed?"

"Ah, yes. There are only three." I led him to the door that led out to the garage. "Can you reprogram the garage door opener too?"

"Yes. That shouldn't be any trouble. I will need your remote opener and a ladder."

Thirty minutes later, as I finished cleaning the baking sheets, Yuri came into the kitchen and handed me an invoice. "I am finished, Mrs. Emory."

"You are fast! I thought it would take a couple of hours."

"My family has owned our business for fifty years since I first came to America." Yuri tapped his chest with pride. "I learned from my father, who learned from his. We are good at our job."

"What an inspiring life you've led. I'm sure you have lots of stories to tell."

"That I do." He pointed at the invoice. "But if you don't mind, I need to get to my next call."

"Is a check okay, or do you prefer a credit card?"

"A check is fine. I know where you live." He chuckled. "Here is the one and only master key. You will need to get copies made."

As soon as Yuri left, I loaded up the cookies and drove to the closest florist. I purchased a bouquet of assorted flowers the clerk assured me were suitable for a sympathy visit and winced as I handed over my credit card. The real murderer needed to be found as soon as possible so I could get another job. My bills weren't going to pay themselves. But I couldn't visit Mrs. Carlton without offering my condolences, and nothing said sympathy like flowers and cookies.

Mrs. Carlton lived in Corona del Mar, a few blocks from the Pacific Ocean. Parking was almost nonexistent during the summer months, unless you showed up early in the morning. I drove up and down streets, moving farther and farther away from the place of my intended visit, until I chanced upon a young family loading sandy beach toys into the back of their SUV. I waited patiently while they cleaned sand from the legs and feet of their two towheaded toddlers and strapped them into their car seats. A twinge of regret hurt my heart, and I wondered if I'd ever have the chance to have children. Philip had always insisted we weren't ready to discuss the possibility, and in hindsight, it was for the best.

Once they pulled out, I started the torturous task of trying to parallel park in the impossibly small space the family had just vacated. After three attempts, I decided it was good enough, even though the front of my car measured three feet from the curb. Too impatient to try again to straighten the car, I gave up and turned off the ignition.

I carried the heavy vase of flowers and the basket of cookies as I trudged downhill. I had several blocks to walk until I came to Mrs. Carlton's snug little home. By the time I reached the house, my feet were screaming, and I wished I could change into athletic shoes. My tired arms couldn't wait to deliver their heavy loads. My once-clean silk blouse stuck to my back, and I was sure my makeup slid down my face. The hot midday sun baked the road, the sidewalk, and my head. I missed the usual cool ocean breeze, which was noticeably absent. No wonder people were flocking to the beach.

A white picket fence lined her property; her yard was covered with roses and other blooming flowers. The yard reminded me of a wild English garden—a bit chaotic but very inviting with the bistro table and two chairs sitting beneath the shade of a large oak tree. The bright, cheery red door complemented the brown-and-cream-colored stonework façade. I hadn't really met Mrs. Carlton before, but she had waved to me from her front steps when I picked Tori up several months ago. I hadn't been invited in since Tori rushed to my car and said she was running late for her manicure appointment. Apparently, the friend she loaned her car to hadn't shown up when promised, so she had asked me to provide transportation service.

I rang the doorbell and my arms sighed in relief when Tori's mom answered the door. I noticed her eyes weren't red or puffy. Dressed in sharply creased gray slacks with a light-pink silk blouse and her white-blonde hair curled around her round face, she looked ready for a luncheon or a visit to upscale shops. A strand of pearls lay wrapped around her neck, and small pearls with diamond accents rested on her earlobes.

"Mrs. Carlton, please accept my most sincere condolences. I am so, so sorry for your loss." I tried to put the vase into her hands, but she backed away from me. Uh-oh. Was she worried I was the killer? Would she call the police?

"Really, Mrs. Carlton, I had nothing to do with Tori's death, and I hate that people think that's the case."

The woman's eyes widened. "Young lady, you have the wrong house."

Chapter 14

O h, dear Lord. Had someone not notified her about Tori's death?

"Are you Mrs. Carlton?" I shifted the vase to rest on my hip and hoped I wouldn't drop the flowers.

"No. You're mistaking me for someone else." Her cheeks turned pink, and she gripped the handle of the door, probably so she could slam it in my face. "I'm Mrs. Landow."

Had Tori's mom remarried and taken a different last name? Clearly this poor woman hadn't been notified, or perhaps she was suffering from early dementia. "Um, I'm sorry to break the news to you, but Tori lost her life."

"Wait a minute, you were here with that good-for-nothing tart a couple months ago." The woman leaned toward me and examined my face. "I'm calling the police."

I backed away and hoped I could make a run for it without dropping the heavy vase of flowers. Did she think I was a murderer too? "I think there's been a misunderstanding. You don't need to get the police involved."

"Zeus! Come!" The woman's sharp guttural command cracked in the hot summer air. "Don't move, young lady, or my dog will attack."

I gulped when the biggest Doberman Pinscher I'd ever seen came to the door and sat by his mistress. No way could I outrun the beast.

"I'm sorry, Missus… really, this has been a huge misunderstanding. I didn't kill her."

"You said that before." Mrs. Landow rested her hand on the top of her dog's head, which came nearly to her waist. "I don't care if you killed her or not. It's probably what she deserved. What I do care about is that you cased my house and, two days later, stole the artwork I had assembled for my exhibition."

"I know nothing about that." My heart pounded. I was terrified she would allow her dog to tear me apart. "I only gave Tori a ride home. She said you were her, uh, mother."

"Right." The woman rolled her eyes. "Why would she say that?"

"If you're not related to her, then what was Tori doing here?" My face flamed. I'd been played by Tori again. Had everything she told me been a lie?

"She offered to come give me a manicure and pedicure, since I'd been too busy preparing for the exhibition to get to her salon."

"You were a client at her salon?" I needed to keep her talking while I figured out how to walk away without bite marks.

"Yes. It's such a lovely salon." Mrs. Landow looked at her nails and scowled. "Tori did beautiful work. I'd been a regular client there for six months before she took advantage of me."

"Why do you think Tori had something to do with the theft?" I eyed the dog, grateful his owner still held onto him. "Maybe it was a coincidence?"

Mrs. Landow's face changed from thoughtful to downright angry. "If it was only a coincidence, then why was her cell phone disconnected, and why haven't I been able to locate her?"

"That's odd. I talked to her almost every day on her cell phone." I thought back and realized I hadn't visited her salon in a long time. Tori always wanted to meet elsewhere. Could Tori have used a different number for clients? "Do you happen to still have her phone number?"

She pulled a slim cell phone from a pocket in her slacks and turned on the device. I was a little worried when she removed her hand from the dog's head to access her phone. But Zeus remained still as a carved statue, except for his eyes. His gaze followed my every move, and I barely dared to breathe.

Mrs. Landow recited a phone number.

"No, that's not the phone number I had for her." I needed to scratch my nose, but my hands were full of flowers and cookies. I scrunched my nose up and down a couple of times, trying to relieve my discomfort. My arms ached to put my load down, but I was afraid to move, so I shifted my feet a little to adjust the weight and kept close watch on the Doberman.

"I still need to call the police so they can sort this out. You're probably involved and know where the artwork can be recovered."

"Please believe me, I had nothing to do with it." My mind whirled, trying to figure out a way to talk her out of calling the police. I didn't need to be arrested again. My mother would kill me. "If I was guilty, would I be here, bringing you flowers and cookies as a condolence for her death?"

The woman sighed and tapped her toe a few times. "You have a good point."

"I really don't know any more than you do, Mrs. Landow. Please, just let me walk away and let the police investigate Tori's death. Maybe they'll turn something up on your art."

"Well, if she really is dead, then perhaps...." She didn't finish her sentence or say anything else.

And then I noticed her eyes were fixated on the flowers. I

realized she wanted to keep them. Great. I'd spent over a hundred dollars on flowers for nothing. However, if sacrificing the arrangement got me away from her terrifying attack dog, it would be worth it.

I thrust the vase out. "If you'd like to keep these, I'd be happy for you to enjoy them, along with the cookies."

She walked down the steps and eagerly grabbed the arrangement and basket from my hands. Then she edged back toward her dog. "If you're sure you don't want to keep them, I'd be delighted to take them. My bridge group is coming later this afternoon, so it's perfect timing, as they say."

"Uh, sure. Enjoy, and I'm sorry to have disturbed you." I released a huge sigh of relief. It appeared she would allow me to leave her yard unscathed. I kept my gaze glued to the beast while I inched my way backward, toward the gate. I couldn't turn my back on him until I was far from the reach of his razor-sharp teeth.

The dog and his mistress stood guard, and the bright-red door didn't close until I started the hot uphill walk to my car. I supposed they wanted to make sure I wouldn't steal anything as I left. Frustration over having more questions than answers about Tori's life poured out of me. So did perspiration as the sun beat down on my head. I didn't think it was possible Tori could be involved in art theft. None of it made any sense, and I still suffered from the heebie-jeebies over my close encounter with Zeus. Mrs. Landow was one strange lady… a wealthy, bridge-playing Newport Beach socialite on one hand and on the other, a woman prepared to watch her vicious dog tear apart an unwanted stranger.

My phone buzzed in my pocket. I saw a text from my sister asking if I wanted to come to dinner tonight. It dawned on me that Carrie could provide Randall's phone number, since she hired him for the party. I kicked myself mentally, realizing that I would have saved money if I had thought this through. Instead, a group of elderly, probably rich, given the location, ladies would enjoy my flowers and cookies.

I sent Carrie a text back indicating I would come to dinner, along with a request for her to text Randall's phone number to me. My phone rang immediately.

"Hey, Carrie." I didn't even need to look at the name displayed.

"What in the world do you need his number for?" Exasperation flooded her voice. "Mother told me about the fiasco last night. He's nothing but trouble."

"Nothing happened. Besides, it's not what Mother might think." I held the phone away from my ear as Carrie jabbered over my attempt to explain. When the phone quieted, I put it back to my ear. "Tori was apparently involved in his brother's murder, and I need to find out the connection. No one is going to clear my name if I don't do something about it."

"No way, Em. You do not need to get tangled up in this."

"But I need to do something. Besides, I'm already involved." I knew my sister wasn't going to like this. "Mr. Hotshot Detective has me as his only suspect and is doing everything he can to support his assumption."

"Let the police do their job. They'll figure it out." Carrie was always the optimistic one. "This isn't like one of those small-town mysteries you like to read. Just get back to work, and it will get resolved."

Oh boy, how did I break the news I didn't have a job any longer? This wouldn't be pretty. "Um, about that…."

"About what?" Carrie mumbled something to one of her daughters. "I need to go. Sophie stuck a raisin up her nose. Talk to Philip. He'll tell you how the investigation is going, and that will put your mind at ease."

With that, Carrie disconnected, but not before I heard her yelling at Sophie. I shook my head. Philip would tell me about the investigation when you-know-what froze over. I was beginning to suspect he might be the one trying to pin the murder on me. Tori had probably fed him lies about me, and he must have fallen for them. But why? Why would Tori do that to me?

Frustrated that I still didn't have Randall's phone number, I trudged to my car and gratefully turned on the air-conditioning. Wondering how to track him down, I sat there for a minute or two while I tried to get cool in front of the blowing air vents. Inspiration struck, and I snatched my cell phone up. The stable venue, where the party was held, should have his contact information on file. I remembered him saying he was trying to get the word out about his band.

After getting the number from information and being connected to the stable, I waded through the list of options, punching numbers as prompted. I finally connected to a live person.

"Hi, I'm interested in hiring the band that played at the Hansen party on Saturday. Can you provide their phone number?" My lies were getting more frequent. It should worry me… but it didn't… yet.

"Oh yes, I have his business card. Hold on a sec and I'll get it." She sounded like an elderly woman with a smoker's voice. Gravelly and a little congested.

I listened to Muzak for a few minutes, wondering if she had forgotten about me.

"Sorry for the delay. The phones all started ringing at once." The receptionist coughed and took a moment to blow her nose. "Are you ready to write this down?"

"Yes, I'm ready." I wondered if I would ever get the number.

After finally writing the phone number down, I was prepared to get off the phone and track down Randall. "Thank you."

"No problem, dear. Let me know if you need anything else." The woman coughed again. "And come by and see us. I'll be happy to give you a tour. Do you realize our facilities are available for private parties, both indoors and outside?

Would you like the information for the caterer? The food was fantastic, and the cake, oh my, was the most darling thing you've ever seen."

"No, the band is all I need. I already have the caterer's number."

"Okay, dear. Give us a call if you want a tour." She sniffed. "My name's Bertha if you decide to drop by."

I finally disconnected from Bertha, who, from the sound of things, had a cold. With trembling hands, I punched in Randall's number. His phone rang four times and connected to voice mail. I hung up, not wanting to leave a message. I'd rather catch him off-guard so he wouldn't have a chance to blow me off or avoid me. Time to talk to the Stoner Dudes, also known as Steve and Stan.

Chapter 15

Traffic crawled along the Pacific Coast Highway toward Costa Mesa, with beachgoers heading to the sand and surf for the afternoon and others heading for lunch with a waterfront view. The drive took far longer than I wanted, and my stomach growled when I realized I hadn't eaten lunch. Too bad Mrs. Carlton had kept all the cookies. I needed them more than she did right now. Steve and Stan probably only had chips in their apartment, and my refrigerator was mostly bare, except for leftover buttercream frosting and baking ingredients. I needed to eat something to hold me over before dinner with Carrie.

A quick request to Siri showed me the closest In-N-Out restaurant, and I detoured to satisfy my craving. I groaned when the drive-thru line wrapped around the parking lot and stopped me out on the street. My mouth watered as I thought about the cheeseburger, fries, and vanilla milkshake that could be mine, but I didn't want to spend that much time sitting in line to order. I steered around the cars in line and drove past In-N-Out. I headed to the Stoner Dudes' apartment instead.

As I pulled up in front of their four-plex, my hands shook once I saw Tori's place closed off with yellow crime scene tape. After parking, I trudged up rickety wooden steps, which looked like an accident waiting to happen. Rumors floated around town that Steve and Stan Miller were supposed to be wealthy. But since they lived in a dump like this, I was sure those were only rumors, probably spread by the brothers themselves as a joke. I knocked on the weathered door, its dull brown paint peeling in several spots.

"Dudette! Revisiting the scene of the crime?" Steve smirked at me with bloodshot eyes after he had flung the door open. "Are you here to gloat over killing your frenemy?"

"Yeah right, Steve. I need to talk to you and your brother."

"Hey, dude, she just confessed! Call the cops." Steve swayed a little. "Wait, hide the weed then call them."

"I didn't confess. That's called sarcasm." I bit off my desire to add the word "idiot." Really, how did these guys make a living? "Someone's framing me, and I wanted to talk to you."

"Oooh, playing Jessica Fletcher?"

"What? You watch Jessica Fletcher?" Why did that surprise me? The guys probably binged on cable all day long, but the Hallmark Mystery Movie Channel being on their radar wouldn't have been my guess. TMZ seemed more their style.

"Dudette, we're up on all that stuff." Steve opened the door wider and gestured for me to come inside. Then he yelled, loudly enough for the entire neighborhood to hear, "Hey, dude, put some clothes on. We have a guest."

I had never been in their apartment. Instead, they visited Tori's place for parties or hung out on their rooftop, which held a few questionable plastic patio chairs. I tried to keep my mouth from dropping open. The inside of their abode was a well-kept secret, and I never would have guessed what the two men had been hiding. It certainly belied the image they portrayed to the outside world.

First of all, the apartment was huge. The brothers

appeared to occupy the entire two upstairs units and must have knocked down walls to open the space further. Second, it was clean. I mean squeaky clean and no clutter. I had expected to spot empty chip bags and beer cans littering the place, but instead, the hardwood floors gleamed with polish, and the masculine and tasteful furniture was artfully arranged in inviting groupings. Several books sat on a glass-top coffee table, and if the titles gave any indication, they were nonfiction philosophical tomes and theories of physics. The great room opened into a gourmet kitchen with granite countertops and high-end stainless-steel appliances.

"I would kill to have a kitchen like yours. It's beautiful."

Steve's eyes bugged out.

"No, not literally kill. I would never kill anyone. Really! You just have an amazing kitchen. Do you use it?"

"Of course." He winked. "I might have even attended culinary school once upon a time."

Stan chose that moment to saunter into the living room, wearing nothing but boxer shorts. I quickly averted my eyes but not before I almost drooled over his amazing bod. Six-pack abs and all. Why had I gotten the impression that both these guys sat around snacking, channel surfing, and gaming twenty-four hours a day, expanding their muffin-top middles? And this apartment? Why didn't they host parties here or let anyone in? Could their public persona be an act?

"Uh, hi, Stan." I still couldn't look at him.

"Dude, I told you to put clothes on."

Stan scratched his head. "Sorry, Em."

"Um, no problem." I admired him covertly as he ambled to what appeared to be a laundry room. Yep, he was pretty ripped… in a good way.

"Dudette, you wanna beer?" Steve motioned at the refrigerator. "Help yourself."

"No thanks. I'm good."

"So, what brings you back to the scene of the crime?"

"I'm not a killer, Steve." I had to remind myself not to call him Stoner Dude to his face. "Can I ask you and Stan if there had been any strangers hanging around? Especially the day when we, um, you know...."

He raised his head and looked at me over the bridge of his nose. "What day?"

"Fine! The day Tori and I got into the fight. The day she died." I got the feeling this guy only played dense. Why did they want people to see them as stoner idiots?

"Nope. Didn't notice anything or anyone who didn't belong." Steve tilted his head at me and squinted his dark hazel-colored eyes again. The gesture reminded me of a quizzical bird. "How did you not know your husband was with Tori? Dudette, it's been going on for months."

"You knew! And you didn't tell me?" Was I the only one who missed the signs of his affair?

"Some chicks are into stuff like that, so it wasn't any of our business."

I shook my head. "Did you ask Tori about it? Did she ever say why?"

Stan chose that moment to join us. He was dressed in pressed blue jeans that fit him just right and a polo shirt. A Ralph Lauren polo shirt. I'd never seen either of these guys wearing anything but baggy, faded cargo shorts and either raggedy flannel shirts or hoodies that had beer logos peeling and fraying from age. Clothes that made them look twenty-five pounds overweight. I was living in the Twilight Zone.

"Tori was all about the party, the fun." Stan leaned back on the sofa and placed a bare foot on the coffee table. "And what Tori wanted, Tori got."

He must get regular pedicures. Buffed nails, no overgrown cuticles, no calluses. I wondered if Tori had been his manicurist.

"True, but she also liked to talk. Did she have any issues with anyone? Could someone else be mad at her for taking something or someone that didn't belong to her? Was anything out of character for Tori the last few days?" I sounded desperate.

"Nope. She didn't say anything, and we noticed nothing." Stan's voice sounded deeper and more polished than I remembered from chatting with him at Tori's. "You're the only one who's caused a commotion and was where you shouldn't have been."

Great, even the Stoner Dudes thought I might be guilty.

"Okay, I have to say it. You guys are blowing my mind." I gestured around the room. "What gives? The outside of the apartment is dumpy, looking like it needs to be condemned, but this? And you? What's up with that? Was Tori privy to your secret?"

"Absolutely not! She was a leech, and while we didn't care if she speculated, we didn't need her kind of drama." Stan chuckled. "We're making an exception for you."

"Why? What if I'm a killer?"

"Are you?" Steve's weed drawl was gone.

I was right. Steve and Stan had an act for their public persona.

"No! I'm being framed."

"Exactly. We'd like to try to help you." Stan stood and straightened one of the physics books on the table. "We've checked out our security camera recordings, but they don't show the entry to Tori's place. We didn't set them up to watch her apartment because of invasion of privacy issues and all that. Unfortunately, we heard nothing that night either."

Yeah, I remembered. Music blasted from their apartment that night. I wondered if they had girlfriends or other guests visiting at the time, although I didn't remember seeing other cars parked in front of the apartment.

"Did you see her supposed cousin Randall at any time? He's tall, with short-cropped hair and amazing blue eyes."

"Oh, you mean the cop?"

"No, he's not a cop. He plays in a country-western band."

"Dudette…." Steve's drawl came back. "I've never met anyone so clueless."

"I am not clueless!" When they both laughed, I had to clarify myself. "Maybe naïve but definitely not clueless."

That made them laugh even harder.

I wasn't happy. "Seriously, guys, help me out here. Did Randall ever come by Tori's place?"

They both wiped tears of mirth from their eyes, and then Stan finally answered me. "He came a few times. He never stayed long, and Tori always slammed the door on him when he left."

Finally, some real information. "We could surmise they were arguing every time he saw her?"

"You could probably surmise that." Steve steepled his fingers together. "Tori expressed her unhappiness about him moving to the area a few times."

"Randall told me she was once engaged to his brother."

The brothers exchanged a look. I didn't know what it meant, but I had the feeling they had more information than they were telling me.

"What else can you tell me about Tori?" If they wouldn't be forthcoming, I would have to play Twenty Questions.

"Rumors. That's all they are is rumors."

"Come on, guys. My freedom is on the line. Tell me what you've learned."

"This is only a rumor, but we heard she was using her salon as a front for money laundering."

Tori and an illegal business? It didn't add up, even after Mrs. Landow's accusations. She wasn't conniving enough. Instead, she was a party girl who loved cosmos and mojitos. She never did anything illegal, aside from exceeding the speed limit every time she got behind the wheel of her car.

"I just don't see Tori being involved in something like that. As her best friend, I would have been aware."

Stan and Steve collapsed into another laughing jag.

I wasn't amused. "What are you laughing at? This isn't funny!"

"Dudette, you are so clueless," Steve sputtered in between guffaws. "I mean, really, your husband is having an affair with her for how many months, and you have no idea? So why would you know if she was doing some laundering?"

Okay, he had a point. Still…. "Fine. Say she did. How does Randall fit in? What's his connection?"

Stan shrugged. "We're only repeating rumors."

"Do you have anything else you can tell me about Tori? That I might have cluelessly overlooked?"

That sent them into another fit of laughter. This scenario was getting old.

"Well then, I guess I'll go track down Randall and get his side of the story if you're not going to be of any more help."

"Be careful, Em. You don't know if he's the killer or not."

Chapter 16

With Stan's warning ringing in my ears, I drove back to my house and decided to whip up a batch of lemonade cupcakes to take to my sister's place. It was the least I could do, since she was feeding me dinner, plus I needed to have her taste-test the recipe because I planned to serve it at one of her upcoming catering events.

Since I wanted to get to Carrie's house early, I took a few shortcuts in making the cupcakes. After turning the oven on to preheat, I used my food processor to grate the cold butter for both the cupcakes and the frosting. That way, it would reach room temperature more quickly. While I gathered the dry ingredients, I used my KitchenAid stand mixer to cream the semi-soft butter together with the granulated sugar. While the mixture whipped, I added eggs, vanilla, lemon juice, and sour cream. When I made cupcakes for the clients, I would use freshly juiced and zested lemons. Today I relied on lemon juice I had frozen in ice cube trays earlier in the summer as well as lemon oil extract to bump up the flavor. After a quick zap in the microwave to defrost, the juice was almost as good as fresh.

Once the ingredients were combined, I stopped the

machine and dumped the leavening, salt, and flour in all at once, instead of adding them in small increments. I tried to keep the flour from exploding from the mixing bowl but didn't succeed when I turned the mixer back on. White powder coated my workspace and the front of my shirt. Once the flour mixed into the butter and sugar mixture, I stopped the mixer. I didn't want to over-mix and make the cupcakes tough.

I lined a cupcake pan with a rainbow of colorful paper wrappers I knew my nieces would like. Then I portioned the batter into each cup with an ice cream scoop. The oven chimed, which alerted me it was hot enough to bake, so I slid the cupcake pan into the oven and set the timer for fifteen minutes. My mouth watered as the scents of vanilla and lemon filled the air.

While the cupcakes baked, I got out a clean mixing bowl and placed softened butter into it, along with half the confectioners' sugar. I pulsed them together using the KitchenAid mixer, and once I was sure I wouldn't be covered with a cloud of white powdery sugar, I turned it onto medium-high speed to whip for a few minutes. I added three tablespoons of defrosted lemon juice and a couple drops of lemon oil extract, mixed them in, then added the remaining confectioners' sugar. A few minutes of whipping created a fluffy buttercream frosting that made me want to lick the bowl clean.

The timer dinged on my oven, and I removed the golden mini cakes and placed them on a wire rack to cool. I would let my nieces pipe the buttercream frosting onto the cupcakes for dessert after dinner. I fitted two disposable pastry bags with large star tips and put enough frosting into each bag to frost four cupcakes apiece. The remaining buttercream went into a plastic container so I could refill the pastry bags as needed for the girls.

I threw the dirty dishes into the dishwasher and wiped down the counters, placed the still-warm cupcakes into an open container, and then headed to Carrie's. I arrived too early for dinner, but I wanted to help her cook and perhaps wheedle information about Randall out of her.

I parallel parked in front of their craftsman-style home in Costa Mesa, narrowly avoiding scraping the rims on my wheels. Their charcoal-gray home had white trim, and Carrie somehow found time to keep the flower beds weeded and flowering bushes alive. I barely kept a philodendron plant alive, and from what I heard, those were next to impossible to kill. My brother-in-law's car wasn't parked in the driveway, but I didn't expect him to get home from work for another couple of hours.

I admired the artistic new plaque that displayed the name The Bergers etched in a scroll font, hanging from the door. My sister must have purchased it recently. As soon as the doorbell rang, I heard the excited voices of two little girls. Upon throwing the door open with abandon, Sophie and Kaylee launched themselves at me. They were dressed in matching pink T-shirts decorated with sparkly Popsicles interspersed with ice cream cones, while white shorts contrasted with their lightly tanned legs. They were proud of their recently pink-polished toes and made sure I noticed and admired them.

"Auntie Em! Did you bring us a present?" Their bright green eyes, so much like their mother's, beamed at me.

"Girls, I've told you it's impolite to ask guests that question," Carrie scolded. "Let Auntie Em come in and relax."

"It's okay." I hugged the girls tightly then examined Sophie's nose. It looked like she'd survived the raisin crisis. I didn't mention the cupcakes and buttercream I had in my tote because I knew my nieces would whine and beg to frost the little cakes and my sister wouldn't be happy. They needed to wait until they ate a good dinner. Plus, my sister would use the cupcakes as a bribe if needed. "I've missed you both, but sorry, no presents today."

"Where's Pipuh?" Sophie peered around my legs, looking for my pup.

I thought my niece's pronunciation of Piper's name was adorable, and I loved how the two girls doted on her.

"She's with Uncle Philip right now."

"Can we go see Uncle Philip?" Kaylee bounced up and down. "Please?"

"I want to see Pipuh. Why didn't you bring her and Uncle Philip?"

My mind went blank. I didn't know how to explain the breakdown of my marriage to four-year-olds. "Uh, they're training. So, they're busy right now."

My sister looked me over and drew her eyebrows together. If she didn't stop that, she would soon have a permanent wrinkle line between her eyes.

"Soph and Kaylee, why don't you go watch *Frozen*? You can have popcorn while Auntie Em and I fix dinner."

My nieces dropped me like a hot potato and raced for the family room. I was relieved the girls had been given a distraction, but I was worried too. My sister never let her daughters have a snack this late in the afternoon, so I was probably in for another lecture or something equally uncomfortable.

I followed Carrie into her cheerful kitchen. The walls were painted buttercup yellow while the pristinely clean white pine cabinets added a nice contrast. Splashes of small red appliances dotted her white quartz countertop. I handed her the tote containing the cupcakes and buttercream frosting. She peered inside the bag then opened a cabinet door and stashed the cupcakes and frosting. I didn't need to tell her the plan for the cupcakes, since we'd done this many times before.

"Let me know what you think about the flavor and texture of the lemonade cupcakes. If you like it, I'll make them for the Chamber of Commerce lunch. I'll try to find some small strawberries to garnish the frosting for the event."

She nodded, retrieved a cupcake from the container, broke

off a piece, and popped it into her mouth. I was relieved to see her grin, especially after she took a second and then a third bite. "I can't wait to try it with the frosting."

Something fragrant bubbled on her industrial-sized stove-top. I picked up the heavy wooden spoon from the red ceramic spoon rest and lifted the lid that perched on her cast-iron Dutch oven. The heady fragrance of rich beef married with a bold red wine, garlic, onions, carrots, and tomatoes filled the kitchen. I might have drooled while I stirred her beef daube Provençal stew.

"Can you turn off the burner?" Carrie finished off the rest of the cupcake and closed the cabinet door. "I took it out of the oven fifteen minutes ago, but it wasn't thick enough. The extra liquid should have cooked off by now. We can reheat it right before dinner."

"Looks perfect." I really wanted to eat a bowl right now but knew Carrie would scold me.

"Would you start the cornbread muffins while I get the girls their popcorn?"

"Uh-hum." I caved in and put a tablespoon-sized bite of stew in my mouth. I needed to make sure she had properly seasoned the stew. At least that would be my excuse if my sister complained.

Since I spent so much time helping Carrie with her cater-ing, I knew her kitchen as well as my own. I busied myself stir-ring cornmeal, flour, baking powder, sugar, and salt together, along with a pinch of cayenne pepper. Thomas would appre-ciate a lot more spice, but Sophie and Kaylee would complain. My sister came back as I whipped eggs and milk together.

"You're off work early today."

"Yep." I gave the batter a quick stir.

Here came the lecture, although I wasn't sure what issue she would tackle first. I considered stalling by asking about her pregnancy but decided to let her vent about my shortcomings first. The evening would be more pleasant that way.

"I got a call from Thomas early this afternoon."

I froze. Someone from my company must have called him. If he knew they had fired me, then so did my sister. Rats! I'd hoped to hide my disgrace for a few days and find another job in the meantime. But deep down, I knew I only kidded myself. No one would hire a murder suspect.

"I didn't believe his news, so I called your office line. Imagine my surprise when your phone had a recorded message to press zero for assistance with no option for leaving a voice mail. What's going on?"

"Apparently, Mr. Wilkins couldn't handle my notorious Facebook photo and being questioned by the police about Tori. I got fired." The more I thought about it, the angrier and more hurt I became. Why had Tori wanted to ruin my life so completely? I couldn't tell my sister someone tried to black-mail my boss from my company email account because that person certainly had been Tori, and I'd never hear the end of her blaming me for my choice of friends.

"What are you going to do? How are you going to pay your mortgage and pay Mother back?"

I whipped my head around so fast to look at my sister that I became a little dizzy. "Wha… what? What do you mean pay Mother back?"

"The money you borrowed when you and Philip bought your condo. How did you forget borrowing thirty thousand dollars?" My sister shook her head. "I was a little hurt you never told me but figured your sense of pride, or Philip's pride, kept you from sharing with me."

The room spun, and I had to sit down or else I would have fallen. I found a kitchen chair as my knees collapsed. "I didn't borrow money from Mother. This is the first I've heard anything about it."

I looked at my sister as we both said, "Philip!"

"That snake! That, that…." I bit my tongue when I remembered my nieces were in the house and had radar ears.

"Why would he do that without even asking me? He's the one who borrowed it, so he will have to pay it back."

Deep down I acknowledged I would be the one to pay. Philip counted on the fact that I'd never skip out on repaying my mother the debt.

"How could he keep it a secret?" My sister stared at me incredulously. "You're an accountant and should have your finger on every penny that comes in and out of your house."

"You're not married to someone like Philip," I whined. "He has this macho image that a man is the head of the household and takes care of everything. Honestly, I got so sick of numbers after working with them all day long, I was happy he wanted to do all the banking and bill paying."

I looked at the statements every once in a while, but I didn't pay close attention. I realized several months had passed since I'd bothered to look. I had been involved in several detailed, brain-numbing audits for my employer's clients. My head swam with numbers by the end of the day, which often included long overtime hours. My weekends had been busy with my baking for my sister's catering contracts, so I didn't do much besides bake and perform general household chores. It looked like I had wrongfully assumed my husband had our finances under control. It was also entirely possible Philip had hidden any incriminating documents in case I went looking.

"How much has he paid her back?" I hoped he had poured the extra cash from my overtime checks into repaying the loan. I'd been hyperaware our mortgage was more than I was comfortable with when we purchased the house, but Philip had insisted on buying it anyway.

My sister remained silent but gave a small shake of her head.

My mouth fell open, and the blood drained from my face again. "He hasn't paid her one red cent?"

"I'm afraid that's the case. He always gave Mother the sob

story that the bank tacked on so many fees that the mortgage ended up being much higher than you expected." Carrie narrowed her eyes. "She never said anything because he told her you were super-stressed out from demanding to buy your condo in the first place. He put the blame all on you."

"That, that… rat! He's the one who wore me down, begged me to buy the place when I was uncomfortable with the price." My face felt hot, and I became short of breath. "I've got to go talk to Mother and explain. What am I going to do? I don't have a job. We're going to have to sell the condo. Where will I live?"

"You can stay with us." My sister gave me a brief hug. "And Thomas can help you find a job."

I pointed at her belly. "You've got a full house with another one on the way. But thanks for the offer."

"There's always Mother. She has plenty of room."

I shivered. Move in with Mother? "Perish that idea! My car would be more comfortable than living with her."

"I'll call Thomas and see if he can find you a job. Hopefully things won't get so desperate."

"No one will want to hire me." I groaned. "I'm a murder suspect. Plus, everyone has seen that photo on Facebook."

My sister laughed.

"It's not funny."

"That photo might be useful if you get an interview with the right person." Her eyebrows wagged up and down.

"Ick. I don't want to work for someone like that." Beggars couldn't be choosers, though.

My sister dished up a bowl of the succulent beef stew and handed it to me. "Eat this then go talk to Mother. She'll know what you should do."

And that was exactly what I worried about.

I MADE a detour home before driving to my mother's house.

If I examined the mortgage and credit card statements, I might have a better grasp of what financial crisis faced me. I hoped I wouldn't find anything else Philip might have hidden from me. A tingly sensation crept down my spine, and I got a terrible premonition about our financial situation, but I shook it off. I would concentrate on the facts once I had them in hand.

When I opened the door, I missed Piper jumping into my arms. I needed to add her custody to my list of things to resolve with Philip. I hoped he would at least let me have joint custody. Full-time would be better, and he could have visitation rights on his days off. How did my life dissolve into this mess? Why did Philip and Tori need to destroy my carefully planned life?

I opened filing drawers in our home office, looking for bank statements and any other documentation that would give me an overall picture of what faced me. Philip would try to stick me with the entire debt, and I had no illusions that it wouldn't take a lot of money for attorney fees to force him to help pay. Money I certainly didn't have and money that needed to go to my attorney to keep me out of prison.

No financial documents were found in our office, aside from paid invoices for utilities and cell phones. I moved on to our bedroom and rifled through drawers but came up empty-handed. Philip had done a thorough job of removing most of his belongings, so there wasn't much to go through. He must have taken all the financial files with him. But why?

I went through my own drawers, just in case he had hidden the files there for some unknown reason. Although I didn't find the files, I came across an old jewelry box that my paternal grandmother had given me as a child. The wooden box, painted a delicate pink shade, was now scratched and marked with age. The box had held the trinkets and coins she gave me on each visit. Those gifts ended with her untimely death right after I turned five, and even though I barely remembered her, I had kept the box all these years. It now held the few photos I had of my grandmother, my dad, and my very young self. A lump filled my throat. People I loved always seemed to leave me.

I wrestled with the jammed tarnished brass latch and opened the cover of the box. Years had passed since I'd thumbed through the photos. They brought up painful memories that were best left buried, but in my current mood, I wanted to see them again. An old black-and-white photo of my grandmother as a young teen sat on top of the few photos. She wore a dark pencil skirt and a white frothy blouse with the requisite pearls wrapped around her neck. Her hair, cut chin-length, had a wave to it. The photo printed in black and white, so I couldn't tell the color of her hair. It wasn't blonde, dark brown, or black. I wondered if it might be red like mine. I set her photo aside and picked up the one of her holding my father, in which he appeared as a toddler. He appeared to be squirming to get out of her arms, and I remembered her telling me he had always been a handful.

A sandwich-sized plastic baggie wedged beneath the remaining photos grabbed my attention. I didn't remember putting anything in my jewelry box other than the photos. I pulled the bag out and saw it contained a small, four-inch-by-six-inch, highly colorful, abstract painting. I'd never set eyes on this painting before. Bold multi-hued blue geometric patterns covered the background, while slashes of red and yellow lines were randomly strewn across the canvas.

I held it up to the light and looked at the tiny signature in one of the corners to see if I recognized it. I didn't, so I pulled my cell phone out and Googled the artist's name. Once the information loaded, along with a photo of the local artist who created the piece, I almost dropped my phone. In fact, I almost fainted.

The painting I held in my hands was titled *Chaotic Zeus* and was valued close to ten thousand dollars. It had been stolen two months before. The artist was Mrs. Landow herself, painting under the name of Arlette Land. In addition to this painting being stolen right before the planned exhibit, twenty other canvases had suffered the same fate and had never been found. The value of the stolen artwork totaled close to half a million dollars.

How did it get into my jewelry box? I certainly didn't place it there, and I was sure Philip wouldn't be involved in stolen art. Had Tori been involved in the art theft like Mrs. Landow had accused her? Did Tori plan on me taking the fall for the theft to get me out of the picture so she could have Philip? My hands trembled while I tried to decide what to do. If the police searched my house and found the painting, I would be in a world of trouble—more trouble than I needed with my current woes.

Unfortunately, my fingerprints now covered the baggie. I didn't want to remove the bag because I feared I might damage the artwork. Then I worried because I'd already Googled the painting. What if the police confiscated my phone? They would find my search. I put my family photos back into the jewelry box and returned it to the dresser drawer.

The stolen art needed to be hidden in case the detective came with a search warrant. The only reasonable thing I could do would be to let my attorney know and follow his advice on turning in the painting without taking the blame for the theft. That would be next to impossible to do now that Mrs. Landow could identify me. I worried, too, that someone else had worked with Tori and would come looking for the artwork.

Chapter 17

I grabbed the ladder and some duct tape from the garage and trudged back to my bedroom closet. After placing the baggie inside a zipper plastic bag, I wrapped it inside a paper bag. The dusty attic, which was really not much more than a crawl space located above the master bedroom, contained the furnace. It seemed like the best hiding place I could find, so I taped the package to the back of the furnace. Since it was August, I wasn't worried about a potential fire. I wouldn't use the furnace for another several months. Even then, it was on for an hour here or an hour there on chilly mornings before work. The package would be long gone by then.

After returning the ladder to the garage, I logged into our bank accounts on the laptop. I hoped seeing the complete picture about my financial health would relieve some of my anxiety. At least Philip hadn't absconded with our laptop, since I couldn't afford to replace it. I tried a variety of user-names and passwords. With each new one I tried, my hands got shakier and shakier. None of the combinations worked, even though I was positive Philip had told me what it was eons ago. Philip must have changed it. What was he hiding?

My only choice in finding answers would be to confront Philip and demand an explanation or visit the bank. I chose the bank. I wasn't ready for a showdown with Philip...yet. Besides, I was never good at confrontation, especially with Philip. It was long past time for me to grow a backbone. It was time to stop being a lemming. Time to step up to the plate and swing the bat. Time to... I rolled my eyes. My mother's clichés were rubbing off on me.

Fighting the habit of putting fresh food in Piper's bowl, I grabbed my keys and headed to the bank. My fingers drummed the steering wheel of my car, the tempo increasing at each stoplight that held me up. I continued to berate myself for becoming so lackadaisical and relying on Philip so completely. Clearly he didn't have my best interests or those of our marriage in mind. He never had.

I glanced at my watch when I pulled into the bank's parking lot. Five forty-five. I had cut it close, but I had fifteen minutes before they closed. Good. That should give me plenty of time to get a recap of my accounts and mortgage. Unless there was a long line, but luck was on my side... this time. The second the young greeter near the door took my name and pointed toward the business side of the bank, a middle-aged man, trying to look much younger than his age by bleaching his short, spiked hair, rose from his glassed-in cubicle and came toward me.

"Good afternoon. I'm Del Blasser." He stretched out his hand to shake mine. "How can I help you today?"

"I'd like to check on my mortgage balance and bank accounts. I seem to have forgotten both my login and pass-words. Unfortunately, my husband isn't available for a few days to remind me what they are."

Del raised his eyebrows for an instant then his profession-alism took over. "Of course, Missus...?"

"Emory Martinez. Sorry, I forgot to introduce myself." I gave him what I hoped was a charming grin, although, with the way I felt, it was probably a grimace. "I have my bank account numbers but forgot to bring the mortgage statement. Can you help me?"

The lies were slipping out of my mouth faster and faster. I should be worrying about my soul.

"Of course, Mrs. Martinez. I'll just need to see your ID and at least one of your bank account numbers." He gestured toward his cubicle. "Please come to my office and make yourself comfortable. Can I get you some coffee or water?"

Given the lateness of the day, I was sure he hoped to wrap this up and get out of here. Even though I was thirsty, I didn't want to prolong this man's workday any longer than necessary.

I handed him my driver's license and my checkbook. "I'm fine, but thank you."

Del exhaled loudly as he clicked away on his keyboard. Obviously, he didn't want me holding him up past six. He glanced at me a time or two before averting his eyes and concentrating on his computer screen situated on the side of his desk. It angled away from where I was sitting, so I couldn't see what he was looking at.

Del blew out a long sigh, shook his head, and then leaned back. "Mrs. Martinez, your mortgage and second mortgage appear to be in arrears, almost to the point of defaulting on the loans."

A buzzing began in my ears the moment I heard "second mortgage," so I almost missed the word "default." I wished he would take that word back. It meant that my life, as I knew it, was officially over. Without a doubt, I would pay for Philip's transgressions for the rest of my days.

I licked my dry lips, which were on the verge of cracking from mashing them so hard together to keep from screaming. "Can you tell me the balances?"

I almost fell out of the chair when he uttered the ungodly figures. This was it. This meant bankruptcy unless Mother pulled strings and sold the condo right away with a real estate agent willing to waive their fee. Even then I would be repaying both Mother and the bank back for years. I was certain Philip would take the easy route of declaring bankruptcy and walk away scot free. Tears stung my eyes, but I blinked several times, trying to keep them from spilling down my cheeks.

"It appears that interest-only payments have been made for quite some time, and then those stopped two months ago." The banker mumbled something I didn't hear, shaking his head. "Am I correct in assuming you weren't aware of the situation?"

I nodded, not trusting my voice to remain steady.

"I can print out copies of the last few months' worth of statements for you."

"Thank you." I closed my eyes. "Can you tell me our checking and savings account balances?"

I dreaded knowing but knew I had to see the whole picture. I briefly wondered if my defense attorney could handle my divorce at the same time and give me a discount on his services. Kind of like a buy-one-get-one-free type of deal.

"Your checking account has one thousand two hundred twenty-nine dollars and seventy-eight cents in it." Del clicked more keys and cleared his throat. "A check for five thousand dollars written to cash cleared yesterday."

What was Philip doing with all our money? What was he involved in? The buzzing in my ears got louder, and my cheeks burned.

"Your savings account balance is five hundred dollars, which is the minimum amount required to avoid fees."

Lucky me. Philip didn't rack up bank fees when he emptied our accounts. My mind was spinning. I needed to check on my 401k account and take him off as a beneficiary. Same thing for my life insurance policy. I didn't want to end up like Tori if he was so desperate for money.

"Mrs. Martinez?" Del had been trying to get my attention.

"Sorry. You can imagine this is a lot to take in."

"I'm terribly sorry. Is there anything else I can do for you?"

I wasn't sure he was sincere when I saw him glance at his desktop clock.

"What does the balance have to be on the checking account to avoid fees?"

"That would be five hundred dollars as well."

"Can you print out the statements for the last six months on both my checking account and savings account?"

"Certainly." He pressed more keys, and his printer hummed again. "Normally there are fees for printouts, but I'll waive them for you."

"I truly appreciate that."

He handed me the warm printouts, which I stuffed into my purse.

"Is there anything else I can do for you, Mrs. Martinez?"

I knew he wasn't sincere but decided I'd take up a little more of his time anyway.

I fumbled to find my blank checks, which had fallen to the bottom of my purse, and wrote a check for cash. "Can you cash this for me, or do I need to visit the teller window?"

I thought I heard another sigh, but Del nodded. "How do you want your cash?"

"Twenties are fine." I was leaving just a bit over five hundred dollars in the checking account, since I figured two could play this game.

Del disappeared for several minutes then returned with a stack of green bills. He counted out the money so fast I couldn't follow but decided to trust him. It was already past six, and I'd overstayed my welcome.

"Thank you for your time, Del."

I shoved the cash into my purse and headed to my car to face my mother.

The drive to my mother's house in Irvine was far too

short. Where was the 405 freeway rush-hour traffic when you needed it? My palms were sweaty by the time I pulled up in front of the guard shack at their development. When the uniformed security guard saw me, he opened the massive wrought-iron gate and waved me through.

I kept my car five miles beneath the speed limit posted within the neighborhood of cookie-cutter mini-mansions. Carrie was right. My mother and Lars had enough room if I needed a place to stay. Given my financial outlook, my options were nonexistent, but the disgrace made me shudder anyway. I pulled in front of their house, which was painted a neutral sand-gray. The color was replicated in varying shades on all the other houses on her block. The brick-red Spanish roof tiles added the only pop of color on the house. Everyone had the requisite drought-resistant landscaping: cactus, succulents, and what I called scrub-brush. In late winter, some of the plants would bloom, but in the heat of August, they looked dusty green and drab.

I squinted at the white Tahoe parked across the street. I hoped the vehicle wasn't Philip's. I glanced at my mother's house then walked to the vehicle and looked in. Fast-food wrappers and sacks littered the floorboard, and a windbreaker with the Chargers logo on it was inside. What was that slime doing at my mother's house?

Chapter 18

I rang the doorbell before inserting my key into the lock and let myself in. Piper barked and whined from the kitchen area. I heard her claws scratch my mother's travertine flooring as she ran full force down the long hallway toward me. My dog jumped and danced in front of me, and I couldn't help laughing at her antics. Her tail acted like a mini helicopter prop, wagging faster and faster. I gathered her up in my arms and let her give me puppy kisses. I missed her as much as she apparently missed me.

"Darling, I didn't know you were dropping by." My mother breezed in and kissed my cheek. She tried to avoid my squirming dog as she placed her lips close to my ear. "Philip is here. Now would be the perfect time to make up and rescue your marriage."

"That is not going to happen, Mother," I hissed. "There's a lot of things you need to know about that... that... creep. He's not the gentleman he's led you to believe he is."

My mother looked shocked. "Now, Emory, that kind of attitude will get you nowhere. Come in here and be nice."

I set Piper down. She pranced beside me, not wanting to

let me out of her sight. "I'm done letting Philip walk all over me. He's betrayed me on so many levels."

I didn't have the chance to tell her because the man I hoped would soon be my ex walked in.

"I thought I heard your voice, Em." He stood there puffing his chest out, and I swore he even sucked in his gut. "Addie and I have been speaking, and I think there's been a huge misunderstanding. We've put too much time in our marriage to call it quits, and I'm willing to overlook your indiscretion and put it behind us."

"My indiscretion?" I sputtered, trying to get the word out. "How about me catching you in the middle of 'it' with Tori?"

"She didn't mean anything to me." Philip ran his fingers through his thick black hair and avoided looking at me.

As if Tori's insignificance to him made his affair forgivable. "Aside from your fling with Tori, let's talk about the money you borrowed from my mother, behind my back."

"What do you mean, Emory?" I had my mother's full attention now. "Philip said you were too embarrassed to ask, but you had your heart set on that condo."

"I just found out from Carrie. I had no idea we owed you money or that this jerk hasn't paid one cent back on that loan."

"Hey, don't be calling me names, you…" Philip bit his tongue when he saw my mother's face. You don't cuss or use crude language in front of Mother.

"Is it true, Philip?" Her voice sounded downright frosty.

Before he answered, I jumped in. I wanted to get all his transgressions on the table before he ran off. I was beginning to see him for the coward he was.

"Not only did he borrow money from you, but he took out a second mortgage on our home and has neglected to make anything but interest payments. Even those payments have stopped, so now we're nearing foreclosure." I took a deep breath. "Would you care to explain how that has happened? We both earned good money."

Like I said, Philip was a coward. He flipped me off and flew through the front door, and his tires peeled as he drove down the street.

"Well, I never…" My mother's voice trailed off. "I never really liked him and thought you could do so much better for yourself."

My eyeballs tried to roll around in their sockets as I picked up Piper. At least my pup was with me now. I wouldn't give her up.

I cleared my throat and tried to stand taller. "Now that you've heard most of the disaster that is my life, I might as well tell you the rest."

"What, there's more?" Mother placed her hand over her heart. "You're not pregnant, are you?"

"No!" I shuddered. I guessed things could be worse than they already were. "I lost my job today."

My mother uncharacteristically put her arms around me and squished Piper between us. "Oh, darling, I'm sorry you're going through such a difficult time. Lars and I are here for you."

Her tenderness made my eyes sting. When she stepped away from me, I put Piper back on the floor and swiped my hands over my eyes. "I know, but I feel like I should be responsible for this mess. I'm not sure where to even start to make it right."

"Let's have a cup of tea and a cookie. We can go over your options and figure this out." My mother patted my shoulder. Apparently, one hug was enough. "There's no way I'll let my daughter get dragged through the mud. We have a reputation to uphold."

There it was. She wasn't as concerned for me as she was for her reputation. At this point I had run out of options, so I followed her into the spacious kitchen, which brimmed with white marble countertops and stainless appliances, and started the kettle for tea.

I made Lady Gray tea and plated store-bought chocolate chip cookies from the glass cookie jar sitting on the counter. My sister and I were both great cooks, but for some reason, that skill eluded our mother. Unless we brought homemade goodies, we made do with pre-packaged ones. My mother ignored her tea and furiously tapped on her smartphone instead. When a chime answered her text, she beamed.

"I've scheduled an appointment with the best real estate agent in Orange County tomorrow morning at nine. She'll meet us at your condo and can show it right away, since she has a buyer who's already been looking in the area." My mother looked at me expectantly. "Don't you agree that the quicker you sell the condo and pay the debt, the sooner you'll get back on your feet?"

I nodded. "Of course, except I don't have anywhere to live. I thought it would take a few months."

"Hmmmm. I have an idea, but I'll need to call in some favors." She tapped her acrylic French-tipped nails on the glass table. "Give me a day or two, and then I'll tell you my plan."

I stared pointedly at the guest bedrooms on the second floor, situated above her kitchen. "No job means no money for rent."

"There's no need to move back home. We can keep that option as a last resort." Mother returned to tapping on her cell phone. "If all goes as planned, you'll have a new job to go with your accommodations."

Why did I feel I had made a deal with the devil? I would be beholden to my mother for the rest of my life, and she would never, ever let me forget about it. Piper snuggled into my lap, and I hugged her close.

"Why was Philip here?"

"He wanted to know if you had given me a new key to

your place. You didn't waste any time locking him out." Mother shook her head. "He's not thrilled about that."

"He's the one who had the affair and moved out. I didn't like him letting himself into my space whenever he felt like it." I nibbled on another cookie, even though the cookies weren't very good. "He wasn't here to rescue our marriage?"

"No. I thought I might help you both see reasons to stay together if I got you in the same room. I had him convinced to work on it, and then you blew up."

"But why? Why would you want me to stay with someone who cheated on me?"

"Men stray, but that doesn't mean they don't love you and can't move forward and have a meaningful relationship with their wife."

"That's an archaic way to look at marriage." I wondered whether Lars had strayed or if she was talking about my father—except that hadn't worked out at all. My dad left us and never looked back. I wanted to ask, but my mother was being unusually open, and I didn't want to risk her clamming up again, since my father was a forbidden subject. "Wedding vows apply to both husband and wife. Besides, Philip has betrayed me on so many levels."

"I see that now." She patted my hand. "Don't worry. I'm on your side."

"I guess I need to talk to an attorney and start divorce proceedings. I want to protect myself as much as possible since Philip got us so far into debt."

Mother was back on her smartphone tapping away. "I told Lars to set up an appointment with his fraternity brother who specializes in family law. Hopefully he can fit you in within the next day or two."

Suggest a task to my mother, and she'd get it done before you'd even finished talking about it. "I can't afford another attorney, and if he's friends with Lars, he will be expensive.

Do you think Mel Shearwood could do a twofer? Keep me out of jail and write up divorce papers?"

"Don't joke about this, Emory. If you want to walk away from this marriage without paying Philip's debt for the rest of your life, you need someone who knows what they're doing." She took a sip of the cooled tea. "You have to wonder how he took out a second mortgage on the condo without your signature. That should clear you of any financial obligation."

Unless he had Tori forge my signature. And then what? Would I press charges against him for fraud? My gut told me Philip was in over his head with something shady. Did Tori get him involved? Could he have killed her over it going terribly wrong?

Mother offered to whip up omelets for dinner, so I stayed until it got dark. Fresh strawberries and honeydew melon accompanied the simple fare. Piper sat at my feet, hoping for a few nibbles of egg, while my mother chatted about inane topics like her golf handicap and the weather.

I finally headed home, loaded down with collapsed boxes and packing tape with instructions to get ready to move. Piper sat in the passenger seat next to me, her tail wagging. She was happy to be going home. At least she looked like she was well fed and recently bathed and brushed. Despite his actions toward me, Philip loved Piper.

I pulled my car into the garage. The second I opened the Honda's door, Piper jumped over me, ran to the door leading into the house, and barked.

Chapter 19

"I know you're excited to be home, Piper. Give me a second to get my things." I remembered that Mother had sent me home with some leftover fruit too.

Instead of quieting down, Piper barked even louder. I unlocked the door leading into the kitchen and set my packages and purse on the counter. Piper raced to my bedroom and barked without letting up. When her bark changed to a deep growl, the hairs on the back of my neck stood up. Was someone in the house? Should I call the police?

"Piper, come, girl." Of course she didn't listen and barked again. Perhaps a rodent had slipped in and she had it cornered.

I tiptoed to the bedroom and came to a sudden halt. Someone had smashed the window and ransacked every drawer then strewn the contents across the carpet. My clothes had been yanked from the closet and various garments piled in heaps on the floor. My heart broke when I saw my girlhood jewelry box smashed to pieces and my treasured photos ripped in half. I knew I had digital copies on my laptop, and I could always reprint the photos, but somehow knowing my grandmother and my father had once touched these same pieces of paper used to bring me comfort.

Philip. It must have been Philip, since he had desperately wanted the new key from my mother. I put Piper in her crate so she wouldn't cut her paws on the glass littering my bedroom floor carpet. After closing the curtain over the smashed window, I wrestled the ladder from the garage into position in my closet and inched my way into the attic. I gave a sigh of relief when I felt the paper bag secured to the back of the furnace. That had to be what he was searching for, and I would do everything I could to keep it from him. Somehow, I knew if Philip got his hands on that little painting, I would find myself framed for another crime.

I shivered, wondering if I had been living with a murderer. Would I be the next victim? I needed to call the police and file a report. Not that they would do anything about this. Nothing had been stolen, but I hoped insurance would cover the repairs. I hesitated. Was Philip involved in this? Or were other cops involved? I was spooking myself and really didn't want to be here by myself when the police sent someone to take a report.

Shutting the bedroom door, I released Piper. She ran to my bedroom door and barked a few times before running to her food bowl. She looked at me and whined while wagging her tail.

"Okay, I get it." I filled her bowl with dry dog food and refreshed her water.

Piper sniffed her dish once then looked up at me and started the whining again. Oh boy. What had Philip been feeding her? She'd obviously been spoiled over the last couple of days. I rummaged in my freezer and found dog treats I had made from a recipe in a cozy mystery book. After quickly defrosting one treat in the microwave, I crumbled it over her food. She sniffed it, looked at me, and chowed down like she hadn't eaten in a month. I would need to work on getting her to eat her regular food, but now wasn't the time.

I called my attorney's cell phone. He answered with a gruff, whadda-you-want attitude.

"Hi, Mel, it's Emory. Sorry to disturb you after office hours, but someone broke into my house, and I'm afraid to call the police." I was talking as fast as I could, so some of my words came out garbled. It didn't help that I had started shivering. Was I catching a cold?

"Whoa. Slow down. Are you safe? Are you sure the intruder is gone?"

"I'm sure no one is here, and I have Piper, so I feel safe." If my husband came after me, though, I wasn't sure our dog would protect me. "But I think it was Philip who broke in, so I'm worried about calling the police."

"Call them to file a report." I heard a huge sigh on the phone. "I'll be there in ten minutes. You'd better call a glass repair company while you're waiting."

I called the main number for the police station closest to my house. It wasn't an emergency, so I didn't want to clog up the 9-1-1 lines. After giving my information, they told me someone would be out within an hour to brush for fingerprints and take a report.

I searched my phone for window repair companies and made a few calls. Not one call was answered. Even the number listed as a 24-hour-emergency repair service went to voice mail. I left a message. Fifteen minutes had come and gone from the time I had spoken to Mel. I had probably interrupted his dinner but was relieved I wouldn't be alone when the police came. I could also give him the painting and let him figure out what to do with it.

When the doorbell rang, I clipped a leash on Piper and then answered the door. Mel stood there, glaring at Detective Jackson. Piper barked at the two men and lunged at the detective. The leash almost slipped from my hand, but I grabbed it before Piper snapped at him.

"I'm so sorry about that, Detective Jackson." I pulled Piper back into the house and wedged her behind me. "This has been an upsetting time for her, and she must feel the need to protect me. Let me crate her."

As I placed a soft chew toy in the crate with my dog, I wondered about the detective. Why had Piper tried to attack him? I thought dogs were good judges of character, and I worried Detective Jackson might be involved, aside from trying to prove I was Tori's killer.

The two men had let themselves in and sat at my dining table. I nodded at them both before choosing a seat next to Mel.

"Detective Jackson, what brings you here?" My voice quivered. "Surely my house being broken into doesn't warrant a homicide detective taking down the report."

"I want to make sure you're not using this as a way to get rid of any evidence." He waved his hand around the room. "I'll need to look around and dust for prints. Not that I expect to find any."

My eyes narrowed. I was ready to give in to my annoyance over his assumptions and tell him off. When a meaty hand squeezed my arm, and I saw my attorney glaring at me instead of at the detective, I clamped my lips together and kept them clamped.

"Fine," I hissed from the corner of my mouth.

"Do you mind if I look around now, Mrs. Martinez?" The detective seemed to be trying to avoid involving Mel.

"Do you have a warrant?" my attorney answered.

"No. Your client called us about a break-in, remember?"

This wouldn't get resolved unless I stepped up. "Fine, the smashed window is in my bedroom. The jerk dumped all my clothes on the floor and destroyed some photos. Nothing is missing that I can tell, but I'd like to file a report for the insurance company just in case."

Mel turned his glare back at me, and I shrugged. "I want to get this over with so I can repair the window and clean up since my mother scheduled a real estate agent to come over in the morning."

I slapped my hand over my mouth. Oh. My. Gosh. My mother would flip if I didn't have this place pristine when she showed up in the morning with the realtor. I realized, with or without a window repairman, I wouldn't be sleeping at all tonight.

"You're not wasting any time moving forward, Mrs. Martinez." The detective sat back down. "Is there a particular reason for rushing to sell your home?"

Again a meaty hand squeezed my arm, except the squeeze was a lot harder this time. Mel must have been trying to make his point and get me to stop opening my mouth.

"My client's reasons are personal, Detective, and have nothing to do with your case."

"I guess that remains to be seen, but it definitely makes me suspicious."

As if I needed anything else to make him suspicious of me. Why wasn't he looking into Philip? Oh yeah, my hopefully-soon-to-be-ex was a cop. They stuck together and protected their own.

Once Detective Jackson was out of hearing range, my attorney turned his glare back to me. "If you weren't Lars's stepdaughter, I would decline representing you. What part of not talking do you not understand?"

Funny thing, before all this murder stuff, I would have said I was a very quiet and shy person. I didn't chat much unless Tori got me wound up. But now, I couldn't be quiet to save my life.

"I don't mean to talk. It's just that I have to make him understand I'm innocent."

"No, you don't have to make him understand you're innocent. Your job is to sit there and be quiet. My job is to keep you out of jail by providing reasonable doubt when you go to trial." Mel leaned in close to my ear and hissed, "Do I make myself clear?"

I nodded and plastered what I hoped was a contrite expression on my face. My stomach felt like a volcano ready to erupt. I didn't want reasonable doubt. I wanted people to know I was completely innocent instead of always wondering how I got away with murder, like they did with O. J. Simpson. It looked like I would have to step up my own investigation, since neither my attorney nor Detective Jackson would clear my name.

Mel cleared his throat. "Emory, please pay attention."

"What?"

"I've been trying to ask you why you're putting the condo up for sale."

"Because I lost my job and I'm in debt, thanks to Philip. I don't trust him to help pay for the loans he took out, so I'm selling."

"I heard about you getting fired. You should have called me."

"Why? There isn't anything you could have done." News apparently traveled fast in our town. I was sure I'd hear from Mother that her bridge club ladies' chatter would be focused on my troubled life. She wasn't going to be happy.

"It's a wrongful termination. I can still file a lawsuit and get your job back."

"Uh, let's not do that yet. My mother thinks she can get me another job and a place to live." I cringed when I said that. I sounded like a loser, but I would be utterly humiliated to show my face back at my accounting firm.

"Just let me know when you're ready." Mel stood to leave.

"Do you have to go now? There's something I want to show you after the detective leaves."

"Oh, you mean this?" Detective Jackson strode into the room, holding up the baggie containing the stolen artwork.

Chapter 20

"How did you…?" My voice squeaked. "That's not mine. I can explain it."

"Detective Jackson, would you give me a moment to confer with my client?" Mel's forehead wrinkles were furrowed so deep from frowning at me, you could have planted seeds in them.

I thought I saw the detective roll his eyes, but at least he nodded. "I need to go through the clothing more thoroughly. See if I missed anything."

"Wait, you were only supposed to take fingerprints and write a report for my insurance company." Once more, the meaty hand clamped onto my arm and squeezed. I was sure I would have a bruise.

"My client is right. We'll have to ask you to leave all of her property here and come back with a search warrant."

"Nice try, Mel. You know I can confiscate items if I happen to think a crime has been committed." Detective Jackson laughed. "By the way, thanks for leaving the ladder set up in the closet. It made my job easier. I'll be back with a warrant to continue my search."

"When will that be?"

Mel gave me another scowl.

"My mother is coming with a real estate agent in the morning, and it would be awkward if you came while they were both here."

Oh boy, it would be beyond awkward. My mother would disown me if that happened. I tried not to think about how it would be even worse when I was arrested for possession of stolen artwork.

"I think you have more serious issues than dealing with your mother, Mrs. Martinez. Whoever broke in showed a lot of rage when they smashed your jewelry box and ripped up your photos. On top of this problem." The detective held up the painting.

I knew what he said was true, but then again, he didn't know my mother.

After the detective left without telling me when he would be back with the warrant, Mel called a glass company, and someone on the phone promised they would replace the window within an hour. I let Piper out of her crate and offered my attorney some tea or coffee, which he declined. After I made myself some hot tea with honey, I popped a dozen frozen Lemon Crinkles into the oven. I needed comfort.

With a sigh, Mel plopped back into a dining-room chair. "You'd better tell me how you got into this fiasco tonight while we wait for the glazier."

I explained how I had found the painting hiding in my childhood jewelry box, which I hadn't opened in years.

"I assume your fingerprints are covering the purported stolen painting?"

"I didn't know what it was, so I picked it up." I shook my head. "It has to be Tori's or maybe Philip's, even though I find it hard to believe. But there's no other explanation."

"It's obvious whoever broke in here is angry the painting wasn't where they left it." Mel looked me over. "You shouldn't stay here, even with the window repaired. Maybe you can stay with a friend—or better yet, with your mother and Lars, since they live in a gated, guarded community."

I shuddered. "Let me call my sister. I can sleep on their sofa."

"Do you really want to put your sister and her children in danger? Someone is angry and might try to find that package again."

"Oh, I didn't think about that. You're right." I shuddered again. "I'll have to stay with my mother."

Even though Mel had declined a beverage, he ate almost the full baking sheet of warm Lemon Crinkles. While the cookies kept him occupied, I hurriedly stuffed clothing into the closet and the drawers of my dresser, not bothering to hang or fold anything up. I kept a few things out to put into an overnight bag to take to my mother's house, but I was more concerned about the condo looking decent for the real estate appointment. After I cleaned up the last bit of broken glass, the doorbell rang. I put Piper back into her crate so she wouldn't bark her head off at yet another stranger entering our home.

"Thanks for coming by on such short notice." I swung the door wide open to admit the glazier. Only it wasn't the glass guy. It was Randall.

"Did I come at a bad time?"

"It might have been appropriate to call before you dropped by." I brushed a cookie crumb from my cheek and hoped I didn't have others clinging to my face. "Someone broke in, so I'm waiting for the glass repair person."

"I called several times and left messages. When I didn't hear from you, I was a little worried. Are you okay?"

"You might as well come in. My attorney is here too."

Randall followed me into the kitchen, where I introduced him and my attorney to each other. I put more frozen cookie balls, chocolate chip this time, into the hot oven, and let Piper back out of her crate. Instead of barking at Randall, she sniffed him, nudged his hand, and insisted he pet her. Interesting. I hoped that meant she was a good judge of character, but then again, my dog adored Philip.

"Is anything missing? Do you know why they broke in?"

"Nothing is missing that I can tell."

Now, if my attorney hadn't been present, I would have spilled the entire story. But one menacing glare from Mel reminded me to keep my lips zipped. I also remembered that he charged by the hour, which made him an expensive babysitter—one I couldn't afford, even under the best circumstances.

"Mel, since Randall is here to keep me company, you don't need to wait around for the glazier." Hint, hint. When I saw him eyeballing the cookies in the oven, I wondered if he'd take cookies as a form of payment. "I'm sure the repairman will be here soon, and I promise to go back to my mother's tonight."

Mel took a long look at Randall and nodded. "Make sure she does that, young man."

"Sure. No problem."

My dog gave Randall a gentle nose nudge to remind him she was being neglected, so he bent back down to give Piper more love.

I walked my attorney to the door and opened it just as the glass guy rang the bell. I cringed. Piper wasn't in her crate. This could get ugly. My dog wasn't a bad dog, but she was protective and acted like she wanted to tear someone's arm off, especially when the doorbell rang and a stranger appeared. Once she settled down, she was fine, which was why the crate training had been helpful. Except, this time, there was no barking and no golden mass of fur barreling through the front door at the unsuspecting man.

Mel had finished giving the glazier instructions, so I led the middle-aged man, dressed in a khaki uniform with the name Cody embroidered on his shirt, to my bedroom. He took a few measurements and asked if I could leave the front door unlocked, since he'd be going in and out multiple times. My dog was being uncharacteristically quiet, so I went back to the kitchen and found Piper on her back, legs splayed out. Randall was giving her a massage. I shivered—in a good way —when I imagined getting a massage like that from Randall. I shook my head. I did not need to go there.

"Are you a dog whisperer? I've never, ever seen her so mellow with a stranger in the house."

He laughed, his voice low and utterly sexy. "Piper's a good dog. She just needs an alpha to show her some attention."

Whoa. It was getting hot in here, and it wasn't because the cookies were baking. I startled when I realized I'd left the cookies in the oven and forgot to set a timer. I rushed to the oven and opened the door, expecting to see smoke roiling out. Instead, perfect golden rounds of cookies oozing melted chocolate chips sat on the baking sheet.

After moving the cookies to a wire rack to cool, I excused myself to call my mother. It took me a while to find my phone, and when I turned it on, sure enough, I saw three voice mails from Randall. I paused and looked back at the man mesmerizing my dog. Why would he show up at my house when I didn't answer my phone? It wasn't like we were close or had even dated casually. Could he have been the person who broke into my house? It made little sense. I couldn't think of how he might be connected to the painting unless Tori had told him she hid it here. All of a sudden, I felt uncomfortable being alone with him.

Chapter 21

I called my mother, who was appalled about the break-in. She immediately asked if she should reschedule the real estate agent. Given the awkward problem of the detective showing up with a search warrant, I didn't want my mother anywhere around when that happened. I also didn't want to warn her of the possibility, so I was glad she brought it up and not me. Nor did she need to hear that a search warrant hung over my head. I hoped the detective would be long gone by the time my mother showed up with the real estate agent.

"We had better reschedule the agent. Besides, Philip is on the title, so I need to get his agreement to sell the condo." I planned to put off talking to him about that until I found out what would happen with the search warrant. "But the reason I called is my attorney doesn't think I should stay here on my own. There's a bit of, um, rage in the break-in. Can I stay with you tonight?"

My mother remained uncharacteristically quiet for a few moments. "Of course, darling. I'll prepare the guest room. What time should we expect you?"

I looked at my watch. Ten already? "The glazier is working on the window now, so hopefully within an hour."

I realized that was late for my parents, but I had no choice.

"Send me a text when you're on your way."

Back in the kitchen, I tried to come up with a plan to get Randall out of the house before the glass guy left, but he hadn't finished telling me the story about Tori and his brother. My curiosity won over common sense. I also couldn't bear to tear Piper away from her personal masseur. She looked like she was in doggie heaven.

"You never finished telling me about Tori and your brother the last time you were here. Would you like to talk about it now?"

Randall sat up, his magic fingers leaving Piper's fur. She glanced at him then closed her eyes and drifted back into nirvana.

"Yeah, we were rudely interrupted. Your husband is a piece of work."

"Soon to be an ex-husband, I hope." I twisted a strand of hair around my finger. "I'm so sorry he tried to hit you. There's no excuse for his behavior."

Randall waved off my apology. "It's not your fault, so don't blame yourself. My brother worked with a few arrogant cops like that. You learn to avoid them as much as possible."

Silence hung between us. I wasn't sure he wanted to talk about his brother, and I didn't want to pry. Well, I did want to pry, but I tried to be sensitive to the loss he must feel over his brother's death. I got up, plated some cooled cookies, and set the plate on the table in front of Randall, while I waited for him to break the silence.

He picked one up and ate half of it in one bite. Once he swallowed, he finished the remaining half.

"Would you like a glass of milk or some tea with the cookies?"

"Water is fine."

By the time I filled a glass with ice and filtered water, Randall had eaten three more cookies. Maybe the cookies were his dinner. I couldn't judge. I'd eaten a dozen cookies for dinner a time or three.

"Thanks. These are fantastic." He sighed contentedly. "I guess I should tell you about Dylan and Tori. Some days are harder than others to talk about it."

"Take your time," I murmured, although I really thought he needed to hurry so I wouldn't get to my mother's house too late.

"Right after Dylan graduated from the police academy, he became engaged to his high school girlfriend, Selena. They wanted a long engagement while she finished her college degree to get a teaching credential. In the meantime, he moved to the vice squad. He was a natural at undercover, since he had a darker complexion than I do and was bilingual, thanks to Selena and her family. Somehow, Tori befriended her, and a few months before the wedding, Selena found her new friend and my brother in bed together."

Randall rubbed his face with both palms then twisted his neck back and forth until I heard a pop.

"The next thing I know, Dylan and Tori were engaged. I always thought something was off about Tori, but I couldn't prove she was doing anything wrong. Dylan started acting different and spent more money, especially on expensive gifts for Tori. Gifts that I was sure he couldn't afford. But he would never talk to me about it."

Randall paused and cracked his knuckles. "His unit planned a big takedown after a reliable snitch told them about an incoming shipment of stolen cigarettes. I'm sure he told Tori about it. She was always asking us questions about our work. Anyway, when the unit showed up to make the arrests, they were met with heavy gunfire. They knew we were coming, and Tori was the one who warned them."

I told myself not to interrupt, but I had to ask after he said "we." "You worked with your brother?"

He nodded. "I convinced my baby brother to join the vice squad with me. Dylan became the first one shot in that ambush and died in my arms. I blame myself for his death as much as I blame Tori."

"There might have been a lot of different reasons they knew you planned the arrests. Why do you suspect it was Tori?"

"The night of his death was brutal on me, on our family, but Tori remained conspicuously absent." Randall's nostrils flared, and his eyes turned flinty. He pressed his lips into a hard line and rubbed the back of his neck. "Aside from responding to the text I sent her about Dylan, she wouldn't answer her phone. I went to his apartment to make sure she was okay. Tori, along with all her stuff, had disappeared. Except for several cases of stolen cigarettes left behind to besmirch my brother's name. Internal affairs got involved and suspected that he had been smuggling stolen merchandise out of the evidence room and selling it. He had far more money in his bank accounts than there should have been on his salary."

"But they had no proof, did they?"

"No. He was conveniently dead and couldn't explain any of it. But I knew my brother. He never, ever would have stolen or sold that stuff. I ended up resigning. I couldn't stand the whispering. My coworkers looked at me, always wondering if I might be dirty like my brother."

"What do you think really happened?"

"I'm sure Tori had someone on the inside stealing the merchandise from the evidence room, and she sold it. My brother became an expedient and dead scapegoat to place the crime on." He shook his head. "I've uncovered a few things while investigating Tori these last two years that make me suspect she was also involved in a money-laundering scheme.

Her salon is a convenient front. I'm sure latching on to law enforcement officers was an amusement, not the main way she made her money."

"But what about the money? How did it get in your brother's account?"

"Tori had access to his accounts and probably put just enough there to throw him under the bus. I'm sure she kept most of the money. Dylan was lax in any kind of paperwork and wouldn't have noticed his balances." Randall chuckled, but his laughter sounded forced to me. "He was always behind in filing reports for work and wouldn't turn them in until our sergeant threatened him with a desk job."

"Still, maybe Tori left because she became afraid for her life?" I wondered why I tried to stand up for her, but I wanted to know the whole story. I thought my questions might prompt Randall's memory.

"The more I looked into Tori's past, the more the same pattern emerged. My brother wasn't the first one, and I'm sure not the last. I'm also sure she never worked alone. She has someone behind the scenes orchestrating the thefts and selling the merchandise."

It made sense. Philip would never get involved in something like that, but Tori probably had been manipulating him, which meant that her handler might still be around and active. Yet, Randall knew a lot about this stuff. Could he be the one who broke in? Tori might have hidden the artwork in my dresser and told Randall where to find it before she was murdered. Did he have the means to kill her? I worried that, if he did, he might hope I'd give him the painting or tell him where it was.

"Apparently, she started up the same process with Philip. I'm not sure exactly what it is, but after he moved out, I found a small painting that Tori might have stolen. Of course, Detective Jackson says I stole it and is coming back with a search warrant." I figured it best to be upfront that the police were in possession of the piece. He couldn't do anything to get it back now... if he was the mastermind behind this.

"I'm happy to talk to the detective and explain Tori's background and my theories, if you think it'd help."

"That would be great!" I hoped he could convince Detective Jackson of my innocence. But doing that would mean throwing Philip under the bus, so to speak. "I found large sums of money missing, plus Philip took out a second mortgage on our home on top of borrowing money from my mother. We're up to our eyeballs in debt."

"Sounds like Tori was taking advantage and bleeding you dry."

"But I had no idea it was happening."

Randall lifted his eyebrows at me. "You never noticed any indication he had an affair with Tori either."

Chapter 22

When I thought about it, I realized I had spent little time with Philip in the last couple of years. He worked the graveyard shift, came home, and crashed into bed as I was getting up and going to work. My husband was generally gone by the time I got home from work, and he worked weekends. Typically, his midweek days off were supposedly spent with buddies. He took me out to dinner occasionally after I complained, but then he slipped right back into his pattern of never being around. I blamed it on his job, but apparently the problem was Tori.

"What will happen to Philip? He'll lose his job, won't he?"

"It depends on if they can prove he was involved in Tori's illegal activities. They'll probably start with a polygraph test and take it from there. He won't be fired just because he had an affair with her."

"I would feel terrible about that. His life revolves around his career as a police officer."

"Wouldn't you feel worse if he used his position to steal from people?"

"You're right. I hadn't thought of it that way." Things were looking bleak for both Mr. and Mrs. Martinez.

"Ma'am, I'm done with the window." The glazier stood in the doorway, a sheet of paper in his hands.

The invoice. I gulped, retrieved my credit card, and handed him the plastic. Peter would have to rob Paul to make ends meet for the time being. While the man swiped the card, I took the invoice from him and glanced at the bottom figure... and gulped again. When did glass get so expensive?

I used the pad of my finger to sign my name on the touch screen of his iPhone and gave him my email address for the receipt. It probably wasn't worth the trouble of turning it in to our homeowner's insurance, but at least I had it if other expenses occurred because of the break-in.

"Would you like a few freshly baked chocolate chip cookies to take with you?"

"No thank you, ma'am. I'm diabetic, but they sure smell good. I'll let myself out. Thanks for your business."

"Thank you for coming on such short notice."

I followed him to the front door. "I'll lock up after you leave, since I'm still a bit worried after that break-in."

"It's completely understandable. Have a good evening."

After locking the front door, I inspected my new window. Everything seemed neat and clean, except for the jumble of clothes I had stuffed in the closet. From appearances, the glazier had even managed to clean up all the little shards of glass I couldn't get. I glanced at my watch and realized my mother would be unhappy with me if I didn't get to her house soon.

When I returned to the kitchen, Piper was still conked out, and Randall was checking his phone. I yawned. The past few days were catching up with me. "I'm sorry for the interruption, but I need to get to my mother's house. She's an early-to-bed, early-to-rise type of woman, so I don't want to disrupt her too much."

Randall grinned. "And I suppose you're a night owl?"

"Not hardly. But I stay up later than my mother." I

yawned again. A big, unladylike yawn. "Thank you for telling me about your brother. It's hard to believe Tori could be the cause of so much grief for so many families."

"She was ruthless, and she finally got what she deserved."

Whoa, this man was bitter. Maybe he killed her, but why was he hanging out with her in the first place when I met him? It was strange he would socialize with her at all.

Once again, my curiosity won out. "If you thought she was responsible for the death of your brother, why did you go to the bar with us and hang out like old friends?"

"Because I'm sure she was the front for the theft ring. She was arrogant enough to think I suspected nothing and made up all kinds of excuses for why she disappeared." He ran his fingers through his short-cropped hair. "I want to take down the people who are ultimately responsible for my brother's murder. Unfortunately, someone killed her before I could find out who that is."

My phone chimed with a text from my mother. I knew what the message said without looking at it.

"I'm so sorry, but I really have to leave. Thank you for telling me about your brother." I patted his arm, wanting to convey my sympathy but not sure what else to do.

I didn't want him to get any ideas if I hugged him. That was too dangerous.

"Please let me know what Detective Jackson says after you talk to him about Tori."

Randall gave Piper one more pat and then gave me a peck on the cheek. "Thanks for the cookies. I'll call you soon."

As soon as I locked the front door behind him, I rushed to pack a toothbrush and nightie. I grabbed food for Piper and her fleece blanket then snapped a leash onto her collar. She was instantly awake, and she half dragged me to the door.

"Sorry, sweetie, no time for a walk." I pulled her toward the door leading to the garage while texting Mother that we were on our way. "We'll go once we get to Mother's house."

. . .

PIPER'S cold nose nudged my hand, pulling me from a dream-less sleep. I had slept deeply for the first since I had stumbled over Tori's body. My stay with Mother and Lars wasn't such a bad thing, although the thought made me shiver when I worried it might be longer than a night or two. I glanced at the bedside clock. It was only seven. Beside me, Piper whined.

"Okay, I'm getting dressed."

I threw on the same clothes I had worn yesterday and stumbled down the stairs, trying to keep up with Piper. When I walked past the kitchen, the aromatic scent of freshly brewed coffee lingered in the air, but I didn't see either Mother or Lars. After grabbing Piper's leash and checking to make sure the house alarm had been turned off, I took my dog for a walk.

The sun was already heating the air. Today would be another scorcher. The rest of the country might laugh at us coastal southern California natives when we complained about summer heat when the mercury hit over eighty degrees. The same was true of winter cold. We complained it was too cold if the temperature dipped below sixty-eight. What could I say? We were spoiled that way and had unreasonable expec-tations for what perfect weather should be.

After Piper did her business, we returned home, and I grabbed a cup of coffee. I settled into a cushy patio chair beneath a sun umbrella and sipped the coffee while checking emails on my cell phone. The soothing sound of the rock waterfall feature on my parents' pool relaxed me. I hadn't looked at Facebook since my notorious photo with Randall went viral, and I wondered if I should delete my account. Unfortunately, that account was the only way I had kept in contact with several old high school and college friends, and I didn't want to lose that connection.

I logged in and scrolled through the news feed, catching

up on baby photos and vacations posted by my various friends. I noticed a private message in my inbox, so I clicked to open it. The message was from Bandboy, a band classmate from high school who played in the clarinet section with me. He had been a nerd back then. Black-framed glasses, buck teeth, terrible acne, and hair that had obviously been cut by his mother. I thought he had been crushing on me throughout high school, but once I made sure he knew we were pals and nothing more, we had become close friends. We lost touch after he moved away to college, and for the life of me, I couldn't even remember where he had planned on attending. Some friend I was.

When he sent me a friend request a few months ago, I had no trouble recognizing him, even though he had registered his name as Bandboy Rules. His real name was Brad Ruller. He used his high school graduation photo as his profile picture. I hoped he had outgrown his geekiness, but I wasn't sure, since most of his posts on Facebook were about marching bands. I knew nothing about his adult life other than his obsession with bands. Curious, I opened the message.

Hi Emory, don't know if u remember me? We were in the clarinet section in band together in hi school. I'm in town for the next few days and wondered if we could grab coffee or a drink. Here's my cell # so text me. 555-555-1234. Btw, great viral pic - u look like ur a party girl now :)

Chapter 23

Why couldn't people just forget they saw that photo? I hoped Bandboy wasn't renewing his crush. I didn't want to hurt his feelings, though, so I sent a quick text saying I'd meet him for coffee. He had been a sensitive teenager, and I remembered his dad had taken off with another woman around the time we started high school. I was sure that was why we bonded so quickly. I had lived through my father doing the same thing, and my heart still hurt from his betrayal.

Bandboy's (I had a hard time thinking of him as Brad) mother had never worked before her husband left, so money was always tight. He confided in me when we were sophomores that all his clothes came from thrift stores and that he and his mother ate a lot of beans and rice because they didn't cost much. The other non-band kids at school were cruel to him, even though he was super-smart. I hoped life had treated him well.

My phone chimed with a text asking if I could meet at Starbucks in downtown Huntington Beach this afternoon. Sure, why not? I didn't have a job, and there was nowhere I needed to be. I hoped I still had money loaded on my Starbucks gift card. It would take some getting used to not shelling out four dollars for a cup of coffee any time I wanted.

My mother stepped out on the patio, so I confirmed the time to meet Bandboy and then put my phone down. She wore cream-colored slacks and a pastel floral silk blouse, while every hair on her head appeared perfectly coiffed and her makeup expertly applied. I felt grubby next to her.

"Good morning, darling." She ignored Piper, who was rubbing up against her, trying to beg for a pat. "I hope you slept well."

"I haven't slept this great since… well, it's been a long time." There was no need to bring up the dead body. "Anyway, thanks for letting me stay here last night."

"You're welcome. I'll have Beatrice strip the sheets and wash the towels later this morning." She finally caved in to Piper's persistence and gave my dog a halfhearted pat on the head. "I'm on my way to a board meeting this morning, but I'm sure you can find cereal or oatmeal on your own, if you're hungry. I also put extra boxes by the front door so you can get your house packed up."

My mother disappeared back into the house, and I realized I'd been dismissed and told to go back to my own home. I sighed and took another sip of my coffee. Time to put my big-girl panties on and hope no one tried to break into my house again.

"There's something I forgot to tell you." She stepped back onto the stone patio.

Startled, I jumped at the sound of her voice and choked on the coffee I was trying to swallow. Once I stopped coughing and wiped the blurry tears from my eyes, I looked at her.

"I talked to Philip last night, and he's agreed to sign the real estate contract right away. A meeting's scheduled with the agent tomorrow morning at nine sharp at the condo. She already has a client slated to see it at ten, so I suggest you hurry home and get it ready for the walk-through."

Her heels clicked back onto the travertine floor, and she closed the front door. I pulled Piper into my lap and buried my face in her fur. How could I explain to my mother that Detective Jackson would tear apart any boxes I packed once he got his search warrant? I wasn't sure who I was more afraid of, my mother or the detective.

"Come on, Piper. Let's go home and see if we can do something to make them both happy."

As I waited for the gate to open so I could leave my mother's neighborhood, my phone chimed with another text. Bandboy wanted to meet now. I drove through the opened wrought-iron gate and pulled to the curb to text him that I was leaving Irvine but needed to drop Piper off at home first.

Brad responded before I could put the car into drive. **Have outdoor table. Bring Piper. I'll get Puppuccino.**

After sending a thumbs-up emoji, I made my way to downtown Huntington Beach. The sky was brilliant and clear, while the bright morning sun made the Pacific Ocean sparkle. I rolled down the windows as we cruised the Pacific Coast Highway. Piper was in heaven sniffing the smells of the sand and sea. The long Huntington Beach pier, with the iconic red-roofed restaurant at the end, attracted numerous tourists and fishermen alike, and the pier looked busy even though it was still early in the day.

As we sat at a stoplight, I caught glimpses of several surfers catching the pounding waves, their wetsuits reflecting the sunlight. Even though it was summer, the water remained fairly chilly, especially if you spent any amount of time in it. I thought about my times spent at the beach as a child and my mother telling me to come out of the water. Even when my teeth were chattering and my skin covered with goose bumps, I had always insisted I wasn't cold.

We circled a few blocks before finding parking. Once I

snapped the leash on to Piper's collar, she pulled me toward the beach. She must have remembered being taken to the dog beach last summer. Piper loved frolicking in the sand and surf with all the other dogs. She had so much fun, but it had taken me weeks to get all the sand out of her fur, even though I bathed her several times and brushed her every day. We hadn't been back since.

We arrived at Starbucks, and I searched the outside tables for Bandboy. Certain he wasn't the same geeky kid I knew in high school, I still saw no one who resembled him. I glanced at my watch when a deep masculine voice called my name.

"Emory!"

I turned around to find a tall, gorgeous man waving me over. His honey-blond hair was a bit wavy. Even from this distance, I could see his eyes were gray and accented his chiseled cheeks and jawline, which had a shadow of a beard growing. A tight T-shirt showed off his impressive pecs. I might have drooled.

I made a mental note to not call him Bandboy. "Brad! I haven't seen you in forever."

He gave me a long hug, and I remembered too late I hadn't done my hair or put makeup on and that I was still wearing the same rumpled clothes from yesterday. I hoped I didn't smell bad.

"You look great." He reached down to scratch beneath Piper's chin. "What would you like to drink? My treat."

"You don't have to do that."

Brad waved my comment away. "My pleasure. Besides, I invited you and Piper, so it's the least I can do."

"In that case, I'll have an iced latte."

"I'll have it right up with a Puppuccino for Piper." He bent back down and ruffled my dog's fur. "You two can wait here and hold the table for us."

Brad opened the door to the store, and I admired his well-muscled backside. He had opted to wear board shorts with flip-flops, and from appearances, he spent a lot of time in the sun. Unlike me, who was pasty white. I quickly dabbed on lipstick and tried to smooth my unruly hair back in a clip I found lurking in the bottom of my purse. Bandboy was nothing like I had expected, and I wondered why he used his nerdy high school photo as his Facebook profile picture.

Once Brad returned with our drinks and Piper had inhaled her Puppuccino, we gossiped about other classmates for a while until I couldn't control my curiosity any longer.

"What brings you back to our area? It's been about ten years since I've seen you last."

"My sister recently had a baby, and my mom isn't getting any younger, so I thought I'd open another office here."

"They have to love seeing you around more." I wasn't sure how to be subtle, but then again, Brad hadn't shared anything on his Facebook page. "So… what kind of business are you in? Your Facebook profile doesn't give any information about you."

"Were you checking me out?" My face warmed, and he laughed.

"No… okay, yes. I like to keep up with all my friends."

"I own a game software-developing company in San Jose. Business is good, and I think now is the time to open another branch down here. I can find employees from new college graduates here in Southern California."

I immediately thought of the Stoner Dudes. "Hey, do you know Steve and Stan Miller? I think they develop game software, and from what I can tell, they are pretty successful."

Brad scratched his head. "No, I don't know them. Maybe they freelance develop and sell to the big guys."

"What games does your company develop?"

Brad rattled off several titles, but they meant nothing to me. My unfamiliarity with them didn't stop me from nodding like I followed what he was saying.

"I'm dying to know…." I grimaced at my poor choice of

words. "I mean, I'm really curious why you use a high school photo and the name Bandboy for your Facebook page."

"I had a stalker a few years ago. She was a former employee who thought I should be in love with her." He ran his manicured fingers through his hair. "I was lucky she physically backed off once I got a restraining order, but she orchestrated a Facebook attack on my account, so I had to close it. I figured this way I could still connect to friends without giving away my identity to anyone looking for me that I'd rather not find me."

"That's scary!"

"Like I said, it happened a few years ago, and she hasn't bothered me in over a year. I'm hoping she's gotten counseling or at least moved on." Brad paused for a moment and took a sip of his coffee. "It looks like you're having some excitement in your life right now."

Oh boy. Here came the conversation I didn't want to have. "I wouldn't really call it excitement. 'Terrifying' might be a better word."

"I didn't mean to make light of your situation. Are you doing okay?"

Gee, how did you answer that question to someone you hadn't seen in ten years? They probably wanted to hear you were managing, but that wasn't an honest answer. On the other hand, it would take an hour to tell the truth. "Um, I'm hanging in there, but it's been a rough few days."

"I'm sure that's an understatement." Brad snorted out a laugh. "I always wondered why you married that cheating, no-good son of a gun. I knew he would break your heart."

"Wait. What? How did you hear about Philip and Tori?" My hands got clammy. "It's not something I've told anyone but my family."

Brad snorted again. "Em, you are so naïve. Just about anyone who knows you was aware your husband has had some side action going on for years. It wouldn't surprise me if one of his former girlfriends did Tori in. She lasted longer than most."

My head swam, and I saw stars. Tori wasn't the first? And everyone else knew about it? That cheating son of a gun was right!

Chapter 24

"Are you okay?" Brad touched my cold hand. "You're not going to pass out, are you?"

"Why didn't anyone tell me? I had no idea."

"We all figured you had an open marriage."

"Ewwww…. Nope. No way!"

"Then what about that Facebook photo of you and that other guy partying it up?"

"First of all, Tori drugged me. Second, she Photoshopped that compromising photo." My face flamed, and my blood pressure skyrocketed. "She was doing everything possible to get my husband to divorce me."

"Seems like she was doing you a favor."

"Now that I know the real Philip, I have to agree with you. But in the meantime, someone is trying to frame me for her murder."

"I wouldn't blame you for wanting to kill her." Brad peered closely at my face.

"I would never do something like that." I shook my head so hard I felt a muscle twinge in my neck. "If anything, I was angry at my husband."

Brad practically guffawed. "That's not what I heard!

Rumor has it you were in a major catfight with an almost-naked Tori."

"What?" I screeched. Several people looked over to our table.

Piper nuzzled my hand.

"Where are you getting these rumors from? I mean, who is spreading these rumors?"

"You didn't get into a catfight with Tori?"

I huffed, and my body deflated into the chair. "I did, but she deserved it. How does everyone in the universe know about my sordid life? Seriously, who is your source?"

It was Brad's turn to shake his head. "Nope. No can tell."

I knew that would be his answer, so I didn't press the issue. Despite my pitiful life being fodder for the rumor mill, Brad had given me a clue to who else might have wanted Tori dead. Maybe one of Philip's other flings killed Tori and tried to frame me.

I needed to talk to his partner, Amy Doyle. I remembered the way she looked at Philip when she found out about his affair. She appeared crushed, but perhaps she had been faking it, trying to cover her anger. I remembered the way she glared at Tori during the barbecue Philip and I held earlier this summer. It was the same way she glared at me when she thought I wasn't looking. Amy also had plenty of opportunities to steal my cake knife during the party or any of the other times she visited my home. She might have hoped Philip would get back together with her with Tori dead and me spending the rest of my life in prison.

"Earth to Em." Brad touched my hand again. "Are you going to be okay?"

"I hope so." I took a sip of my latte. "You gave me a lot to think about, like who else might have framed me for Tori's murder. I need to talk to Amy, Philip's partner, before I make any accusations."

"Whoa! Don't be putting yourself at risk. Tell the police and let them handle it."

Yeah right, like Detective Jackson would actually consider one of his own was a murderer. Nope, I was his number-one suspect, and I was sure he was doing everything possible to prove my guilt. It was up to me to prove my innocence by finding the murderer.

"The police aren't looking at anyone other than me. I've given the detective means, motive, and opportunity." I quickly told Brad why I thought Amy was a good suspect.

"You don't need to do anything dangerous. Let the police do their job. It'll work out eventually."

"I don't have the time to wait for them to do their job when they only want to focus on me. I'll talk to Amy at her place of employment with lots of people around. That will be safe enough." I didn't want to give Brad too much information. For all I knew, he would repeat our entire conversation back into the rumor mill. Plus, he seemed awfully connected to what was happening in my life. Was he somehow involved in Tori's murder and wanted to make sure he wasn't a suspect? Nah. Now I was imagining things.

"You really need to let the police handle it and stop thinking you can be an amateur sleuth." His phone beeped, and he glanced at the screen. "I hate to run, but my real estate agent finally got an appointment for the building I want to lease."

"That's okay. I have things I need to get busy with too." Like pack my house. "Thanks for the coffee and Puppuccino."

"My pleasure. Since I'll be in town more often with my expansion, maybe we can have dinner next week?"

"Sure. That sounds nice." That is if I wasn't in jail already.

Once Piper and I made it home, I unloaded and reconstructed the boxes my mother had sent with me. While mindlessly taping boxes together, I thought about Brad and his offer for dinner. While he was gorgeous, I didn't want him to get the wrong idea that I was looking for another relationship. I was done with men for a long time. I hoped I wouldn't end up hurting his feelings, since he was a nice guy. Well, at least he was a nice guy in high school, and we'd had a lot of fun in band together. Memories came flooding back, and I realized I had forgotten how much the two of us had bonded. With our emotional connection back then over being abandoned by our fathers, we had shared a lot of our innermost fears and feelings with each other. I berated myself for letting our friendship wither away after high school.

Not feeling like packing, I called my sister to check on the upcoming catering events that she needed help with. The call went straight to voice mail, but almost immediately I received a text from her stating she was at the doctor's office for a check-up. After that, she had party duty at the twins' preschool, so she would call me later.

I glanced at the clock and wondered if Philip was still on desk duty and if Amy worked another shift. Or perhaps another officer had been assigned graveyard duty with her. If I trolled the streets around the precinct at the beginning or at the end of every shift, I might find a chance to talk to her. I doubted Philip would do me the courtesy of giving me her personal phone number. There were still a couple hours before the morning shift ended and the swing shift started, which gave me plenty of time to shower, do something with my hair, and perhaps pack a couple of boxes.

However, I really needed to talk to Steve and Stan again and tell them what I had found out. They might be able to give me some background on Amy. I wondered if they might have noticed her around Tori's house before. Packing procrastination was a wonderful motivator to take another drive and investigate.

. . .

I CLIMBED the rickety stairs once again. The door opened before my fisted hand had a chance to knock.

"Hey, dudette, whatcha doin' back at the scene of the crime?" Stan looked frumpy and hungover.

"I know your secret, Stan. You can stop playacting." I laughed but then paused when Stan's eyes suddenly looked cold, almost reptilian. "I mean the secret where you want everyone to think you and your brother are partiers? And stoned most of the time."

Stan laughed, and the feeling he was hiding something other than his wealth passed.

"I have no idea what you're talking about," he answered with an exaggerated slur and waved me in. "Me 'n' Steve are the ultimate party boys. We try to live up to your and Tori's nickname for us, 'Stoner Dudes.'"

Uh-oh. "How did you… oh never mind. I'm really sorry about that. Tori was a bad influence. It was just easier to go along with her."

This wasn't going like I had planned, and I was getting a little uncomfortable. "Is Steve around?"

"Nope. He's out scoring more weed." Stan had plopped on the sofa and was now watching me from half-closed eyes.

I got the feeling I was a mouse and he was the cat. "I wanted to give you both an update on what I've found out in my investigation and see if you know anything about Amy Doyle. Philip's graveyard partner."

Stan leaned forward and motioned me to sit down. "She's petite and has short brown hair?"

I nodded. "Yes, that sounds like her."

"She drove down this street several times a week and always slowed down right in front of Tori's apartment."

"Do you think she might have been stalking Tori?"

"Sounds like it. Do you think she's the killer?"

"If looks could kill, Tori would have been dead at the last

couple of barbecues we had when Amy attended. I'd be dead too." I shivered.

"Let me guess. She had an affair with your darling husband?"

"I'm pretty sure. I wanted to see if you had heard anything about her and if you can find her address for me." It would be much easier to confront her at her home, where I wouldn't be surrounded by a dozen uniformed cops who all wanted to arrest me.

"You don't want much, do you?" Stan flicked imaginary dust off his colorful board shorts. "We're gamers, not hackers. People in law enforcement are harder to find because of the layers of privacy. Plus, I don't want to be caught messing with something like that. Go ask Philip."

I tried giving him my sad-dog face. My lower lip came out, and I hung my head and opened my eyes wide. My ploy worked.

"Fine. I'll see what we can do, but don't get your hopes up." He shook his head and rolled his eyes. "You should just follow Philip when he gets off work. Chances are he shacked up with her after you kicked him out."

Technically, I didn't kick Philip out. Truth was, he packed up his things and left after seeing the horrible fake photo of me with Randall. At least I came to my senses and changed the locks not long after that. However, I was fine letting Stan think I had been the one to end things. His suggestion wasn't a bad idea, either, although that snake would probably spot my car a mile away. "Okay. I'll try to find her that way first, but if it doesn't work, I'll let you search for me."

Stan checked his watch. "I hate to run you off, but I have an appointment I need to get to."

"Sure, no problem." I headed to the door. "Thanks for your help."

The door closed quickly behind me as I stepped over the

threshold. Had I been dawdling, the door would have slammed into my behind. I sensed something was going on with Stan, and it wasn't a good something. Still, he had given me a decent idea of how to track down Amy without confronting her at the police station.

Chapter 25

I parked across the street from the station, where I had a fairly good view of the gated parking lot the officers used for their personal vehicles while on duty. I didn't want to broil in my car, but since I needed to conserve gas, I rolled down the windows and turned off the engine. Even though only a little while passed before Amy walked down the steps and got into a parked white sedan, I felt sticky, and perspiration rolled down my back.

I glanced at my watch and saw the shift wasn't ending yet, and she wasn't in uniform. Perhaps it was her day off, or maybe she had visited Philip. Grateful to start my car and crank the air-conditioning up, I made sure all the vents pointed directly toward me. I impatiently waited for the electric gate to open and then waited an additional few seconds. Finally, I pulled my car out of the parking space and followed her.

Amy drove a new Toyota sedan that still had the paper tags on it. My Honda was already fifteen years old, and I experienced a twinge of jealousy, realizing it might be decades before I could afford a new car. I shoved my feelings aside and focused on following Amy but not so closely she would notice.

She stayed on busy streets, and I felt lucky the red-light-green-light god smiled on me so I wouldn't lose her.

About fifteen minutes into my surveillance, Amy finally pulled into the parking lot of a grocery store. This situation was even better than confronting her at home, since there were people around. It felt safer, somehow, so I pulled into the empty parking space across the aisle from her. I waited while she collected her reusable shopping bags then opened my door as soon as she locked her car. For a cop, Amy wasn't at all observant about her surroundings. I was three steps behind her, and she never turned to see who was there.

"Amy, can I talk to you a minute?"

She startled at the sound of my voice.

She turned around with a pleasant look on her face then immediately scowled when she saw it was me.

"I only need a minute of your time." I was lying. I had a lot of questions that would take time to answer, but I wasn't sure she would accommodate me.

"What do you want?" she hissed at me. "Are you following me?"

Yeah, I was, but I would never admit it. "No. I wouldn't do something like that. But I really need to ask you a question."

Amy huffed and rolled her eyes. "Fine, whatever."

Now I had her attention, I panicked. None of my questions were happy, good-vibes, "how ya doin'" questions. Nope. The questions were accusatory, and I would make her mad. "Um, were you or are you having an affair with Philip?"

"How dare you ask me that." Her face turned beet red, and her eyes narrowed into little slits. "I don't need to listen to that kind of crap from you."

She was seconds away from either stomping off or maybe smacking me. I reached out and laid my hand gently on her arm. "I'm not blaming you, and at this point, I don't even care if you are or aren't. Someone tried to frame me for Tori's murder, and I need to find out why."

If Amy was mad before, she was furious now. She jerked her arm away from me. "Now you're trying to find out if I killed the tramp? You've got a lot of nerve, Emory. You're lucky I don't sue you for slander."

This wasn't going well. Granted, I didn't expect a heart-to-heart chat, but I was getting nowhere, except for pissing off a very dangerous woman who carried a gun. I raised my hands in a position of prayer and supplication. "I'm not accusing you of anything. You spend a lot of time with Philip at work. I'm trying to find out if he mentioned other women who might have wanted both Tori and me out of the picture. Please, I'm desperate."

Amy exhaled a long sigh and looked around the parking lot. "Sure, there were a lot of other women. He never mentioned names, though, and none ever came around when I worked with him… except for Tori."

Well, this wasn't helpful. "He mentioned no one in particular?"

"I can't believe you're really that clueless, Mrs. Martinez." Amy stuffed her reusable shopping totes into her purse and turned back toward her car. "I'm done with this conversation. If you ever approach me again, I'll slap a restraining order on you faster than you can spell it."

I waited until Amy had peeled out of the parking lot, disregarding the speed bumps and stop signs as she did so. I thought it was interesting she didn't deny having an affair or deny killing Tori. Instead, she did everything she could to intimidate me. I wondered if Steve or Stan could find out any background information on this cagey policewoman.

Before I reached my car to head home, my phone rang. I didn't recognize the number but answered it anyway. As soon as I heard the voice, I wished I had ignored the call.

Detective Jackson, parked in front of my house with a search warrant in hand, wanted to know whether he should break down the door or if I would unlock it for him. Since I had just spent too much money changing the door locks already, I asked him to have patience and said I would be there in ten minutes or less. I hurriedly sent my attorney a text and then crossed my fingers, hoping to hit green lights all the way home.

His unmarked sedan blocked my driveway, so I had to parallel park down the block. It usually took me three and often four tries to fit my car into a space, but this time I left the back end of my car hanging way out in the street. I hoped no one would hit it, but at this point, I had more important things on my mind.

My hands shook as I fumbled with the house key, trying to unlock the front door. Detective Jackson grunted a brief greeting, shoved the warrant into my hands, and started breathing down my neck. Was he worried I would try to hide evidence in the nanosecond I had before he entered my house? After I dropped the key and tried to pick it up from the floor, he rushed by me.

Piper whined, and I apologized to her for making her spend extra time in the crate. I grabbed her leash and clipped it on before she could morph into attack mode. The last thing I needed was for her to get aggressive with the detective. She'd never bitten or even snapped at anyone, but she certainly sounded like she was going to. I walked Piper to the sliding glass door and let her out into the small space. After I removed her leash and told her to be good, I stomped back inside to make sure the detective wouldn't have a chance to plant evidence.

He removed the drawers in my dresser, inspected the inside edges and inside the shell of the dresser, then slammed them shut. I felt violated… and angry.

"You don't have to stay here and watch me." His gruff voice matched the scowl on his face.

"Yes, I do." I glared back at him. My voice rose louder than I had intended, and I refused to be intimidated any longer. "I can't believe you're doing this. You have to realize I'm innocent, yet here you are again, harassing me."

"I'm not harassing you." He pulled another drawer from my bedside table. "If you have nothing to hide, this shouldn't be a problem."

"Not a problem?" I crossed my arms tight against my chest. "You're invading my privacy, even though I'm innocent!"

The detective didn't respond. He kept his back to me. I bit my lower lip, trying to calm my racing heart. It was thudding so hard in my chest I was sure he heard it clear across the room. I was innocent, but what if someone planted more stolen artwork? I couldn't stand the suspense any longer.

"Did you get the results back on the painting you found yesterday?"

"You know exactly what it is," he answered, his voice sharp.

"Um, no, I don't know what it is, since it's not mine."

"Here's the thing, Mrs. Martinez. The only reason I haven't arrested you yet is because that painting is a bad forgery of artwork that was stolen a couple months ago." He stood and did his best to look imposing. "You're hiding something, and I will find it. I'm not going to let you get away with murder and theft."

My eyes might have bugged out. I saw stars and began to worry, and then my head spun. Passing out in front of this arrogant detective would be mortifying, so I took a deep breath. I suspected he had already convicted me in his mind from day one, but I had erroneously hoped he would have an open mind to investigate other people. With a sigh of relief that the painting was a forgery, I exhaled the breath I had been holding. It was one less problem to worry about—except why had a forgery been hidden in my jewelry box?

"Here's the thing, Detective Jackson. You won't find anything because one, I'm not a killer and two, I've never had anything to do with anything illegal in my entire life." My eye twitched, but I needed to shove his accusations back at him. "Can you possibly entertain the idea for just a moment that someone is trying to frame me?"

He narrowed his eyes and gave a small shake of his head before sifting through the piles of clothes I had shoved onto the closet floor. When he pawed through my panties, my ears felt like they were on fire. I twirled the ends of my hair around my index finger and examined my shoes, but I wouldn't leave the room. At least the detective kept his head down and didn't make eye contact or say anything. He seemed just as embarrassed as I felt.

"Hello!" Mel hollered from the front door I had forgotten to lock.

"Come in. We're in my bedroom." I didn't want to take my eyes off the man digging through my belongings.

"Do you have the warrant?" Mel asked.

I hadn't heard the large man sneak up behind me, so I jumped. "It's on the kitchen counter."

He grunted and left to find the paper. When he returned, Mel patted my arm. "Has our good detective found anything yet?"

"Nope and unless someone planted something incriminating, he won't." Part of me knew my attorney wouldn't have wanted me to ask the detective about the artwork, but since I had, I thought I'd better tell him the results. "An interesting result showed up when the painting was examined by experts."

"And how do you happen to know this?"

I wanted to talk to my attorney in private, but I didn't dare turn my back on the detective. He might be so desperate he would fabricate evidence and arrest me. "Detective Jackson gave me the information when I asked."

Mel's ears turned red, but I had to hand it to him for not bawling me out. "And what did you find out?"

"It's a forgery. A bad one at that."

"What? That's it?"

"Yep." The big question of the day was why someone would put a forgery in my jewelry box then come back and tear my room apart looking for it. Even though I dreaded the thought, it was time to talk with Philip and find out what kind of mess he had gotten himself into.

It didn't take long for the detective to search through the rest of my bedroom and bathroom. Philip had taken most of his belongings, which cut down on the number of things he needed to paw through, and I wasn't much of a packrat. The kitchen, however, was a different story. I'd collected various flours, more decorative sprinkles than I could ever use, and all kinds of pans in numerous shapes and sizes. I had packed every square inch of space in my cabinets and small walk-in pantry with baking items.

When he opened the cabinet holding the containers of eight different flours and five different sugars, I thought I heard him cursing under his breath.

"Can you please be careful to not cross-contaminate the flours? There are a couple gluten-free blends that have to remain that way." The sealed containers were clearly marked and stored on different shelves, but I didn't want to risk the expense of having to replace supplies.

I watched as he examined each container. All the while, I was ready to jump in and make sure he contaminated none of my flour blends. "Thanks for being careful with the gluten-free ingredients. Most people don't realize how devastating a tiny particle of gluten can be for some people."

"No problem. My son is celiac, so I understand the risks."

Wow, the man might be human after all. "How old is your son?"

"Ten."

"That's such a fun age. What's his name?"

"Adam."

The detective might have been only answering with only one word, but at least he was talking to me. "Does Adam have any other siblings?"

"No."

This conversation reminded me of playing Twenty Questions. I glanced at his left ring finger and saw a tan line. Perhaps he was recently divorced, which was why he acted so cranky. I wasn't usually nosy, and I was definitely not pushy, but this man had been making my life miserable. It gave me a little pleasure to invade his privacy like he had mine.

"Sorry about your divorce."

"What?" When Detective Jackson turned to stare at me, his emotional pain was evident. "How did you find out?"

I tapped my bare ring finger. The absence of the gold band that used to encircle it felt odd. "Your tan line."

He shook his head and turned back to continue the search of my cupboards.

"For what it's worth, I am sorry. Especially for your son. It must be hard on him." I remembered all too well when my dad left.

"I think I'm done here for now, Mrs. Martinez." The detective washed his hands and ignored my attempt at sympathy. "Can you think of anyone who might try to pin the murder on you?"

"No. Well… maybe." I exchanged a glance with Mel, who was uncharacteristically calm. Maybe he had given up on trying to rein in my nosiness. "I'm finding out that Philip was a player, and perhaps one of his girlfriends wanted me out of the picture. What better way than to kill the current girlfriend and frame the wife?"

"If that's the case, you're lucky they didn't kill the wife and frame the girlfriend."

Chapter 26

I gulped. That possibility had never entered my mind.

"Do you have names of other potential girlfriends?" The detective pulled his notebook from his pocket.

"I don't have proof, but Philip might be involved with his partner, Amy Doyle." If she hated me before, she would really want to murder me after this. However, had she been honest with me when I questioned her, I wouldn't have said anything to Detective Jackson. I almost chuckled. Who was I kidding? Of course I would have told him, especially if she admitted to having an affair.

The detective scribbled in his notebook while my attorney glared at me. I looked at him out of the corner of my eye and shrugged.

"I'll let myself out." Detective Jackson slid the notebook back into his pocket.

He left without saying he would talk to Amy and didn't even say goodbye. And here I thought we were finally bonding.

"You realize you made a mortal enemy, if not two, by throwing Officer Doyle under the bus."

"Yeah, I figured it might happen. But someone tried to

frame me, and she wouldn't answer my questions about her relationship with Philip. You should see her mooning over him!"

Mel's eyes bugged out, and his face turned even redder than usual, which wasn't an attractive look on his puffy face. "You talked to Ms. Doyle? Do you realize if she is the murderer, your life is in danger? I won't even get into the legal ramifications your actions could have."

Apparently, my attorney wasn't quite as resigned about my involvement in the investigation as I had hoped. "I had to do something, since Detective Jackson is so focused on me."

"No, you don't have to do anything. Your job is to trust the process and let law enforcement and the court system clear your name." He rubbed his hand over his whisker-stubbled cheek. "Just give it time."

Time wasn't something I had a lot of. No one would hire me with this murder case hanging over my head. Creditors were breathing down my neck. My mother was mortified. And I was losing my home.

"Do you understand what I'm saying? Don't get involved."

"You're right." I couldn't say I wouldn't keep asking questions, but I knew to let my attorney think I was going to stop.

"Call me if Detective Jackson comes back and be careful. No more talking to potential murderers or even witnesses." The large man lumbered toward my front door. "You're making my job a lot harder than it needs to be."

As soon as Mel drove away, I brought Piper back into the house and called Philip.

My soon-to-be-ex answered on the first ring. "What do you want?"

"We need to talk."

"I have nothing to say. Papers will be served to you tomorrow."

"What? What papers?"

"Divorce papers."

A month ago, that statement would have devastated me. Today I was relieved I'd be free from this snake. Eventually I would grieve over what my marriage could have been and angry over what it had become. I had once loved this man enough to take his last name, but now it was time for the relationship to end.

"Em, are you still there?"

"Sorry. It's just a lot to process right now." It wasn't a good idea to tell him how I really felt right now, so I softened my voice. "But we still need to talk. In person. Please?"

"I don't think we should." Philip was silent for a moment. "It would probably be better if we met with our attorneys present."

"This has nothing to do with our marriage ending. I'm in serious trouble, even though I'm innocent." Laying on the damsel-in-distress act might appeal to his macho self. "Maybe you can make sense of what's going on, since everyone seems to think I killed Tori."

I heard him sigh. "Okay. I'm busy until after seven tonight. I can drop by after that."

"How about we meet at the Costa Mesa dog park? Piper's been cooped up a lot lately and needs to burn some energy off." Besides, I didn't want to be alone with Philip. He might be the killer. Even if he wasn't, I was sure Tori's death was tied to him somehow. Plus, in the past, Philip had been able to charm me no matter how angry I had been. I didn't want to give him the opportunity to get me to fall for his moves again.

"That works. I'll be there a little after seven."

PIPER WAS IN DOGGIE HEAVEN, running her heart out with the other half dozen dogs at the park. I laughed at her puppy antics and felt my spirits rise… until Philip came into view. He looked like he had lost weight. His face was haggard, and it appeared he wasn't sleeping well. His T-shirt and jeans looked rumpled and dingy, like he had slept in them for several days. For some reason, that gave me a small degree of satisfaction.

When Piper saw Philip, she barreled toward him for a few seconds, but then a black poodle distracted her. Guess she didn't miss him much either. I had placed two of the cheap plastic chairs in a far corner of the dog park so we could talk without anyone listening in.

Philip nodded at me and sat precariously on the cracked chair. "What's so important that you couldn't talk about on the phone?"

"I thought you might like to see Piper. She misses you." Not really, but I wanted to soften him up.

"Yeah, that's obvious." His gaze followed our dog as she romped with an Australian Shepherd and then stopped to roll in the grass. "You look good, by the way."

"Uh, thanks." I self-consciously smoothed down my hair, which blew in the gentle breeze. "It's no secret everyone thinks I killed Tori, but you have to recognize I'm innocent."

He grunted but didn't agree I was innocent. That worried me, but I pushed on. "Someone broke into our condo and ransacked it. When Detective Jackson searched the condo, he found a painting which was supposedly stolen. I'm sure that's what the intruder was after. Plus, there are all the loans you've taken out and the fact we're flat broke. What kind of trouble are you in, Philip?"

"What do you care?" He bent forward, resting his elbows on his knees, and rubbed his face with both palms. "You're probably happy I'm on my way to crashing and burning."

"Not at all." I tentatively placed a hand on his arm and felt him trembling. "Are you involved in the thefts? Do you need legal advice?"

Philip took a ragged inhalation of breath then straightened up and brushed off my hand. "I'm fine. I'm sure you'd like nothing more than to watch me lose my job and my friends."

"That's not it at all!" I was afraid he'd try the macho, I'm-so-tough line. After seven years of marriage, I guessed I knew him. "Somehow, I think this is all tied in to what happened to Tori, and I'm trying to figure it out. Preferably before I get sent to prison for something I didn't do."

"Let the detectives do their job, Em, and leave me out of it." Philip stood and watched Piper. "I guess the dog is yours. She doesn't care about me either."

He walked away from me and toward the opening.

"Wait, I need answers!" I yelled at him, not caring who overheard me. "I need to understand what's going on."

My soon-to-be-ex didn't stop and instead picked up his pace. I wondered what he was up to, and I was determined to find out. I whistled for Piper, and for once, she instantly came to me. After her leash was clipped on, we headed to my car. I wanted to find out where Philip was staying and what he was doing.

It didn't take Philip long to reach the freeway and head east on the 55 and then north on the 405 Freeway. I worried I would lose him in traffic, but luckily there were only pockets of slowing, so I kept him in sight. He was in the far left non-carpool lane when suddenly his white SUV darted across traffic and took the 605 Freeway exit. I almost couldn't merge into the exit lane but managed it at the last second, leaving several cars honking their horns at me. I crossed my fingers, hoping Philip didn't notice.

Ten minutes later, when I realized where Philip was heading, my heart sank. The building was brightly lit with a flashy sign inviting people to play the tables and eat delicious buffet food. I would have no way to recover all the money he had lost there. It was gone forever, and I would be paying his debt for the rest of my life.

Chapter 27

I parked several rows over from Philip and watched as he ambled toward the casino entrance. He seemed focused, and in his hands, he fondled what appeared to be a credit card. I berated myself for not canceling our credit cards sooner. I dug through my purse and pulled out the one credit card I carried. After calling the toll-free number on the back of the card, I waded through the menu, punching number after number until I reached a live person. Once I explained the situation, they closed the account and promised I would receive a final bill within a few days. I almost wept when I was told the balance due. A balance that had been a few hundred dollars the last time I glanced at the statement, a few months ago, was now a few thousand dollars. I only used the card for groceries, gas, and other mundane household items, and I was sure Philip had said he paid it off every month.

I knew we had two other joint credit card accounts for emergencies, but since I didn't carry them in my wallet, I promised myself I would cancel them as soon as I got home. I worried over the amount of money he might charge on one of those cards tonight, but right now, unless I wanted to make a huge scene, I couldn't do anything about that.

Piper whined, and I petted her head. My mind played out scenarios, wondering if I had jumped to conclusions. What if he wasn't gambling? Could he be meeting another mistress? Or moving stolen artwork? I snapped the leash onto Piper and opened the trunk of my car. I was sure the casino would frown on me bringing my dog in, but it was too hot to leave her in the car.

Right after we adopted Piper, I enrolled us in a service dog training program. Piper did great. Me? Not so much. In fact, I was the one who caused us to flunk out. The instructor told me that if I would learn to be more commanding, we were welcome to come back. Plus, I was really lax about working with Piper, aside from the five minutes before classes. I found her service dog vest tucked into the back corner of the trunk of my Honda. I hated to take advantage of the system that allowed service dogs into public places, but desperate times called for desperate measures.

A beefy security guard, buttons straining on his tight shirt, was standing by the glass doors leading into the casino. He gave us a cursory glance before turning his attention back to the gaming tables. On the far side of the huge, open room, I spotted the side of Philip's head as he sat at one of the card tables. He had a stack of chips in front of him and intently studied the cards in his hand. I knew nothing about playing poker or gambling, but I could tell he wasn't happy. From the way he was rubbing his jawline, he didn't like what he saw in his hand. Sure enough, he threw the cards down, and the dealer swept away the pile of red and yellow chips from the table's center.

Not wanting Philip to see me, I walked alongside the far wall until all that was visible was the back side of his head. No one was paying any attention to Piper or me, so I stood a few more minutes. My stomach plunged when he lost more money. As much as I didn't want to cause a scene, it was time to stop him from putting us further in debt.

I wove around the crowded tables and then pulled Piper to a stop. Officer Amy Doyle, dressed in a yellow floral-print sundress, had her arms around Philip's neck and was kissing him on the lips! Now I had proof they were involved. My suspicions about Amy killing Tori bubbled up. It made perfect sense. Kill the competition and frame the wife. She had motive, opportunity, and means. In several of my favorite mystery books, I read that detectives looked for those qualities. I turned around and made my way to the exit as quickly as I could without calling attention to myself. Detective Jackson needed this information right away.

I gave Philip and Amy another quick glance. She was trying to lead him away from the gaming table, and they seemed to be arguing. The same security guard who had stood at the casino entrance marched up to them. He grabbed them both by their arms and escorted them in the direction of the exit. When I saw them coming straight toward me, I darted behind a large pillar, hoping it was wide enough to hide both me and my dog.

"You have no right to tell me what to do," Philip said in a low and menacing voice.

"When you keep borrowing money from me, I have every right to make sure you don't piss it away," Amy answered, her voice low and cold. "You need help. You're addicted, Philip. I won't stand by and let you ruin your life or my life either."

"That's enough, you two. Wait until you're in private to hash this out." The security guard didn't seem fazed, so I assumed he ran into this situation fairly often.

I waited until I was sure Philip and Amy had left before I walked to my car. I worried that Tori had gotten him involved in something illegal to support his gambling. That forged painting had me concerned I was overlooking something because I sure didn't see Amy having anything to do with it. From what Randall had told me, Tori was the one involved in theft and money laundering. I needed to talk to Randall and the Stoner Dudes again, but those conversations would have to wait until tomorrow.

Once Piper and I arrived home, I called Detective Jackson and told him what I had seen.

He was dismissive. "It's not illegal to gamble. Nor is it illegal to have an affair."

"I know, but this gives Amy Doyle motive, opportunity, and means." I liked the way I could rattle it off. It sounded impressive, to me at least.

Detective Jackson laughed—not in a "this is funny" way but a condescending way. "Mrs. Martinez, I'm investigating, so go back to your mystery books and leave the real work to the police. Don't forget, I know you have motive, opportunity, and means too. It's late, so unless it's an emergency, please don't bother me with any more wild theories."

Suddenly I didn't feel so sure of myself. As much as I had learned, I still knew nothing. I would have to find proof Amy was the killer and then present the evidence to Detective Jackson.

Chapter 28

After dealing with the credit card companies, I put Piper in her crate and tumbled into bed. I was exhausted, but my mind was working overtime, trying to solve the case. Every time I drifted off to sleep, giant playing cards chased me, and by the time dawn broke, I was more than ready to get up to end my nightmares.

Since it was too early to track down Randall or visit the Stoner Dudes, I assembled some of the cardboard boxes my mother had sent home with me. I started in the garage and packed the nonessentials, like tools and the car-washing products Philip had left behind. I left household paper products out, since I was sure I would need them over the next few weeks. Next, I started packing my bookcase. I left out recipe books I thought I might need but boxed up the fun decorating books that I had collected by the score. I got distracted and browsed through a couple cupcake cookbooks I had bought the previous year and never looked at. My phone rang just as I finished my second cup of coffee.

It was Mother. "Darling, the realtor is bringing over a client at nine this morning. Please tell me you're packed and the condo is clean."

I was glad I had gotten up early so I wouldn't have to lie to my mother. "I've got quite a bit packed, but it's taking longer than I expected."

She sighed. "Well, I suppose that can't be helped. Put all your boxes in the garage and make sure everything is tidy. You can finish packing once they leave."

"Okay." There was no use arguing with her, but I'd finish packing when it fit into my schedule. I had a murder to solve first. "Are you meeting the realtor here, or am I on my own?"

"About that...." She was silent for a few beats. "We thought it would be best if I was there and you were, uh, elsewhere."

"You mean leave?"

"Thank you for understanding, darling. We don't want to make the prospective client nervous around someone who has been arrested for murder."

"I wasn't arrested for murder!" Technically I had been arrested, just not charged, but I would never admit I had been arrested.

"Well, you know how the media blows everything out of proportion, so we thought it was for the best."

I ended the call after half-listening to my mother's mindless chitchat and jumped into the shower. If the client was showing up in two hours, I needed to get a move on. After pulling my hair into a wet ponytail, I made my bed, shoved all the boxes containing my books into the garage, downed breakfast, and took Piper for a quick walk. She would have to hang out with me while they showed the condo, but I didn't think the Stoner Dudes would mind her visiting. I wanted to get their phone number the last time I dropped by, especially after Stan's strange expression, but had forgotten to ask by the time I left.

To sweeten them up after showing up on their front doorstep yet again, I stopped by the donut shop and bought a half-dozen donuts and coffee. It wasn't easy juggling the coffee cups and box of donuts while trying to keep Piper from wrapping her leash around my legs as I climbed the rickety stairs, but I made it without spilling anything. I set the coffee down and knocked on the door.

Stan answered a minute later, shirtless, breathing hard, and covered with a light sheen of sweat. I hoped he had been exercising and not involved in another activity.

"Oh, it's you again." Stan wiped his brow with a blue hand towel. "Don't you believe in calling before dropping by someone's house?"

"Sorry. I really meant to get your number the last time but forgot." I bent down, picked up the coffee cups, and shoved them into his hands. "Here, coffee and donuts for you and Steve."

Stan looked unhappy, but he opened the door wide and gestured me inside. After Piper was secured and lying down by the front door, I followed him to the kitchen. Stan sniffed the coffee and put both cups in the sink before turning on his high-end espresso machine. I should have known better than to buy cheap donut-shop swill for the guys.

"Where should I put the donuts?" I held out the box to him.

"Any apple fritters in there?"

"You bet! There's old-fashioned and glazed yeast donuts too. Oh, and a maple bar and a jelly donut." I placed the box on the counter then handed him the apple fritter.

He grunted and took a huge bite. Stan padded to the living room, eating his fritter, and I stooped to pick up a few crumbs he dropped along the way.

"Don't worry about it. Steve will clean it up."

"That's okay. I'm the one who brought the donuts."

"To what do I owe this unexpected visit?"

I gathered I had annoyed him by dropping by, again, without calling. At least he wasn't with a woman or still sleeping. "Is Steve here?"

"Nope."

"Okay, I'll fill you in on my investigation, and you can tell him." I thought I saw Stan roll his eyes, but honestly, my mind was only seeing Amy kissing Philip. I wondered how long they'd been involved and if Philip had moved in with her. From the sound of it, she had already given him money a few times, so chances were their affair wasn't a new thing.

"Earth to Em. Are you going to share, or did you come over here to space out in my living room?"

I quickly told him about following Philip, his affair with Amy, the break-in, and the forged painting confiscated from my condo. "Do you think all these things are tied in together? Even though Philip has a gambling problem, I don't see him being involved in art theft and forgery."

Stan smirked. "You must admit you're pretty clueless and had no idea he was having affairs. So why not theft too? Especially if the rumors were true about Tori."

"You might be right, but Philip never seemed like he was involved in anything shady." I rarely saw him, so what did I know? "On a different subject, I'm dying to know why you and Steve have the surfer-and-stoner-dude persona. Why hide what you have?"

"If I told you, I'd have to kill you."

I laughed at his quote from *Top Gun*, but somehow, Stan didn't seem like he was kidding, and I felt vulnerable. I tried to joke. "Are you in the Witness Protection Program or something?"

"Or something."

Now I was getting uncomfortable again. The guys obviously didn't want me prying into their lives, but that only made me want to know all the more. "I don't mean to pry, but you make me curious. You're not trying to hide from the government or something?"

"Or something." Stan's eyes turned dark as he watched me

through half-closed lids. "You know what they say. *Curiosity killed the cat.*"

Uh-oh. This time I didn't think he was kidding around. I tried to give my naïve, happy laugh, but the tremor in my voice told me I hadn't pulled it off. "Oh, Stan, you're so funny! Don't worry. Whatever secret you have is safe with clueless little me."

This time, Stan let out a real laugh, and I felt instantly relieved. "You should have seen your face. You really are gullible, aren't you?"

"Yep, that's me. Miss Gullible." I stood. "I'll be on my way and let you get back to hiding from the government."

Stan stood and opened a drawer on a side table. After rummaging around, he pulled out a business card and flipped it to me. "Here's my cell number. Call instead of dropping by."

I glanced at the card and saw his name and a phone number. That was it. No business name, no address, nothing. "Sure, and sorry about coming by this morning."

Once Stan's front door slammed behind me, Piper and I headed to the car. I checked my phone but saw no message from my mother, which meant we couldn't go home yet. I called Randall. When his voice mail recording answered, I hung up without leaving a message.

"Well, Piper, maybe we should go for a walk on the beach."

By her yelps and the way she wagged her tail, I was sure she said a resounding "yes."

Chapter 29

We were early enough that summer crowds hadn't clogged the parking lot close to the iconic Huntington Beach pier. After I leashed Piper, we headed for the broad paved bike path that bordered the sand. I stopped for a moment to watch several wetsuit-clad surfers balance on their boards and ride the pounding waves. Piper would be thrilled to go for a swim, but I didn't want the added chore of grooming her and trying to get the sand out of her curly coat of fur. She would have to be content with a walk.

As we headed away from the pier and walked toward Newport Beach, I was mindful of the colorful bikes whizzing by and kept Piper to the side. I loved watching the families, parents with kids in tow, bicycling down the wide path, the kids ringing the bells on their bikes or honking attached clown horns. Their faces all had looks of pure joy, and their laughter and shrieks of delight filled the air. A touch of sadness enveloped my heart when I recalled memories of all I had missed out on after my dad abandoned us. Shaking off my blues, I picked up my pace and collided with Bandboy.

"Are you okay?" Brad reached out to steady my arm. "You

need to watch where you're going, or you'll hurt yourself one of these days."

"I'm so sorry, Ba... Brad! You're not hurt, are you?" Aware I was standing on his flip-flop-clad foot, I took a hasty step back.

"I'll survive." He chuckled while rubbing the top of his bare foot. "Want some company on your walk?"

"Sure. We just got here." I glanced at my gorgeous walking partner and wished I had taken time to put makeup on and do something with my hair besides putting it in a ponytail. "Did you come down for a walk, or are you on your way to breakfast or coffee?"

"I had an interview with a potential employee at the coffee shop across the street and decided to take a walk while I was down here." He stretched his arms wide. "God, I have missed this place. Northern California beaches aren't the same."

I had to agree with him. I was very lucky to live in this area. Piper stopped to sniff interesting smells every so often while Brad and I chatted nonstop about high school and mutual friends. Once again, he surprised me with his knowledge of local gossip, which he was all too willing to share. I laughed often at his colorful stories about starting up his business and his travel adventures. He was an entertaining guy, and I began to relax.

We had walked about a mile when my phone chimed with a text from my mother. **Meet at condo 10 min.**

Did she think I had parked around the corner from my home, just waiting for the client to leave?

At beach walking Piper. There in 30. She wouldn't be happy with my reply, but it was the best I could do.

"Sorry to rush our walk, but I need to go home." I rolled my eyes. "Sometimes it's like I'm still a kid, running at my mother's every beck and call."

"No problem. I need to get back for another interview, anyway." Brad bent down to scratch Piper's ears. "I'm so glad we reconnected. Do you want to have dinner with me tomorrow night? There's a new seafood place that just opened in Seal Beach that I've wanted to try."

Uh-oh. I didn't want to, but I needed to be honest with Brad before he thought there was a chance at something more than friendship between us. "Um, that sounds nice."

"If you don't like seafood, we can go somewhere else." Brad straightened and looked me in the eyes.

"It's not that. Seafood is fine." My face burned, and I let the words tumble out of my mouth as I rambled on. "It's just, um, I don't want to give you the wrong idea. You're a great guy and I've enjoyed getting reacquainted with you again. But I'm not ready to date. I'm not even divorced, so I can't even think about anything like that yet...."

Brad's guffaw was so loud that several walkers turned to see what was going on. "Oh, Em, you really are naïve, aren't you? I assumed it was an act."

"What? I don't know what you're talking about." Did I miss that Brad was married? His ring finger was bare when I bent down to look at it.

"That's not the team I play for." He wiped tears of laughter from his eyes. "I was sure you knew that in high school."

His words puzzled me at first, and then I started putting the pieces together. Brad never dated and had never made a pass at me, even though I thought he had a crush. I assumed he had been ultra-shy. He shared all the gossip about movie stars and about our peers. He even critiqued my outfits from time to time and made helpful suggestions on hairstyles to try. Brad had been a good friend.

"Oh! No, I never knew, but it wouldn't have mattered anyway."

"That's exactly why we were friends in high school." He paused a moment. "It surprised me you didn't stay in touch once we graduated. It hurt my feelings when you didn't respond to my letters once I moved to the Bay area."

"On our pinky-promise swear, I never received any letters from you. I supposed you had moved on to new friends and didn't have time for me." A deep frown furrowed my brow. "My mother… she wouldn't have hidden them from me, would she?"

Brad didn't reply but instead raised his sun-bleached eyebrows and shrugged.

"I'll bet she did. She loved Philip and wouldn't have wanted any other guy to come between us." I stomped my foot, startling Piper. "Most mothers say, 'Finish college before getting married.' Not my mother. She pushed me down the aisle before I could even legally drink. And look where that got me."

Brad pulled me into a warm hug while Piper nuzzled my hand. "Put it behind you and live your life like you want. Trust me, hanging on to anger isn't going to help."

"Thanks. I'll try to remember your advice." My smile was weak, but I thought it was better than nothing. "I'd better go see what Mother wants. One of these days I'll give her a piece of my mind, though. She almost ruined my chance at having you as a friend."

"So, about that dinner. Are you in?"

"You bet."

I needed friends now more than ever. I was lucky Brad had come back into my life just when I needed friendship most.

Chapter 30

I walked into the condo to find my mother packing the kitchen supplies. Her normally well-coiffed hair was out of place, and she had a coffee stain on her cream-colored slacks.

"What took you so long?" she snapped at me. "Grab more boxes and start packing. I wish you had gotten it done like I asked you two days ago."

"What's the rush? Even if someone puts in an offer, it will take a month for escrow to close." I bent over one of the packed boxes, removed the containers of flour and baking powder, then placed them back on the shelf.

"What do you think you're doing? This needed to be packed up yesterday," Mother said with a huff. "The real estate agent is getting Philip's signature accepting the offer. She waited here as long as possible for you to sign first. Honestly, why did you take off like that?"

"I need my baking supplies. I'm supposed to provide four dozen cupcakes for a Chamber of Commerce meeting next week. I don't see what the rush is. I can finish packing the kitchen later." I bit back a retort. "Besides, I didn't expect someone to snatch it up with the first showing. Don't I need to sign the contract?"

"Yes. She'll bring the contract here in about an hour." She pushed a wayward strand of hair from her eyes, leaving a smudge of something on her forehead. "The buyers have relocated from Texas, and they took the asking price without blinking. I guess they're tired of living in a hotel room."

"Still, what's the rush with packing up? I have thirty days for escrow, don't I?"

"No. You have three days, to be exact."

"What? Why?" No way could I move out in three days. "Even though I'm not an expert, I'm aware escrow doesn't move that fast."

"No, but they offered a five-thousand-dollar cash bonus if they could move in during that time frame. If escrow hasn't closed in a month, they'll rent the condo from you on a month-to-month basis." Mother hauled another collapsed box to the table and assembled it.

Something seemed off, but it could be because I was dragging my heels on moving. This was my home and my security, and it had signified my independence. Now I was giving it up, with no place to go.

"They're paying cash for the condo, too, so escrow will move fast. Philip has agreed to let you put the cash bonus toward paying Lars back for your loan."

"You're forgetting one tiny little problem. I have nowhere to live now." I gestured around the room. "We'll need to get a storage unit for everything. Maybe Carrie will let me sleep on her sofa if you don't want me staying with you. Besides that, where am I supposed to bake the cupcakes?"

"Don't worry about it, darling. We have an appointment at three this afternoon with your new employer and landlord."

"Wait, what?" I was confused. My mother had mentioned none of this before. Besides, who would hire a murder suspect? "What job? How did I get hired when I haven't even interviewed? Please tell me it's not flipping burgers at McDonald's."

"Calm down, dear. I called in a favor from an old friend of mine."

Her cheeks turned pink, making me suspicious.

"You'll be doing accounting work and some light cooking. Things you excel at, so they'll be pleased to have you."

"What about my living arrangements? Is this mystery employer going to be my new landlord?"

"Oh, they've agreed to let you and Piper live in the pool house."

I almost choked. A pool house? With pool chemicals and cleaning equipment cluttering a slimy concrete floor? "Do I need to bring my own cot, or am I sleeping on a stack of pool towels? Have you even seen the place?"

"Honestly, darling. Be grateful you have a place to move to with your dog. I'm sure it will be lovely or at least comfortable." She wouldn't look at me. "Which reminds me, they would like to meet Piper during the interview."

Easy for her to say. My sister's sofa was beginning to sound acceptable. Perhaps I could barter babysitting duties for a few hours of sleep time on the sofa every night. "Okay… so who is my new employer and landlord?"

"David Skyler and his mother, Matilda."

I almost fainted. David Skyler was one of the richest men in Orange County, thanks to all his real estate development projects, and one of the most well-known philanthropists in Southern California. I'd never known my mother to mention either of their names. "How… how the heck did you manage that?"

"Oh, David and I went to school together, and we've been friends ever since." Mother waved her hand in a loop, like knowing him was no big deal. "He's realized he needs help after that tragic accident."

I puzzled for a moment then remembered Mr. Skyler's

very young third, or it could've been fourth, wife had been killed a while back in a hit-and-run accident. To my knowledge, the police had never arrested the culprit.

"How come I've never heard you talk about him?"

"I guess it never came up." She almost giggled and then blushed. "You need to make sure you dress in a nice suit with heels. I want you to make a good impression. I'll bring a choker strand of pearls to hide that… that thing on your neck. And brush Piper. She needs to charm them as much as you do."

My mother was hiding something. Could she be involved with Mr. Skyler? Was that why she was able to "call in a favor" and find me a job and a place to live? Poor Lars. He'd been good to our family, and now my mother was treating him like this.

I tried to ask more questions. Well, it was more like prying into what my mother's relationship with Mr. Skyler was. But she wasn't going for it, and she cut me off.

"You need to focus on packing, Emory." She looked at her watch. "I've got to leave if I'm going to make my appointment on time. As soon as you sign the contract, get ready for your meeting. I'll pick you up at two thirty, so don't be late."

I was being dismissed, so after Mother let herself out the front door, I rummaged around in the pile of clothes that still sat on the floor of my closet, looking for something suitable to wear. Then I set to work ironing the stubborn wrinkles out.

As expected, my mother showed up promptly at two thirty, dressed in a navy pantsuit with four-inch stiletto heels. Her makeup and hair looked salon perfect. Beside her, I felt dowdy. Sure, I'd put on my now-wrinkle-free chocolate-brown silk skirt suit with a demure cream-colored blouse, as well as the choker of pearls she had so thoughtfully offered. At least the choker covered the mark on my neck. But I didn't wear heels, especially stilettos, so I was short and downright plump next to my svelte mother. I'd swiped on a dab of mascara and lip gloss, but that was the extent of my makeup. I'd clipped my unruly hair into submission at the base of my neck, but a few strands were already springing loose. Grimy after packing as fast as I could, I'd had every intention of taking a shower and relaxing before my interview. Unfortunately, the real estate agent hadn't gotten there in time, and it was more important to get the contract signed than to take a shower.

"Don't be nervous, darling. The job is yours." She patted my hand then cleared her throat. "This is more of an introduction between you and Matilda, since you'll be living in her pool house. I should warn you, though. Matilda isn't thrilled with the arrangement."

I groaned. My new employer didn't even want me there, so I would probably be out on the street, homeless within a week. "Then why are we even going?"

"David gave her a choice between an assisted living facility or having a caretaker stay at the house."

"What? This is supposed to be accounting and some light cooking." I shook my head. "I don't know a thing about taking care of an invalid!"

My mother laughed. "You're being dramatic. Matilda isn't an invalid. She fell last week and broke her arm, so David wants someone to prepare meals for her and check in on her a couple times a day. She insists she's fine on her own, but we know she really isn't."

"And I'll be doing accounting for Mrs. Skyler?"

"No, that will be for David. It's accounting and some social secretary things too."

Why did I get the feeling I wasn't getting the full story?

Chapter 31

I looked out the window as we drove south on the Pacific Coast Highway toward Newport Beach. Quaint little restaurants, boat yards, upscale shops, and tourist joints lined the narrow highway. I saw glimpses of Newport Harbor in between buildings as we inched south. It was summer, high tourist season, and the streets were packed with cars, people on bikes, and tourists milling around in front of shops. I tried to avoid this area during this time of the year, but now it looked like I'd be living in this jungle... in a pool house, no less.

We turned off of the PCH, as it was known around here, and onto the Balboa Peninsula. It wasn't quite as crowded here as the main road, and I sighed in relief. I didn't like to be surrounded by people. The tightly packed, narrow houses blocked any views of the bay or the beach. A lot of the homes were valued in the mega-millions, but it didn't seem like you got much square footage for your money. I worried that my pool house would turn out to be a pool hut. My mother parked the car down a narrow street that dead-ended at the bay. I stepped out and heard the honks of seals and the screams of seagulls. A warm breeze carried the smell of seawater.

My mouth fell wide open as my mother directed us toward the mini-mansion sitting adjacent to the bayside, dead-end street. The white edifice towered above us and seemed to fill the entire lot all the way to the water's edge. I began to think the pool house was an illusion meant to lure me here, since no pool or even a teeny-tiny structure could possibly fit at the back of the house.

After being buzzed in through a wide security gate that swung open silently, we made our way to a massive wrought-iron and frosted-glass front door. David Skyler was standing just inside the open door, smiling. He was tall and dressed in an impeccable custom-made suit, complete with a red power tie and crisp white shirt. Even though nothing stood out about his clothes, they screamed money. His full head of blond hair had turned silver around the temples, adding a distinguished look to his well-chiseled, tanned, unwrinkled face. I wondered if he'd had plastic surgery then remembered this was Newport Beach. Of course he had. Everyone did plastic work or at least Botox.

I let my mother take the lead while Piper and I followed behind.

"Addie, you look stunning." David lightly kissed her on each cheek, European style. "And this beautiful young lady must be your daughter."

He reached out to shake my hand. I was holding Piper's leash in my right hand and my purse in my left. As I tried to switch the leash to my left hand, Piper interpreted it to mean we were moving forward, and she collided with my legs. Thrown off balance, I pitched into my new boss's solid chest.

Heat inflamed my cheeks, and I took a huge step back, almost squishing Piper, who let out a yelp. "I'm so sorry about that. It's nice to meet you, Mr. Skyler."

He dropped his hand without giving me another chance to

muck things up. "Please call me David. If you follow me, I'll introduce you to Matilda."

Interesting. He called his mother by her first name. My mother glared at me and then motioned for me to follow her into the house.

I stepped into the wide, two-storied foyer. On one side a curved stairway with a wrought-iron railing reminiscent of crashing waves led to the second floor. Straight ahead of the foyer led to an equally wide hallway featuring a view of the bay through an entire wall of glass doors. With the generous number of windows and an overhead skylight, the house was bright and airy. Art, and I mean museum-quality, famous works of art, lined the hallway walls. It worried me since I was a klutz. I didn't want to be responsible for somehow knocking one of these million-dollar-or-more paintings off the wall. I hoped they were well insured. Nervous, I pulled Piper closer as we walked into the grand living room. I was glad to see the flooring was polished stone. I would have hated to be responsible for Piper scratching an expensive wood floor with her nails.

An elegant, silver-haired woman sat erect in a wingback chair. She wore a floral silk dress and had a generous amount of makeup applied to her fairly unlined face. Like I said, this was Newport Beach, so the level of makeup and her smooth face didn't surprise me. Her lips pursed together. She met my gaze by looking over the tops of her tortoiseshell glasses, and her head dipped slightly to the side. I was certain she didn't like me. Her left arm, encased in a colorfully tattooed cast, was cradled close to her body.

"Matilda, you remember Addie? And this is her daughter, Ann Marie." David waved his hand toward me.

"Emory. My name is Emory." People misspoke my name often, and I corrected the mistake a couple of times before answering to whatever they wanted to call me. "It's nice to meet you, Mrs. Skyler."

"Likewise." Matilda sniffed and stared at Piper.

"And this is Piper." I prayed my dog wouldn't do anything rude like bark or flop on her back to share her girlie parts with these strangers. "She's well trained and won't cause any problems for you."

Matilda nodded but didn't say a word.

David jumped in and recited what my duties would require and what my very generous salary would be. Then he described what his mother could and couldn't eat. If looks could kill, David would be a dead man from the angry glances Mrs. Skyler was giving her son. But she still didn't say a word. My attention had wandered off from what my new boss was saying. Not the best way to make a good impression. My mother gave me angry looks as well, since she was all too aware of my mind wandering away instead of staying focused.

"Here's a printed list of things Matilda can't eat and recommendations for what you can cook." He handed me several sheets of paper. "I think, for now, just have her breakfast on the table by eight. Dorie will tidy up after she's done eating. You're free to prepare her evening meals whenever it's convenient, and she can reheat them when she's ready for dinner. Please check on her around nine before she goes to bed. A phone call will be sufficient. Do you have any questions?"

Why yes, I did have a gazillion questions. Foremost were 'Where is the pool house?' and 'How horrid is it?' But I thought I'd better leave those questions unsaid and focus on the job aspect. "Should I use existing food in the pantry and refrigerator, and where should I prepare the meals?"

"You can use Matilda's kitchen. We'll get you a key to the house and a security alarm code." He paused and scribbled something onto a notepad. "Leave a list of grocery items you need, and Dorie will purchase them. Feel free to cook enough for your own meals as well."

"Thank you. I appreciate your generosity." I resisted the

urge to scratch my nose. "My mother mentioned I'll be doing some accounting work for you. What will that entail?"

He waved off my concern. "Let's get you settled in with Matilda then worry about that. I'll have my business secretary schedule an appointment with you to meet at my house and go over some things next week. After you get up to speed, I shouldn't need you to work more than ten or fifteen hours a week. You can fit those hours in whenever it's convenient for you. I'm dividing my time between Newport Beach and Washington, D.C., so you'll be on your own a lot."

"That sounds fine. Thank you." I was dying to know about my living accommodations but didn't know how to mention them. I looked over at my mother, hoping she'd get the hint, but she was too busy smiling into David's pale-blue eyes. My heart dropped. Poor Lars. "When would you like me to begin cooking for Mrs. Skyler?"

"How about right now?" He looked at his wristwatch. "I'd love to stay and sample what you prepare, but I need to leave for a meeting."

I gulped. Now? Talk about trial by fire. "Uh, sure. Except I came here with my mother, and I don't have a ride home."

Again, he waved his hand in dismissal. "Matilda will have her driver take you and your dog home once you're done. I want you both to get to know each other."

Driver? This was a whole new world to me. "Thank you."

Mrs. Skyler didn't say a word as her son kissed her cheek goodbye. He gave me a quick wave and took my mother's arm as they walked to the front door. Without a backward glance, my mother left me to face a woman who clearly disliked me and wanted nothing to do with me. Silence hung in the air after they left. Mrs. Skyler sighed and then walked gracefully toward me on high heels I never would have been able to manage. She stopped when she stood a foot from my face. I had to tilt my head up slightly to meet her gaze.

She held out her hand. "May I?"

I was confused until she pointed at the lists of foods her son said she could and couldn't have. I handed them to her. "Of course."

She sniffed. "Limited to four ounces of red wine served with dinner each night. No gimlets, no processed sugar, no white bread, no cheese." She flipped through the pages, and her eyes narrowed to mere slits. Then she turned abruptly on her heels and marched toward the closed French doors.

Unsure what she expected of me, I sat still and tried not to worry I would be fired before I even began my new job.

Matilda was halfway through the French doors when she whirled around. "Young lady, follow me."

I told Piper to stay and then trailed Matilda into a library turned office. Books lined two walls, from floor to ceiling. In the corner, a rolling librarian ladder sat parked between shelving. The wall facing the bay was lined with French doors, and I watched a sailboat float by. A large, ebony-colored desk sat in the room's middle atop a colorful Persian rug. A computer monitor and keyboard were the only items on top of the desk. On the remaining wall was a matching credenza complete with a printer and other office paraphernalia.

She walked to the credenza and pulled open the door to a cabinet. Hidden inside was a paper shredder. She fed the offending list into the machine and looked at me with twinkling pale-blue eyes. "Rules are meant to be broken."

Chapter 32

Mr. Skyler was paying my salary, but while I had an obligation to him, I was the one who had to live with Mrs. Skyler. Not sure what to do, I tried to appeal to her sense of well-being.

"Your son is trying to keep you from getting lightheaded and falling again." I pointed at her broken arm. "Eating healthy can keep your bones strong and help your balance."

"There's absolutely nothing wrong with my balance, young lady. I'm strong as a horse." She snorted. "Serves me right for walking down the stairs while sexting that hunky new silver fox I met at the ballroom dance studio."

My mouth fell open. I was sure I misheard her. She didn't say "sexting," did she?

"You can close your mouth, dear. That's not an attractive look on you."

"Yes, Mrs. Skyler."

"It's five o'clock somewhere, isn't it?" She glanced at her watch. "Do you know how to make a gimlet?"

"No, I'm sorry, I don't."

"Don't tell me you're a teetotaler?" Her tone made it sound like avoiding alcohol would be a cardinal sin.

"No, but I tend to stick to wine."

"Hmph." She motioned for me to follow her.

We went back to the grand living room, where she opened an eight-foot-tall by five-foot-wide cabinet door. Hidden behind it was a bar that slid out. "Let me teach you how to make a gimlet."

Mrs. Skyler filled a cocktail shaker with ice from a small refrigerator at the back of the cabinet. Then she poured a few healthy glugs of gin over the ice, along with some Rose's Lime Juice. I was worried because she measured nothing, and it looked like a lot more gin than lime juice was going into the cocktail shaker. After shaking the mixture vigorously, she strained the cocktail into two frosty martini glasses pulled from the refrigerator.

She garnished each one with a lime twist, handed me a glass, and downed half of her drink. "Cheers!"

"Uh, cheers." I took a tentative sip. It surprised me how smooth and flavorful the drink was. Still, it wouldn't do to get loopy in front of my new employer, so I didn't take another sip.

Mrs. Skyler refilled her drink and motioned me to follow her again. "I might as well give you the grand tour. Honestly, my son needs to stop worrying about me. Even with my broken arm, I can manage on my own."

If he knew she was drinking in the middle of the day and sexting while walking downstairs, I suspected he'd be a whole lot more worried.

I followed my new employer around on her tour, starting with the upstairs. There were five bedrooms and six bathrooms. I was distraught when I peered out the windows and didn't see a pool or a pool house anywhere. Was I going to have to sleep in my car? I wasn't sure how to bring up the subject.

Mrs. Skyler and I paused for a few minutes on the balcony of her upstairs master bedroom and watched the sun reflecting on the waterway as it descended on the western horizon. Gulls cried, and pelicans skimmed the surface of the water in a V-shaped formation, hunting for fish. Colorful boats with sunburned passengers glided by the house. Some people took a second look to examine us standing on the balcony, and I wondered what they were thinking.

With her son out of the house, the elderly woman's personality was on full display. She had a biting wit but was affectionate with my dog and courteous to me. And she loved her gimlets. After the upstairs tour, we stopped by the bar for another refill, but she never appeared inebriated. When I called her Mrs. Skyler for the third time, she halted in her tracks.

"Please call me Tillie. Why my son has to be so formal is beyond me." She took another sip of gimlet and motioned to my almost-full glass. "Don't you like it?"

"It's delicious." Surprisingly, I meant it. "I had a bad experience with alcohol recently…."

She winked at me. "Ah, yes. So, dearie, how are you going to get away with murdering that tramp?"

I had taken another small sip of the gimlet just as she asked me that question, and I inhaled the cocktail down the wrong pipe. Coughing and sputtering, I put my glass on the bar so I wouldn't spill it. Piper nudged my knee as I bent over at the waist and coughed more. The question wasn't one I had planned on hearing. My mistake had been hoping this elderly woman was out of the local gossip and news loop, but instead, she was in the thick of things.

Once I caught my breath, I straightened up and smoothed out my skirt. "I truly am innocent."

"That's a shame." Tillie *tsk*ed. "I was so excited to tell my bridge group that my new caretaker and chef is a murderer. Are you sure you didn't kill her? She deserved it."

"No!" I didn't mean to raise my voice, but there was no

reason for anyone to get the idea I was a killer. I lowered my voice back to a normal volume. "I mean, no, of course I didn't kill her, but someone is trying awfully hard to frame me for it."

She didn't say a word for several moments while she tapped a manicured aqua-colored nail on her lower lip. Tillie leaned toward me and broke the silence. "What are we going to do about it? We need to investigate."

Under no circumstances could I allow that to happen. Mr. Skyler would fire me if he found out his mother was getting involved in a murder investigation, so I did what I'd been doing a lot of lately—I lied. "The detective is doing a good job investigating, and I'm sure he'll find the murderer soon."

"Please, don't mollycoddle me," she said with a snort. "I'm aware you're their prime suspect and they're only looking for evidence that proves you killed her. Granted, you've got a good attorney, but he's not putting enough time into your case."

When my mouth dropped wide open again, she tapped my chin. "What are we going to do about that?"

I took a huge swallow of my gimlet. "How? How do you know so much about me and what happened?"

"Dear, you're famous, or perhaps it's infamous." Tillie's eyes glinted. "All of us women who have been cheated on and lied to applaud you for doing in that husband-stealing hussy. We hear things and share with the group when we play bridge."

She really meant they gossiped while playing bridge, and lucky me, I was the current fodder for the gossip mill. After another slug of the gimlet, Tillie topped off my glass, and I ended up telling her about my investigation. I didn't doubt for a moment she would broadcast the details at the next bridge gathering. I hoped the extent to which I had been meddling in Detective Jackson's investigation wouldn't get back to him.

After I spilled my guts to Tillie, she patted my hand. "I'll get my friends together, and we'll brainstorm ideas on who you should investigate next. I think the most likely culprit is that Amy gal, so we must find a way to get her to confess."

Chapter 33

Matilda would get me fired for sure if Mr. Skyler found out about this. "While I really appreciate you trying to help, you shouldn't get involved. Your son will probably sue me, or worse, if he finds out I've put you in danger. Beside, losing one job already this week is more than enough."

"Mr. Wilkins is nothing more than a sanctimonious hypocrite!" She ground her teeth and narrowed her eyes. "Why, my best friend and I saw him at one of those nudie bars in Vegas last month. He was stuffing dollar bills into a stripper's thong, so how does he think he can get away with firing you for that picture floating around the internet? Or because you had the misfortune of finding that hussy's body?"

My eyes bugged out, and my mouth dropped open again. I quickly closed it before Tillie could say anything. Nudie bar? I shook my head and decided not to tell her I was fired because of the blackmail threat. "It's probably for the best. I hated working there, anyway. Honestly, I've never really enjoyed accounting."

"Then why in the world would you ever make a career doing it?"

"It was the path of least resistance." I shrugged. "I needed to do something, and early in our marriage, Philip talked about transferring to northern California. If I earned an accounting degree, it would be easy to find a job no matter where I ended up. Police don't make a lot of money, and I had to work."

"If you could have any job in the world, what would you do?"

"That's easy. I'd open a bakery specializing in cupcakes and birthday cakes."

"Then what's stopping you? Why haven't you followed your dreams?"

"To be honest, it's the money." I didn't want to share the information about Philip's gambling addiction. "We were always short on money and couldn't afford for me not to have a steady paycheck. Plus, it takes a lot of money to open a bakery."

"Doesn't your sister do catering?"

"Yes, and I work with her sometimes. I'm trying to establish a portfolio of my cakes and create specialty cupcake recipes."

"Why don't you become a cupcake caterer?" Tillie looked at me like I was dense for not coming up with the idea myself. "At least to start out. When business grows, you can add in custom cakes."

I shook my head. "I don't have a licensed kitchen, and to pass inspection, I'd have to give up Piper. My condo is too small to keep her isolated."

Tillie stood up suddenly. "Follow me."

Now what? I followed the tottering woman down a long hall on the opposite side of the house from where we had been sitting. I was tottering just as much as she was. The gimlets had finally caught up with me.

When I walked through a wide archway and turned the corner, I gasped. An industrial-sized kitchen greeted me. An eight-burner stovetop and professional-sized stainless double ovens beckoned me to bake. The enormous refrigerator and separate freezer took up almost half of one wall. An eight-foot butcher-block island sat in the middle of the kitchen. Copper pots and pans hung from a rack above the island and gleamed in the pinpointed lights. I ran my fingers lightly across the wood surface and swooned.

In a small alcove outfitted with a bistro table and two chairs, a large bay window afforded a partial view of the waterway while allowing in ample light. A skylight over the butcher-block island brought in natural light while soft fluorescent lights, recessed into the high ceiling, chased away any shadows hiding in the corners of the room. The room was perfect for creating recipes and then bringing them to life.

"Use my kitchen and get your catering company going. You won't have a problem passing inspection here."

I turned to her, tears in my eyes. "Really? But I'm sure my caretaking job for you is only temporary until your arm heals."

"This kitchen is rarely used, except at Christmas. Even then, the caterers bring in the food already prepared and don't cook here." She waved away my concerns. "If my son relents and decides I don't need help, there's no reason you can't still use my kitchen."

I wanted to hug her but was afraid I'd hurt her arm, so I patted her uninjured arm instead. "If you're sure, I'd love to try it." I gave an inward sigh of relief. I would be able to bake the cupcakes for the Chamber meeting like I had promised Carrie.

"Wonderful. I'd like to hire you to make cupcakes for my bridge group next Wednesday." Her eyes sparkled mischievously. "Can you make gimlet cupcakes?"

After assuring her I could make just about any cupcake flavor, I suggested it might be time for both of us to eat. The alcohol had gone straight to my head, and since Tillie had drunk more than I had, I assumed she should eat too. While I perused the contents of her massive refrigerator and her free-standing side-by-side freezer, my mind whirled with ideas on how to create the gimlet cocktail cupcakes. I was sure they would be a hit, given the refreshing citrus and botanical notes of the gin. The trick would be to layer the flavors so they didn't get lost or muted from the flour and sugar.

Tillie excused herself and said she needed to text her friends. I hoped she really meant she wanted to catch her friends up on the gossip rather than engaging in sexting. I shook my head. Tillie acted like a wild twenty-something, and I acted like I was an octogenarian. It made me a bit melancholy to think I had somehow missed out on life all this time without knowing it.

Chapter 34

I sautéed chicken cutlets and created a pan sauce with lemon juice, capers, and a bit of butter. With the fresh lettuce and cucumbers I found, I made a salad with a simple oil and balsamic vinaigrette seasoned with French whole-grain Dijon mustard. In the walk-in pantry, I located half a loaf of a crusty baguette. After slicing it, I rubbed the surface of each piece with a clove of garlic and toasted them. I set the small bistro table with placemats, utensils, and glasses of ice water. After our food was plated, I called Tillie back to the kitchen. I expected her to complain about the lack of wine or alcohol with dinner, but I thought she'd had enough.

Instead, the elderly woman dug into the chicken and salad like she hadn't eaten all day and then drank most of her water. I offered to refill both her plate and glass, but she declined.

"If you cook like that all the time, I'll gain weight." Tillie wiped her mouth with the cloth napkin I had placed by her plate. "My son won't be happy with you. Don't forget he wants me on an austere diet."

"Don't worry. This is a healthy meal with a decent level of calories." My mother had drilled healthy eating into me my whole life. "Healthy food doesn't have to mean bad-tasting food or no flavor."

"Well then, I'm looking forward to you cooking for me." She sighed contentedly. "I was tired of the fried chicken and gravy Dorie always brought me to eat. Don't get me wrong, I love fried chicken. Just not several times a week."

I nodded in agreement and cleared the table. Piper was lying just outside the kitchen. She looked at the plates and whined. I needed to get her home and fed soon.

"Oh my, where are my manners? Poor Piper, you're probably hungry." Tillie motioned for my dog to join her at the table. "There's a new bag of dog food I can open for Piper. It's left from my sweet dog, Tatum. I lost her a couple months ago and haven't cleaned up her things yet."

"That's okay. She can wait until we get home."

Tillie's face fell. "Of course. You probably have special food you give Piper."

"It's not that. I didn't want to cause any extra work for you." Now I felt bad. This feisty lady was lonely and had obviously been missing her dog. "I'm sure Piper would be grateful if it's not any trouble."

"No trouble at all. I'll be right back." She disappeared, and within a few minutes, she was back bearing a bowl of heaped-up food. She filled another empty dog dish with water from the prep sink located in the middle of the island.

We chatted while Piper wolfed down the food. I knew she wasn't deprived of sustenance and couldn't be all that hungry, but when Piper was given a new brand of food, she thought it was treats and chowed down. She acted like I'd take it away from her if she didn't eat fast enough. Once Piper had licked the bowl clean, Tillie stood up.

"I called my driver, and he'll be here in thirty minutes. You probably want to take a look at the pool house so you can see what you need to bring with you." She retrieved a set of keys from a drawer in the island and then motioned for me to follow her. "If there's anything you need, I can furnish it for you."

We went out the massive front doors, through the gate, and across the alleyway. Well, Tillie called it an alleyway. I called it a street. Dusk was nearing, and streetlights flickered on. She unlocked a decorative privacy gate adjacent to a garage. Once the gate swung open, we stepped onto a Spanish-tiled courtyard that surrounded an Olympic-sized swimming pool. The pool lights were on, which made the water glow a bright turquoise-blue. White fairy lights twinkled in the trees dotting the area and on the ceiling of an outdoor patio room. Where I thought the garage ended, another L-shaped structure started with several French doors positioned at regular intervals.

Tillie unlocked a door and motioned me inside. This? This was a pool house? It was almost the size of my condo! The open floor plan showed the pool house was charmingly decorated and furnished in what I would call a French provincial style.

My mouth must have dropped open again because Tillie tapped my chin.

"Will this be adequate for you and Piper?"

I burst into tears. Never in a million years, after all that had happened with Philip, did I dream I would find somewhere I could call home.

"Oh, dear, is this not to your liking?"

"No. I mean yes. I mean, this is so beautiful, and you've been so nice to me. I'm afraid I'll wake up and find myself in jail or back in the nightmare that my life has become." Through my tears, I saw Tillie's concerned face. Piper nudged my hand. "You're like a fairy god-mother!"

"Now, now, it's going to be okay." She patted Piper, who had thrust her head in between us. "Come on. I'll show you around."

After finding tissues for me, she led me around the two-bedroom, two-bath pool house. She showed me the outside bathroom and shower and told me to help myself to the pool towels and enjoy the pool whenever I wanted. Dorie, who I gathered was the housekeeper, would clean the pool house once a week and launder all the linens and towels.

I was sure I was dreaming when a brand-new town car pulled up and a magazine model-worthy blond man, appearing to be in his forties, introduced himself as Andrew. He wore a black suit and tie and told me he had parked in front and would wait for me until I was ready to go. I pinched myself, and when it hurt, I decided maybe fairy tales did come true.

Tillie scratched Piper behind the ears. The woman wore a forlorn look on her face. "Would you mind if Piper spent the night with me? She can have Tatum's bed, or if you prefer her to sleep crated, I have that too."

Piper looked at me then placed her head back into Tillie's hands. I gathered Piper wanted to sleep over too.

"That's fine. It will give me a chance to get some packing done." I brushed hair that the evening breeze had blown onto my face out of my eyes. "Is there a specific day you'd like for me to move in?"

"Whenever you're ready."

"Okay. I'll drop by tomorrow morning to pick up Piper and bring you some breakfast. We can talk about timing then." I was careful to not smoosh Tillie's broken arm and gave her a hug. "I can't thank you enough for giving me this chance to start over."

"Nonsense. You're the one who will have to put up with me." She waved me off before winking. "Go on. Get out of here, or I'll have to pay Andrew overtime."

Tillie's driver dropped me off, and as he sped into the night, I walked toward my brightly lit condo. I didn't remember leaving the lights on, but then again, I had hurried to get out the door for the interview. Promptness was important to my mother, and I knew I was rushed to get dressed and apply enough makeup to pacify her. I was placing my purse and keys on the entryway credenza when a shiver ran up my spine. Stan was sitting on my living room sofa, arms crossed, with his flip-flop-shod feet resting on the coffee table.

Chapter 35

I wished Piper had come home with me. She would have warned me that an uninvited guest had made themselves at home in my condo.

"Stan, what a surprise!" Did I forget to lock the door when I left with Mother? "Do you have new information to nail Amy with?"

Quietly, he sat there, watching me. I walked to the kitchen and got a glass of water. I could still feel the effects of the gimlets a bit. He just stared at me, and I was getting creeped out. "Can I get you anything? Water, soda, coffee?"

"Naw, I'm good."

I guzzled a glass of water then rummaged in one of the packed pantry boxes, looking for something sweet. Nothing inside was edible except sprinkles. Briefly, I wondered if Stan had taken drugs. "I'm going to bake cookies. Would you like chocolate chip or lemon?"

"Em, we need to talk." Even though his voice was quiet, it sounded ominous.

I walked into the living room, and he gestured for me to take a seat. "What's going on? Am I going to be arrested? Did the detective find something else that incriminates me even more?"

"Just drop the act, okay?" He ran shaky fingers through his unruly blond hair. "We know you've figured it out, so what do you want? Money? A cut of the action? Do you want to take over Tori's business?"

Huh? Figured what out? I sat there and mulled over Stan's questions for a minute. The entire time, he looked at me through cold, reptilian eyes and never said a word. Then the pieces of the puzzle clicked into place. Stan and Steve lived in luxury while showing a completely different persona to the public. They wanted people to think they were broke, stoner losers, chubby misfits, when, in reality, they were the exact opposite. Tori lived right below them and had more money than she should. The two men almost never socialized, yet Tori seemed to be a part of their inner circle. Steve and Stan claimed to be successful game software developers, but Brad had never heard of them. Randall said Tori had warned a theft ring operator in Florida that an arrest was coming, and when his brother died, she fled here. It all came down to theft and money laundering. How did I not see it before? Because I wanted Philip's lover to be the killer. I wanted him to suffer, since he'd caused me so much pain.

"What did I figure out, and why do you think I figured out whatever it is?" I tried to be coy, but my voice quavered.

"You're a terrible actress, so don't even pretend." Stan pulled a gun from the crack between the sofa's cushions and pointed it at me. "I asked you what you want."

"The truth? Justice? Not going to jail." When Stan's hand shook, my voice squeaked. I worried he would accidentally fire that thing. "Can you tell me what happened with Tori?"

Stan started to sweat. Large drops of perspiration rolled down his forehead and cheeks. Was it stress, or could drugs be causing this behavior? Whatever it was, I was beyond worried he would be careless and the gun would go off. I didn't want to get shot. I didn't want to die.

"Really? No one can be that naïve." He wiped his forehead with his free hand then laid the gun on the sofa beside him.

An audible sigh of relief escaped my mouth now that the gun wasn't pointed my way. However, without an obvious route of escape visible, I didn't yet see how I would get away. Perhaps if I kept him talking, I could figure out something. "I'm guessing you met Tori in Florida, and she was a front for moving merchandise for either you or your informant. When her fiancé was killed, you moved here and started up your business again."

"That's the gist. Tori's spa shop was a good cover for laundering the money." He shook his head. "Stupid girl had to get involved with a cop, especially when she could steal one away from another woman. Said she loved men in uniforms. I think she was just an adrenaline junkie, and they made her feel like she was living life on the edge."

"What happened? Why did you kill Tori?" I didn't want to ask that question, but I needed answers.

"She skimmed the cash. I'm not sure why, since we've always paid her an exorbitant amount. But then again, she was a greedy witch and loved a good thrill. When we confronted Tori, she threatened to blow the whistle on our operation."

"But what about the painting I found in my condo? Did she put it there?"

"Yeah, she had a good laugh about that one. She wanted Philip to dump you, but he wouldn't, so she staged it so he would think you were involved in stealing artwork."

"But she set the thing up with Randall first then plastered my picture all over Facebook. Why involve the art theft?"

"The painting was a backup plan if Philip didn't care about seeing you with another man. She knew he'd go ballistic if he found out you were involved in something illegal."

Apparently, Tori hadn't bothered to understand Philip. His fragile ego couldn't and wouldn't stand for his wife to be in another man's company, so there was no reason for a backup plan. "Did you know the painting was a forgery?"

Stan chuckled. "Smart, huh? We were aware she was stealing from us, so we substituted real paintings with forgeries. She never caught on. Although, down the road, when she sold them, she'd have ended up with some very angry clients."

"If you knew it was a forgery, why did you break into my home looking for the painting?" I was still upset that my treasured photos had been ripped up.

"We didn't break in."

"Are you sure? Someone did, and it looked like they were searching for it."

"No. It wasn't us."

Perhaps it was Philip after all. I supposed he could have been involved in the art theft to pay for his gambling addiction. Maybe he knew Tori had stashed one of the paintings at our house and wanted it for himself. "So you decided you needed to kill her and tried to frame me?"

"Yeah. She threatened us and became too much of a liability. You and your catfight over Philip made you the perfect scapegoat." He picked the gun up again and pointed it at me. "What's it going to be?"

I was sure his question was rhetorical, and I had become a liability just like Tori. My mouth turned dry, making it hard for me to swallow. "How much money are you offering to buy my silence?"

"You're not an actress. I can read every thought you have on your face." The hand holding the gun shook again, so he rested the gun on the sofa. "I've always liked you, so this isn't easy for me to do."

"Where's Steve? Why are you here and not your brother?" Not that it mattered which one was here, but I wanted to keep him talking while I figured out how to get away.

"He blames me for you figuring out our connection to Tori's death, so I have to clean up my mistake." Stan rubbed his face with his free hand. "Why did you have to stick your nose in where it doesn't belong? Why couldn't you leave it alone?"

Duh, because I didn't want to go to prison for something I didn't do.

He motioned for me to stand up. "Time to go."

"Go? Where are we going?"

"We'll take a boat ride down toward Mexico. A little chum in the water to call the sharks, and... well, you get the picture."

"You won't get away with this." I needed to find a way to stall so I could get out of this horrific situation.

"Of course we will. Once you're taken care of, we'll take our boat and head to a new city to set up our operation." Stan's laugh was chilling. "This isn't the first time we've had to move because of inconvenient, meddling people. It's time to go, so stop stalling."

This wasn't good. The Stoner Dudes weren't on anyone's radar for being the bad guys. They certainly hadn't been on my radar. Heck, I'd been giving them an update on everything I had discovered in my investigation. I pushed myself off the chair, my legs weak and my knees wobbly.

I guess I wasn't moving fast enough because Stan shoved me forward. "No funny business. Walk straight to my car and keep your mouth shut."

When I reached the front door, I was momentarily confused. It was cracked open about four inches. I thought I'd closed it earlier, but perhaps, in the shock of finding Stan here, I hadn't latched it properly. I pulled the front door open and screamed when Philip appeared right in front of my face. He pushed me to the side, raised his Glock, and pointed it at Stan.

222

"Drop your weapon!" Philip yelled in the scariest voice I'd ever heard him use. "Do it now!"

Stan's gun shook, but he didn't lower it.

From the corner of my eye, I saw Philip's partner, Amy, had her gun drawn, ready to back my husband up.

"Put the gun down, Stan," Amy said in a gentle voice, her tone pleading for the man to listen. "It's not worth it."

Stan looked back and forth from Philip to Amy then lowered his gun slightly. Before I barely registered what was happening, he swung the weapon toward me and pulled the trigger.

The cacophony of simultaneous gunfire rang in my ears, and I scrunched my eyes closed, not wanting to see where I'd been hit. I felt no pain except for a small scratch on my cheek and wondered if I was in shock. The screams coming from Stan's lips made me drag my attention back to what was happening in front of me.

Blood oozed from Stan's shoulder while Amy turned him over and cuffed him. I touched my cheek, and my hand came away with a streak of red. Then my knees gave out, and my head hit the wall. Stars floated in front of my eyes, and I shook my head to clear my vision. Philip squawked into his radio and requested an ambulance. Both Amy and Philip glanced my way then ignored me and took turns applying pressure to Stan's wound.

The paramedics were the first to arrive, followed by Detective Jackson and other uniformed officers.

Detective Jackson bent down next to where I still sat on the floor. "Are you okay, Mrs. Martinez?"

I nodded, not sure I could trust myself to speak.

"Do you need medical attention? Did you get injured?"

"I'm not sure." I showed him the palm of my hand, where I had wiped my cheek. "Did I get shot?"

Detective Jackson looked from my cheek to the wall beside my face. He grimaced. "You are one lucky lady. If that bullet had been two inches to the right, we wouldn't be talking."

"Then why am I bleeding?"

"The drywall splintered when the bullet struck. It scratched your face." He motioned for a paramedic to assist me. "You won't even have a scar once it's healed."

My head dipped toward Philip. "Did he hear Stan confess to murdering Tori? Am I cleared?"

"Both he and Officer Doyle heard every word."

I sighed in relief and relaxed against the wall while the paramedic cleaned my scratch and applied ointment. The detective left me sitting there and talked to the crime scene technicians who had arrived. The paramedics loaded Stan onto a gurney and took off.

"Hey, are you okay?" a familiar voice asked. "That's only a scratch, right?"

"I'll be fine." I opened my eyes and saw Philip crouched down next to me. "Why were you here? Not that I'm complaining because you saved my life. Thank you."

Philip gestured at the scene in front of us. "I came to apologize. This entire mess is all my fault."

Philip apologizing? The skepticism must have shown on my face.

"I've started seeing a counselor. It's one of the things they highly recommend doing." He ran his hand through his wavy black hair. "Amy is adamant I follow all their suggestions and get my life back on track. Otherwise…."

I gathered Officer Doyle would make Philip toe the line if he wanted any kind of relationship with her.

"Were you the one who broke into our house?" I was puzzled because I was sure the culprit was one of the Stoner Dudes, but Stan had denied it.

Philip blushed. "Uh, yeah. I'm really sorry about that."

"But why? Why did you have to rip up my pictures and make such a mess?"

"You changed the locks." His voice grew louder, and I could sense his anger. "You had no right to lock me out of my own house."

I stared at him, hardly able to believe he would let his rage destroy something that was so precious to me. Amy loudly cleared her throat.

Philip glanced at Amy and nodded. "Sorry. I've got some things to work through. I guess I'll be attending anger management classes too."

Even though my heart was heavy, I nodded. "I hope you find whatever happiness you're looking for."

And I meant it. Looking death in the face made me realize I hadn't been happy with my life or the choices I had been making. I was floating along, letting Philip, my mother, my boss, and even Tori tell me what to do. The upheaval in my life and getting over my heartbreak wouldn't be easy, but I had new friends and new goals. I was going to succeed my way and find out what I wanted out of life.

Chapter 36

Philip called my mother to come pick me up. He didn't trust me to drive, and for that, I was grateful. She arrived holding hands with Lars, and they both enveloped me in a huge hug. I still didn't know what was going on with her and David Skyler, but that would wait for another day. For now, I was glad to see her smiling at Lars, and he seemed happy with her.

My mother insisted I sleep in as late as I wanted. When I mentioned the amount of packing that needed to be completed before the move-out deadline, she told me Lars was paying someone to do it for me. So, I slept in… until six and remembered I was supposed to bring Tillie breakfast and pick Piper up.

I crept downstairs, intending to make a batch of blueberry muffins before anyone got up. Lars and Mother were in the kitchen already, drinking coffee and reading the newspaper. When they saw me, Mother came and gave me a hug.

"Darling, good news. They caught Steve just as he was leaving the marina for the open sea."

Again, I sighed in relief. I had worried he would seek revenge if he remained on the run. Lars turned the newspaper over to hide the front-page headlines, which, I assumed, were all about my misadventure. But I didn't care anymore.

"I need to make muffins and take them to Tillie this morning for breakfast."

"Tillie?" Lars asked. "I thought you were caring for Mrs. Skyler."

"She likes people to call her Tillie."

Mother and Lars exchanged a glance, and his eyebrows arched into his forehead.

"What? What was that look for?"

"Nothing. I'm glad you're getting along with her so well." She took another sip of coffee. "How are your living arrangements? Does the pool house have a cot for you, or will you have to make do with a pile of towels?"

I had the good grace to blush. "No, it's quite beautiful."

They returned to the business section of the newspaper, carefully hiding the front section from my view. I mixed batter for muffins then gently stirred in frozen blueberries, divided the batter between the muffin cups, and popped them into the oven. I sat down at the table.

"Okay, what gives? What is going on with Mrs. Skyler?" My new-and-improved self wouldn't be put off so easily. Tillie was my friend, and I had been hired to care for her, so to speak.

My mother sighed and glanced at Lars again. He gave a small nod.

"David is concerned she's suffering from dementia. She refuses any tests to check for signs of Alzheimer's and gets angry when he brings it up." My mother twisted her coffee cup around in her hands. "She's changed her name from Matilda to Tillie. You've seen what she did with her cast. It looks tattooed! And wearing aqua nail polish? What eighty-something-year-old does that? What really concerns him is she takes off for Vegas without telling him. Who knows what kind of trouble she might get into?"

I knew exactly what kind of trouble she could get in. "I spent a lot of time talking with Tillie yesterday, and I'm pretty sure she doesn't have dementia. She's realizing she only has a few years left in her life and wants to live every single minute to its fullest."

"I hope you're right. It's tearing David apart." My mother looked back down at her now-empty cup. "He wants you to report on everything Tillie does and who she sees. If she's doing something inappropriate for her age and her position in society, he wants a phone call right away."

My mouth dropped open. I wouldn't betray my new friend like that. If I thought she was a danger to herself or to others, it would be appropriate to say something to Mr. Skyler. But everything I had seen and talked about with her indicated she was simply enjoying life. I snapped my mouth shut and decided I wouldn't put my mother in the middle of this.

"If Mr. Skyler would like to discuss his job requirements with me, that's his prerogative. But I will let Tillie know what his requirements are." I was enjoying the new me.

This time it was my mother who had her mouth hanging open, but she quickly recovered. "Good for you, darling."

I wrapped up four warm muffins and headed to Tillie's house. She buzzed me in when I rang the gate bell and met me at the front door. Piper bounded out and greeted me with yips and kisses. I handed the muffins to Tillie and gathered Piper in my arms to hug her.

"I've got coffee on. Come in and tell me all about your near-death experience last night." Tillie's eyes were bright with excitement. "The gals at bridge will be so jealous you're living here!"

Three cups of coffee, two muffins, and one hour later, I took my leave to head home and collect my personal toiletries and some clean clothes. I didn't want to spend another single night in my condo, so Tillie agreed I should move to the pool house right away. She no longer drove so the garage was empty, which left it free for the boxes and furniture the moving company would deliver. That'd give me a chance to go through them and decide what I needed to keep and what I could donate to charity.

Halfway home, my cell phone rang.

It was Randall. "I heard about your excitement last night. Are you okay?"

"A little shaky, but I'll be fine."

"My flight leaves for Tampa this afternoon. I wanted to say goodbye before I left. Can we meet for coffee?"

I'd had more coffee than my jittery nerves could handle, but I was sure Randall needed closure over what had happened to his brother because of Tori, Stan, and Steve. "Sure. Where would you like to meet?"

He named a place close to the John Wayne Airport in Santa Ana, so I took the next exit and returned the way I had just come.

Randall was sitting at a sidewalk table. He jumped up and hugged me before asking what I wanted to drink. When I said water, he raised his eyebrows.

"I just had three cups of coffee with an eighty-something-year-old lady. Water is all I need."

"Hang on and I'll grab you some, and then you can tell me about it."

As he strode into the shop, I watched his jean-clad back-side, which I could have watched all day long. I shook my head and reminded myself I was finished with men, at least for a while. Once Randall came back, he made me tell him every single thing that happened with Stan and Steve, and when I had exhausted all those details, he asked me about my new friend.

He laughed when I described her antics, but his laughter wasn't condescending. "I hope I'm that full of life and adventure when I get old."

We sat and chatted another few minutes before Randall

looked at his watch and stood up. "If I want to make my flight, I'd better get to the airport."

Following his lead, I stood, unsure if I should shake his hand. "I'm glad you were able to find out who killed your brother, and I hope you find closure."

"It helps, and it's all thanks to you." Randall cleared his throat. "I've been giving it a lot of thought, and I'm going to leave Tampa for good. I've had a job offer in Irvine, so I'll be moving back in a month or as soon as I can wrap up my business in Florida."

"Oh, I thought since you had a band, you were already here permanently." I wasn't sure why he was telling me this news. I was just a random chubby person that Tori had thrown at him, unless he felt a connection because I had inadvertently discovered his brother's killers.

"Naw. I was a band fill-in when I was available. I've been floating around the last couple of years hunting down Tori but kept a home base back in Tampa."

"That's a big move, so good luck." Those words sounded lame, even to my ears, but I didn't know what else to say.

"When I come back, I'd like to take you to dinner." He met my gaze. "Like on a real date."

What? Did I hear right? Why would this gorgeous guy want to date me? My face warmed, and then I reminded myself I was finished with men. "Uh, yeah, here's the thing. I'm not going to date for a long time. I need to get over Philip and find out what I want."

Randall stepped toward me, put his arms around my waist, and pulled me close. He leaned his lips into mine and gave me a sizzling kiss that made my toes curl.

He stepped away, smiling. "You were drugged the last time we kissed, so I thought you should experience it properly. I'll call you when I'm back in town."

With that, he strode toward his car while I admired the view.

Chapter 37

O nce I got settled into the pool house, Tillie suggested we throw an end-of-summer party. Together we pored over my recipe books and settled on an Italian-themed dinner. I wanted to make tiramisu cupcakes for dessert, but in the end, Tillie convinced me to make her new favorite: gimlet cupcakes. Since my family hadn't sampled them yet, I capitulated, and I had to admit, I had developed a taste for Tillie's favorite cocktail. The golden cupcakes with specks of lime zest were moist and refreshing from the citrus flavors. Perfect for a warm summer evening.

Since my nieces were coming to our dinner party, I made a batch of citrus-flavored sugar cookies and cut them into summer cookie-cutter shapes. Beach balls, flip-flops, ice cream cones, and surfboards. Once the baked cookies cooled, I frosted the tops with white royal icing and allowed them to dry until hardened. After dinner, the girls could use edible markers to decorate their cookies before eating. I made plenty of extras in case other guests wanted to join in the artistic fun by coloring cookies.

The night of the party arrived, and my entire family

came. The pool house captivated Sophie and Kaylee's imagination, and they wanted to spend the night. I promised to schedule a sleepover for the following weekend, since I would be kept up late tonight cleaning up after the party and couldn't keep my eye on them. Brad came alone, and my mother and Lars brought Tillie a beautiful bouquet of roses. They never said another word about dementia, and Mr. Skyler never brought it up either. I still hadn't quizzed my mother about her friendship with David.

Tillie's two dearest friends, Lucy and Sarah, attended, and they were busy hatching another plan to head to Vegas the following weekend. They argued amongst themselves about which strip clubs to visit, while I pretended not to listen. I was pleased to see that the three women all had an equal zest for living and Sarah had even dyed her hair a fashionable pink ombre. I squirmed a little when she tried to convince Tillie to dye her hair a shade of aqua and Sarah a shade of purple for their trip. I knew that idea wouldn't go over well with Tillie's son, but I bit my tongue and decided to cross that bridge later if the event happened.

I had been in heaven the previous week, working in Tillie's kitchen. She had drummed up enough cupcake business among her friends to keep me baking several batches every day. The gimlet cupcakes she took to her bridge club had clinched the deal for me. Her friends tried to stretch my creativity with their unique cocktail cupcake requests, and I wondered if a few of them used Pinterest to hunt for obscure drinks to test me. I enjoyed every minute, though, and so far, I had delivered all the requested cupcakes on time.

Carrie was green with envy, not from morning sickness, when she saw my kitchen. She gave me a hug. "I've missed you! Now that this kid isn't making me so sick, we need to spend time together."

I readily agreed, and she helped me carry out the platters of food to the long table set up in the courtyard. Soon the wine flowed… okay, it had been flowing for quite some time, but we passed around more wine with the food. Soon nothing but the strains of classical music and the clinking of silverware and glasses sounded as my family and friends ate platefuls of manicotti, Italian chopped salad, and homemade sourdough rolls. Tillie caught my eye and raised her glass, and I raised my glass to her. This was what life was all about: friends and family. I was right where I belonged.

Recipes

Potluck Rootin' Tootin' Beans

This recipe is adapted from a very good friend's recipe. Thank you, Janet Clause, for all the wonderful gatherings spent in your home and for sharing your recipes with me!

Ingredients

1 pound lean ground beef (you can substitute ground turkey)

1 medium-sized onion, chopped

2 cloves garlic, minced

1 (3-pound) can pork & beans

1 (15-ounce) can chili beans, drained

1 (15-ounce) can butter beans, drained

1 (15-ounce) can kidney beans, rinsed and drained

1 (15-ounce) can black beans, rinsed and drained

1 cup ketchup

3 tablespoons white vinegar

1/4 cup brown sugar

1 tablespoon liquid smoke

1 teaspoon freshly ground pepper

Salt to taste

Garnish Suggestions:

Cooked and crumbled bacon
Chopped red or green onions
Grated cheddar cheese
Sour cream
Pickled jalapeño slices
Sliced black olives

Instructions

In a large soup pot or Dutch oven, cook the ground beef (or turkey) with the chopped onion over medium-high heat, until the meat is no longer pink. Drain off any grease.

Add the remaining ingredients, except salt, and stir until thoroughly combined. Bring to a simmer then turn to low and cover the pot. Cook an additional 30 minutes, stirring often.

Remove from heat and season with salt before serving, if desired. Allow guests to garnish their bowls of beans with a variety of choices.

Cowgirl Cookies

Ingredients

1-1/4 cups (6.25 ounces) all-purpose flour
1 teaspoon baking powder
1/4 teaspoon baking soda
1/4 teaspoon ground cinnamon
1/2 teaspoon salt
1-1/2 cups (10.5 ounces) packed brown sugar
3/4 cup butter, melted
2 eggs
1 teaspoon vanilla extract
1-1/4 cups (3.75 ounces) old-fashioned rolled oats
1 cup (4.4 ounces) walnuts, chopped
1 cup (3 ounces) sweetened shredded coconut
1 cup (6 ounces) semisweet chocolate chips
1 cup (2 ounces) mini marshmallows

Instructions

In a medium-sized bowl, whisk together and set aside the flour, baking powder, baking soda, cinnamon, and salt.

In a large bowl, combine the sugar, melted butter, eggs, and vanilla. Mix in the flour mixture and, once it is fully incorporated, stir in the oats, walnuts, coconut, marshmallows, and chocolate chips.

Refrigerate for 1 hour.

Preheat oven to 350 degrees (F).

Portion the dough into 2 tablespoon-sized scoops and place on parchment-lined baking sheets. Make sure there is at least 2 inches between cookies to allow room to spread.

Bake cookies, one sheet at a time, 12-15 minutes, until edges start to turn golden brown. The centers should remain slightly undercooked. Rotate the baking sheet halfway through baking.

Remove from oven and allow cookies to cool on baking sheet for 5 minutes then place on a wire rack to cool completely.

Store leftovers in an airtight container for up to 4 days.

Cowgirl Caviar

Ingredients

Salad:

1 (15-ounce) can black beans, rinsed and drained

1 cup fresh yellow corn kernels (or substitute frozen)

1/2 cup bell peppers, chopped (you can use a mixture of red, yellow, and green if desired)

1 jalapeño, seeded and finely chopped

2 tablespoons red onion, finely chopped

1/4 cup cilantro, chopped fine

1/2 large avocado (or 1 small avocado)

2 small tomatoes, seeded and chopped

Vinaigrette:

4 tablespoons olive oil

4 tablespoons lime juice

1 clove garlic, minced

1 teaspoon sugar

1 teaspoon salt

1/4 teaspoon freshly ground black pepper

1/2 teaspoon cumin

Pinch of cayenne pepper (or more to taste)

Instructions

Cook the corn kernels over medium-high heat, stirring occasionally. Once the kernels exhibit some char marks, remove from heat and place in a large serving bowl.

Add the beans, bell pepper, cilantro, jalapeño, red onion, and tomatoes to the corn.

Whisk the vinaigrette ingredients together in a small bowl and pour over the bean mixture.

Toss all the ingredients together then refrigerate for 2 hours before serving.

Right before serving, chop and fold the avocado into the bean mixture.

Season to taste with additional salt and cayenne pepper if desired.

Serve with tortilla chips and/or pita chips. This also makes an excellent topping for grilled chicken or fish.

Baked Jalapeño Poppers

Ingredients

12 jalapeños, halved and seeded with membranes removed
4 ounces cream cheese, room temperature
1 cup cheddar cheese, finely grated
1 cup Monterey Jack cheese, finely grated
3 scallions, green part only, finely diced
1 tablespoon cilantro, finely chopped
1 egg yolk
1 teaspoon ground cumin
4 tablespoons panko breadcrumbs
2 tablespoons grated Parmesan cheese
1/4 teaspoon paprika
Sliced limes and cilantro for garnish

Instructions

Preheat oven to 500 degrees (F).

Place a wire rack in a rimmed baking sheet that has been lined with aluminum foil. Place halved jalapeños cut side down on wire rack and bake 5 minutes, just until they begin to soften. Remove from oven and cool while preparing the remaining ingredients.

Reduce oven temperature to 400 degrees (F).

In a shallow bowl, mix together 4 tablespoons panko breadcrumbs, Parmesan cheese, and paprika. Set aside.

In a mixing bowl, stir together the cream cheese, cheddar cheese, Monterey Jack cheese, cilantro, green onions, egg yolk, and cumin until thoroughly combined.

Portion the cream cheese mixture between the jalapeño halves.

Working with 1 half jalapeño at a time, turn upside down and place cheese mixture in the panko breadcrumb mixture. Press down to adhere breadcrumbs.

Place the coated jalapeño onto a baking sheet lined with parchment paper. Repeat with remaining jalapeños.

Bake 7-9 minutes, just until cheese begins to bubble.

Switch the oven to the broil setting and broil for 1-2 minutes, until the breadcrumb coating turns golden brown. Watch the jalapeños carefully and don't allow the crumb topping to burn.

Remove baking sheet from the oven and cool for 5 minutes before placing jalapeños onto a serving platter. Garnish with cilantro and serve with sliced limes.

Mama's Cornbread Muffins with Honey Butter

Ingredients
Muffins:
1 cup (4.8 ounces) all-purpose flour

1 cup (4.5 ounces) cornmeal, fine ground

4 teaspoons baking powder

1/3 cup (2.5 ounces) sugar

1 teaspoon salt

Pinch of cayenne pepper

2 large eggs

1 cup milk, whole or 2%

1/4 cup vegetable oil

Honey Butter:
1/2 cup butter, room temperature

1/2 cup honey

1/2 teaspoon vanilla extract

Instructions
Muffins:
Preheat the oven to 425 degrees (F).

Spritz a 12-cup muffin tin with nonstick cooking spray or line with paper wrappers.

In a large mixing bowl, whisk together the flour, cornmeal, baking powder, sugar, salt, and cayenne pepper.

In a medium-sized mixing bowl, whisk the eggs, milk, and vegetable oil until completely blended.

Add the milk mixture to the cornmeal mixture and stir until incorporated. Be careful to not overmix.

Divide between the prepared muffin tin cups.

Bake for 15-17 minutes, until a wooden skewer inserted into the center of a muffin comes out mostly clean. A few moist crumbs attached to the skewer is fine.

Let cool for 5 minutes and then remove from the pan and cool on a wire rack. Serve warm or at room temperature, spreading honey butter on muffins.

Honey Butter:

Using an electric mixer on medium-high speed, whip the butter until light and fluffy.

Add the honey in 4 increments, beating well after each addition.

Add in the vanilla extract and whip the mixture on high speed until fluffy, about 5 minutes.

Use immediately and store leftovers in the refrigerator. Before reusing, whip with an electric mixer for 2-3 minutes until texture is fluffy.

Cowgirl Quencher Cocktail

Serves 1

Ingredients

1 ounce coconut rum
1 ounce peach schnapps
3 ounces orange juice
3 ounces pineapple juice
Grenadine

Instructions

Place rum, schnapps, and orange and pineapple juices into an ice-filled cocktail shaker. Shake until well chilled then strain into a margarita glass. Float a teaspoon of grenadine to the top of the cocktail and serve.

Cowgirl Quencher Mocktail

Serves 1

Ingredients
2 ounces peach nectar
3 ounces orange juice
3 ounces pineapple juice
2 drops coconut extract
Grenadine

Instructions
Place peach nectar and orange and pineapple juices and extract into an ice-filled cocktail shaker. Shake until well chilled then strain into a tumbler or kid-friendly glass. Float a teaspoon of grenadine to the top of the mocktail and serve.

Cowgirl Quencher Cocktail Cupcakes

Ingredients

Cupcakes:

1 box yellow cake mix with pudding in the mix

1/3 cup pineapple juice

1/3 cup orange juice

3 tablespoons coconut rum

3 tablespoons peach schnapps

3 eggs, room temperature

1/2 cup vegetable oil

Glaze:

2 tablespoons confectioners' sugar

2 tablespoons butter

2 tablespoons coconut rum

2 tablespoons peach schnapps

Frosting:

1/2 cup unsalted butter, room temperature

5 cups confectioners' sugar

1/4 teaspoon salt

1/2 teaspoon coconut extract

1 tablespoon grenadine

1 tablespoon orange juice

1-1/2 tablespoons pineapple juice
1-1/2 tablespoons peach schnapps
Pink gel food coloring, optional

Garnish suggestions:

Pineapple or orange slices
Maraschino cherries
Decorative sprinkles
Decorative straws
Decorative paper umbrellas

Instructions

Cupcakes:

Preheat oven to 350 degrees (F).

Line cupcake tins with 16 paper or foil liners.

Place all the cupcake ingredients into a large mixing bowl and blend with an electric mixer for 30 seconds on low speed. Increase speed to medium-high and beat an additional 2 minutes.

Divide the batter equally between the cupcake liners.

Bake 18-20 minutes, rotating cupcake tin(s) halfway through baking. A wooden skewer inserted into the center of a cupcake should come out mostly clean. A few moist crumbs clinging to the skewer is fine.

Cool cupcakes in the tin for 5 minutes then remove and place on a wire rack. Proceed with glaze while the cupcakes are still warm.

Glaze:

Place all the glaze ingredients into a microwave-safe bowl and microwave on high for 30 seconds. Stir and heat for an additional 20 seconds, then stir until butter has melted. Use caution as the mixture can bubble over if overheated.

Prick the tops of the cupcakes with the tines of a fork, piercing at least halfway through the cupcake.

Brush the glaze over the top of each cupcake. Allow cupcakes to completely cool before proceeding with frosting.

Frosting:

In a small bowl, stir together the coconut extract, grenadine, orange juice, pineapple juice, peach schnapps, and 1-2 drops of pink food coloring if using. Set aside.

In the bowl of a standing mixer, beat the butter with the salt until creamy, on medium speed.

Reduce speed to low and gradually add half the confectioners' sugar to the butter, beating until incorporated.

Slowly add half the liquid mixture to the sugar and butter mixture, beating well until incorporated.

Gradually add the remaining confectioners' sugar, and once it's been incorporated, add the remaining liquid.

Increase mixer speed to medium-high and beat for 4 minutes, until the frosting is light and fluffy.

If the frosting is too thick, add additional orange or pineapple juice, 1 teaspoon at a time, until desired consistency is reached.

Frost completely cooled cupcakes and garnish as desired.

Makes 16 cupcakes.

Cowgirl Quencher Mocktail Cupcakes

Ingredients

Cupcakes:

1 box yellow cake mix with pudding in the mix

1/3 cup pineapple juice

1/3 cup orange juice

1/3 cup peach nectar

1 teaspoon coconut extract

3 eggs, room temperature

1/2 cup vegetable oil

Glaze:

2 tablespoons confectioners' sugar

2 tablespoons butter

1/2 teaspoon coconut extract

2 tablespoons peach nectar

2 tablespoons pineapple juice

Frosting:

1/2 cup unsalted butter, room temperature

5 cups confectioners' sugar

1/4 teaspoon salt

1/2 teaspoon coconut extract

1 tablespoon grenadine

1 tablespoon orange juice
1-1/2 tablespoons pineapple juice
1-1/2 tablespoons peach nectar
Pink gel food coloring, optional

Garnish suggestions:
Pineapple or orange slices
Maraschino cherries
Decorative sprinkles
Decorative straws
Decorative paper umbrellas

Instructions

Cupcakes:

Preheat oven to 350 degrees (F).

Line cupcake tins with 16 paper or foil liners.

Place all the cupcake ingredients into a large mixing bowl and blend with an electric mixer for 30 seconds on low speed. Increase speed to medium-high and beat an additional 2 minutes.

Divide the batter equally between the cupcake liners.

Bake 18-20 minutes, rotating cupcake tin(s) halfway through baking. A wooden skewer inserted into the center of a cupcake should come out mostly clean. A few moist crumbs clinging to the skewer is fine.

Cool cupcakes in the tin for 5 minutes then remove and place on a wire rack. Proceed with glaze while the cupcakes are still warm.

Glaze:

Place all the glaze ingredients into a microwave-safe bowl and microwave on high for 30 seconds. Stir and heat for an additional 20 seconds, then stir until butter has melted. Use caution as the mixture can bubble over if overheated.

Prick the tops of the cupcakes with the tines of a fork, piercing at least halfway through the cupcake.

Brush the glaze over the top of each cupcake.

Frosting:

In a small bowl, stir together the coconut extract, grenadine, orange juice, pineapple juice, peach nectar, and 1-2 drops of food coloring if using. Set aside.

In the bowl of a standing mixer, beat the butter with the salt until creamy, on medium speed.

Reduce speed to low and gradually add half the confectioners' sugar to the butter, beating until incorporated.

Slowly add half the liquid mixture to the sugar and butter mixture, beating well until incorporated.

Gradually add the remaining confectioners' sugar, and once it's been incorporated, add the remaining liquid.

Increase mixer speed to medium-high and beat for 4 minutes, until the frosting is light and fluffy.

If the frosting is too thick, add additional orange juice, 1 teaspoon at a time, until desired consistency is reached.

Frost completely cooled cupcakes and as desired.

Makes 16 cupcakes.

Gimlet Cocktail

Serves 1

Ingredients

2 ounces gin

2/3 ounce Rose's lime juice

Garnish:

Lime twist

Instructions

Chill a cocktail glass and rim it with a lime wedge.

Add the gin and Rose's lime juice to a cocktail shaker filled with ice.

Shake vigorously then strain into the cocktail glass.

Garnish with a lime twist.

Gimlet Cupcakes

This cupcake recipe has earned one of the highest ratings from my taste testers.

Ingredients

Cupcakes:

1-1/4 cups (161g) cake flour

1-1/4 teaspoons baking powder

1/2 teaspoon baking soda

1/2 teaspoon salt

2 eggs, room temperature

1 cup (200g) granulated sugar

1/2 cup vegetable oil

1/3 cup gin

3 tablespoons fresh lime juice

Zest from 1 lime

1/8 teaspoon pure lime oil (optional)

Glaze:

1/2 cup (64g) confectioners' sugar

2 tablespoons gin

2 tablespoons lime juice

Zest from 1 lime

Frosting:

4 cups (506g) confectioners' sugar

1/2 cup (113g) unsalted butter, room temperature

1/4 teaspoon salt

1 tablespoon fresh lime juice

3 tablespoons gin

1/8 teaspoon pure lime oil, optional

1 drop mint green and 2 drops yellow gel food coloring (optional)

Garnish Suggestions:

Fresh lime wedges

Candied lime peel

Lime fruit gel candies

Instructions

Cupcakes:

Preheat oven to 350 degrees (F).

Line cupcake tins with paper liners.

Whisk flour, baking powder, baking soda, and salt together in a small bowl. Set aside.

Whisk the gin, lime juice, and pure lime oil (if using) together. Set aside.

In the bowl of a standing mixer, whisk the eggs on medium speed for 30 seconds.

Add the sugar and the lime zest and continue to whisk an additional minute.

With the mixer running on low, slowly add the vegetable oil. Increase mixer to medium and whisk an additional minute.

Reduce mixer speed back to low and add half the flour mixture to the sugar mixture. Beat on low until mostly incorporated.

Add half the gin mixture and stir to combine.

Repeat with remaining flour and gin mixture and beat

until smooth, about 30 seconds, scraping down the sides of the bowl as necessary.

Fill cupcake liners about 1/2 full and bake 12-14 minutes. Batter is quite thin, and I like to use 1/4 cup measuring cups for filling liners.

Remove from oven and allow to cool in the cupcake tin for 5 minutes.

Move the cupcakes to a wire rack and immediately proceed with glaze.

Glaze:

Whisk together the confectioners' sugar, gin, lime juice, and lime zest.

Pierce each warm cupcake 4 times with the tines of a fork.

Brush the glaze over the cupcakes, allowing the liquid to soak in before applying more. Be sure to use all the glaze.

Allow the cupcakes to cool completely before proceeding with the frosting.

Frosting:

Place butter and salt into the bowl of a standing mixer and whip until the butter is creamy, approximately 2-3 minutes on medium-high speed.

With the mixer running on low speed, add confectioners' sugar a little at a time, mixing until sugar is coated with the butter.

Whisk the gin and lime juice together along with the pure lime oil and gel food coloring if using.

Once the butter and sugar mixture is creamy, slowly add the gin mixture.

Increase the speed to medium-high and whip for approximately 5 minutes until the frosting is light and fluffy.

Frost the cupcakes and garnish if desired.

Makes 15 cupcakes.

Dedication

For my husband, Dan, who gives me the support and encouragement to create and believe in myself.

And for my granddaughters, Jaidyn, who bravely fights the Rett Syndrome monster every day, and her sister, Emory, who is tenderhearted and caring of her sister. They both inspire me to find joy and laughter in the simple things in life.

Acknowledgments

It's true that it takes a village to create a book. I'd like to thank my husband, Dan, for reading and editing my manuscript several times. Not only that, he also toted my pink cupcake carrier to his golf group on numerous occasions to collect a wide variety of comments and critiques on my cupcake recipes from his peers. And to all my taste testers, thank you for your suggestions and encouragement with each tweak I did on the recipes.

I also have to give a shout-out to Lisa Kelley of Lisa Ks Book Reviews for coming up with the title. I am in awe of her quick wit and way with puns! In addition, she kindly read an early version of my manuscript and provided several worthy suggestions. Dawn Dowdle, owner of Blue Ridge Literary Agency, deserves my gratitude for her suggestions which made my story so much better! She was also instrumental in fixing those pesky grammar and punctuation errors. And last but not least, thank you to my other beta readers, Janet Clause and Kathy Keith.

A huge thank you to Catherine Bruns, Linda Reilly, and Paige Shelton for reading my book and offering me their encouragement! I'm so grateful for the support and friendships of the cozy mystery writing community and feel blessed to be a part of of it both as an author and a reader.

I greatly appreciate the talents of cover designer Karen Phillips. She captured the spirit of my book and made it come alive.

A special thanks to all of the lovely people who follow my blog, Cinnamon, Sugar, and a Little Bit of Murder, and share in my love for delicious food and mysteries! You inspire me to create stories and recipes to share with family and friends.

About the Author

Kim Davis lives in Southern California with her husband. When not chasing her two granddaughters, she can be found at her computer writing or blogging at Cinnamon, Sugar, and a Little Bit of Murder, or in the kitchen baking up new treats to share.

Kim Davis is a member of Sisters in Crime and Mystery Writers of America.

She has also published a suspense novel, *A Game of Deceit*, under K.A. Davis.

 facebook.com/Kim-Davis-Author-1532277473479031

twitter.com/Kookiesandbooks

pinterest.com/kimdavishb

SPRINKLES OF SUSPICION

Cupcake Catering Mystery Series Book 1

Cinnamon & Sugar Press

ISBN 978-0-9990688-2-3

ISBN 978-0-9990688-3-0

Cover Design by Karen Phillips

Edited by Red Adept Editing

 Created with Vellum

One glass of cheap California chardonnay cost Emory Gosser Martinez her husband, her job, and her best friend. Unfortunately, that was only the beginning of her troubles.

Distraught after discovering the betrayal by her husband and best friend, Tori, cupcake caterer Emory Martinez allows her temper to flare. Several people witness her very public altercation with her ex-friend. To make matters worse, Tori exacts her revenge by posting a fake photo of Emory in a compromising situation, which goes viral on social media. When Tori is found murdered, all signs point to Emory being the prime suspect.

With the police investigation focused on gathering evidence to convict her, Emory must prove her innocence while whipping up batches of cupcakes and buttercream. Delving into the past of her murdered ex-friend, she finds other people had reasons to want Tori dead, including Emory's own husband. Can she find the killer, or will the clues sprinkled around the investigation point the police back to her?

Printed in Great Britain
by Amazon